Mirror, Mirror
at 1600 D.C.

by
Edward Galluzzi

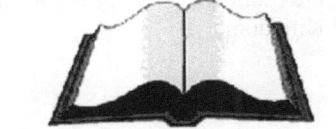

CCB Publishing
British Columbia, Canada

Mirror, Mirror at 1600 D.C.

Copyright ©2008 by Edward Galluzzi
ISBN-13 978-0-9810246-1-5
Third Edition

Library and Archives Canada Cataloguing in Publication

Galluzzi, Edward, 1951-
Mirror, Mirror at 1600 D.C. / written by Edward Galluzzi.
ISBN 978-0-9810246-1-5
I. Title.
PS3607.A423M57 2008   813'.6   C2008-904161-5

United States Copyright Office Registration # TXu-916-174

Publisher: CCB Publishing
              British Columbia, Canada
              www.ccbpublishing.com

Dedication

*I would like to thank my parents, William and Roberta,
and my family and friends for their support.*

*In appreciation, their names, in one form or another,
appear throughout this novel.*

Acknowledgements

I wish to thank Brandon S. Jeffress of *JeffressStudios* (www.jeffstudios.com) for his creation of the cover design for *Mirror, Mirror at 1600 D.C.* I also wish to thank Patricia L. Demaree for her careful proofing of this manuscript.

Contents

Introduction

Under any circumstances, the role of the President of the United States is arduous and replete with challenges. The enduring patriarchy of presidents had ended with the first woman elected to this high office in the United States. This pioneering leader is delighting her supporters and readily converting her critics when she is kidnapped suddenly. But by whom? And for what reason? The unfolding plot is a matter of survival…not only personal survival, but also hanging in the balance is the endurance of the Presidency and the privilege of democracy in America. It will take a very special agent to expose this sinister plot. But whatever the costs, the President must be recovered…dead or alive.

Chapter 1

Spia

It was a particularly warm day, even for the dog days of August, as the bright sun radiated sufficient heat to singe just about every living thing. Apparently nobody told Mother Nature that autumn was around the corner. However, everybody told Hannah with disbelief in their voice, "Hannah, this is not like you!" Hannah's friends and colleagues were right. This was not like her—not like cautious, predictable, prudent, and planned to the minute detail—Hannah. She was having her wedding gown fitted to join a man that she has known only for four months. Four amazing months! No, this was not like Hannah, but then again, Harrison was certainly like no other man.

It was a chance meeting for Hannah and Harrison. Hannah was on assignment in Vatican City, an enclave of Rome, Italy, as a journalist for the *Washington Sun*. Pope Joseph Josetta, who has reigned as the patriarch of the Roman Catholic Church for these past thirteen years, was in failing health. Harrison, who was on special assignment for the President of the United States, was also in Rome. Harrison, the consummate man of duty, has never to this day confided the details of his special assignments to Hannah. She admired him for that. She knew nothing beyond that he was in sensitive negotiations with the leadership of Italy.

Harrison traveled to Vatican City during breaks in the negotiations. He was concerned about the health and emotional well being of Pope Josetta. He had numerous contacts with Josetta as part of his duties to the President over the past seven years. Harrison knew Josetta for many years

1

even before his reign as pontiff during the time of his bishop and cardinal years when he was known by his birth name, Josepha Modesta. Despite their divergent vocations and lifestyles, they often shared common points of view given their mutual Italian ancestry. Harrison's mother was born in Carrara, Italy, a small region northwest of Rome. The holy man Josetta was born in Venice. Carrara has long been known for its marble and it is still mined there today. Venice has historically been the city of romance with its winding waterways and canals. Rome is a tourist's delight, a sightseer's dream that includes St. Peter's Basilica, the Colosseum, the Pantheon, Fountain of the Four Rivers, Castel Sant' Angelo, Piazza Venezia, the Roman Forum, *Piazza* del Campidoglio, the Catacombs of San Calisto, the Baths of Caracalla— the historical sites go on and on.

Josetta has been one of the most popular Popes among the Catholic clergy and laity in recent centuries. As the Pope of the *people,* he has warmed the hearts of all Christians around the world. It was also Josetta's divine directive that altered the traditional vow of celibacy among Roman Catholic priests. For the first time in centuries, priests who were so inclined can now marry and still celebrate the holy sacraments. The shortage of priests and vocations as well as the voice of the people fanned the historical debate of ordaining women priests or rescinding the vow of celibacy for the *men* of God. Such an edict was remarkable given the zealous affirmation of the vow of celibacy for priests that the then enlightened Ecumenical Council of the early-to-mid 1960's espoused *via* the documents of Vatican II.

Harrison and Josetta seldom argued matters of faith and dogma, not that the humble man could debate eloquently theological issues with the venerable man of God. Yet, these good men shared their faith and lineages in Italy. These elements sustained the driving forces in their lives and spiritually bounded their friendship.

Harrison knelt by the bedside of Josetta. He sometimes looked away from the frail man. This was one of those times. Out of the corner of his eye, Harrison saw the flag of Vatican City in the corner of the room. The Vatican flag has two vertical bands of yellow on the hoist side and white with the crossed keys of Saint Peter. The papal miter was centered in the white band. The holy man was conscious and peering at Harrison as if to say, "Do not pity me." Their eyes met as Josetta spoke in a barely audible voice: "Spia" [the Pope's Italian term of endearment for his friend and literally translated as "spy" in reference to Harrison's many covert operations for his President]. "Spia," he said for a second time. "I am an old man and have lived a long life for God. I am ready…" Josetta took a long, deep breath and continued, "Ready to go home." Harrison, who witnessed many deaths in his line of duty, was unable to hold back the tears swelling in his eyes. He grasped the holy man's hand as the man of God continued in his weakening voice, "Remember me, remember God."

Josetta's wry smile did not escape its translation to Harrison. His faith and the nature of his assignments conflicted many times. Harrison called upon "situational ethics" way too often. Yet, his devotion to duty and his President necessitated the delicate compromise.

Harrison's attention returned to the holy man as Josetta weakly spoke, "You are troubled, yes?" Harrison grinned, "I am troubled, always!" The comment brought a smile to the dying man's face. Harrison brought the gift of a smile frequently to their relationship. It was a good time for the humble and holy man to smile. The inevitability of Josetta's death weighed heavily on Harrison, perhaps more so than for the holy man himself.

Josetta spoke, "Who is going to take care of you, Spia, guide you when I'm gone? You will be..." Josetta coughed vigorously for several minutes and then continued, "You will be lost without me." Josetta managed a painful grin and said, "Who will absolve you of all your multitudinous sins?" Before Harrison could defend himself, the holy man anticipated his protest and interrupted quickly, "You, God and I know that you are a sinner. However, when I meet Him, I will put in a good word for you, Spia." Harrison grinned widely and replied, "I think it will take more that a good word, even from you, Josetta." The two friends managed a restrained laugh.

In an effort to assure Josetta that he would be cared for, Harrison spoke, "I want you to know that I met someone, someone I've grown to care for very much in the past few months." The news seemed to energize His Holiness and he asked excitedly, "A woman? You are taking time out to fall in love with a woman, Spia?" Harrison, pretending he was hurt at the pontiff's remarks, said to his beloved friend, "You don't think a woman could become interested in me?" The men smiled and Josetta said, "Interested? Yes, for you are indeed a captivating man." The holy man chose his next words carefully and shook his index finger of his right hand, "Spia, does this woman know, shall we say, the details of your vocation?"

Harrison raised his eyebrows momentarily as if to ask 'My vocation?' without stating the words. He thought to himself, 'my vocation? Who would believe my vocation?' Before Harrison formulated his response, the holy man said confidently, "I thought not." Harrison spoke in a somewhat defensive voice, "Hannah is aware that I conduct special assignments for the President." "And I'm the Pope," said Josetta. "Hannah?" Josetta appeared delighted at the sound of her name. "Conduct?" the pontiff commented in his typically subtle manner, "Perhaps you mean to say 'execute'?"

Harrison chose not to argue the aesthetics of his livelihood, something they had deliberated on many occasions anyway with no productive resolution. "Besides," said Harrison, "I have you to thank for meeting Hannah." "Me, Spia? Cosa intende, io?" It was common for Josetta to lapse to his native tongue, a language quite familiar to Harrison. "Hannah is a journalist for a Washington newspaper. Like most journalists, she is here to cover your health," said Harrison. "You mean my death," the holy one corrected.

Harrison gave his old friend a look of indifference and continued, "You are not going to die." However, the words sounded hollow even to Harrison given the state of His Holiness' health. This time Harrison spoke before Josetta formulated his thoughts, "Hannah has a great deal of respect for you. She considers you 'progressive' you know." "Progressive?" queried Josetta. The holy man heard the descriptive adjective before, but dismissed it with a wave of his hand. "Progressive?" said Josetta with some disdain. He protested, "I'm only the servant of the Lord and His word." Harrison was acutely aware of Josetta's longstanding humility in his papacy, but his impressive list of accomplishments as servant of his church and his dogmatic encyclicals belied his modesty.

In dismissing the cosmopolitan label, Josetta said with a noticeable twinkle in his eye, "Tell me about this Hannah, Spia. Cosa è piace? What is she like?" Harrison observed that his holy friend sparkled a bit over the idea that not only could he have a girl friend, but also that somebody might actually marry him. Perhaps even take care of him.

"As I said," Harrison noted, "she's a journalist for the *Washington Sun* out of Washington, D.C. She has the most beautiful eyes…" "It's always the physical with you first," interjected Josetta. "'The lust of the eye' the Bible speaks" added the holy man. Harrison raised his eyebrows giving him that boyish charm and resumed, "Hannah has the most beautiful hazel eyes and the most angelic face..." "Oh, fratello!" mused the holy man placing his right hand to his right cheek. "Oh, brother yourself," echoed Harrison while mimicking his friend's hand movement. "I'll spare you Hannah's other incarnate qualifications," said Harrison. Josetta only smiled as Harrison continued, "She's a bright woman, very smart, but doesn't flaunt it. Hannah is dedicated to journalism, 'truth from the pen' as she puts it. She has your sense of humor..." Josetta again smiled, but then coughed uncontrollably for a minute or so. "Can I get you anything, Josetta?" The holy man waved his hand 'no' and coughed once again. "Is it my description of Hannah or that she loves me that you can't take?" smirked Harrison. He continued, "You need your rest. I have to get back to work while you lay here with all your servants waiting after you!" Josetta smiled once again although weakly this time. "Good evening, your excellency." At that, Harrison bowed his head, as he was accustomed for Josetta's blessing: "Maggio che Dio benedice Lei nel nome del Padre, e del Figlio e del Spirt Santo." "Amen," responded Harrison. With that, he placed his hand on Josetta's, squeezed lightly. "Don't worry," Harrison said, "You are not going to leave this world of ours until after you meet Hannah." The Pope managed a smile and a nod of his head as Harrison left the room.

Harrison stood in the corridor outside of Josetta's room. He took a deep breath in an attempt to compose himself. Harrison drew strength from his holy friend and it hurt deeply to watch him slip away. He vowed to keep his promise that Josetta would meet Hannah while he remained conscious and alert. With that certainty, Harrison worked his way out of the

Vatican and the multitude of Swiss Papal Guards who protected the Holy See.

Chapter 2

Remembrance

Hannah twisted and turned for almost an hour as her wedding dress was tailored to the curves and lines of her elongated, beautiful body. She bit slightly and pulled down her upper lip as she addressed her seamstress: "Rosella, are we about finished?" The seamstress nodded and smiled, "Uno minuto." Hannah has waited through numerous "uno minutos." 'After all, my wedding day will only happen once' she prayed as she crossed her wedding ring finger of her left hand. As she did so, Hannah admired the diamond engagement ring given to her by her betrothed Harrison. She extended her ring toward Rosella and asked for a second time that day, "Isn't this the most beautiful engagement ring you ever saw?" Rosella eyed the ring for a second time and responded politely as she did before, "Si, bello." Hannah turned her hand toward herself and cherished the ring that she believed would be on her finger forever.

Rosella was a family friend of Harrison's and it was in her home in Carrara that Hannah's wedding dress was being tailored. The home was nestled in the side of a small mountain. It was a two-story structure set in white stone and red brick. The home was set between two large verandas. The main front porch was screened and contained a variety of comfortable outdoor furniture utilized for chat, cards and other table games. The rear porch was rectangular and the wide base lent itself to an extended dinner table. The traditional Italian grapevine draped the perimeter of the porch causing the sun's reflection to appear as moving dots on the table.

"Finito," Rosella said finally. The seamstress stepped back

to admire her work and again repeated, "Bello." She helped Hannah out of her wedding dress and remarked that she would have the alterations completed in two weeks. Hannah thanked Rosella for her exquisite tailoring and apologized for her impatience during the fitting.

Hannah stepped out of Rosella's home into the hot summer day. Like most homes in Carrara, air conditioning was rare. Yet, the humming of many fans kept the home sufficiently cool so that Hannah gasped slightly from the sudden intake of outdoor heat. She was off to the train station and headed for Rome to meet Harrison for dinner. It would take several hours on the Italian railway before arriving at Rome's Saint Peter station.

The train ride to Rome was mundane leaving Hannah to her quiet thoughts and the anticipation of being with her beloved. She thought about their first meeting in Rome and how the Pontiff, Joseph Josetta, intersected their lives. Hannah was covering the failing health of the Pope as a journalist while Harrison was comforting his old friend Josetta. The man of God was their bond, the cornerstone of their first meeting.

Hannah smiled to herself as she recalled her first glimpse of her handsome Harrison. He was a lean, tall man, 'four inches above six feet' he always informed her. His hair was dark brown with some distinguished graying at the temples. Harrison was a muscular man, but not grotesquely so. He often trained to sustain the physical demands of his employment.

'His employment,' the words echoed in Hannah's mind. She knew that Harrison conducted special assignments for the President of the United States. 'Similar to the Secret Service' he had said. It was not the danger inherent in Harrison's assignments that permeated her thoughts at the moment, but the fact that the President of the United States was Elizabeth Ashton, the first woman President in the history of America—

and her husband-to-be conducted 'special' assignments for madam President. Has jealousy reared its ugly head so early in their relationship? Hannah dismissed the thought with a confident, quiet laugh.

Hannah's thoughts returned to the attractiveness of the man. She certainly was not the only woman who buckled under the spell of the suave Harrison Rossetti. Elizabeth Ashton was no slouch even for a bureaucrat. Harrison, the man, certainly did not escape the eye of madam President. 'Hmm?' Hannah thought rhetorically. She shook her head as if the act itself would magically jar the thought from her mind.

The lives of Hannah and Harrison intersected near St. Peter's Basilica about four months ago. Hannah was on her way to Vatican City for a news briefing on the health of Pope Joseph Josetta. Harrison was leaving the Vatican after visiting his holy confidant. He was somewhat dejected and out of sorts as he leaned against the wall. Neither Harrison's attractiveness nor his demeanor escaped Hannah's observant eye. Her heart raced as she approached the disconcerted man and asked with genuine concern, "Are you all right?" There came no immediate response as Harrison was immersed in his own deep thoughts, oblivious to the sights and sounds that surrounded him. Hannah repeated her question; however, this time she tapped the preoccupied man on his shoulder. Harrison gazed up for the first time and the once indifferent surroundings sharpened into focus. He was aware of a woman's presence, but not what was asked of him. Harrison said uncertainly, "Excuse me?" Hannah repeated for a third time, "Are you OK?"

Harrison managed a terse smile. He looked deeply into the eyes of the questioner noticing for the first time the beauty of the woman before him. "Yes, yes I am" he managed to interject. Hannah smiled and seemed relieved that she did not have to begin emergency procedures. Harrison's disposition brightened as he gazed beyond Hannah's eyes. She was indeed a stunning woman. She was tall and slender with pleasing features and a most endearing smile. "Steady Harrison," he said barely aloud. "I'm sorry?" returned Hannah. Harrison gathered himself and extended his hand as he introduced himself, "I'm Harrison Rossetti …and you are?" "Hannah, Hannah Littleton" she offered and shook his hand firmly.

"You seemed troubled," said Hannah. 'Troubled, always' Harrison mused to himself. "My friend," he paused, aware of some swelling in his eyes, "Pope Josetta is quite ill." "You know personally the Holy Father?" asked Hannah. "Yes, I have known him for a long time" Harrison managed to reply. "I am very sorry," replied Hannah. He looked at the beautiful woman and nodded gratefully in response. The pause grew into an uncomfortable silence that shrouded the two strangers.

The stillness was broken by the bells of St. Peter's Basilica chiming out their noonday hymn. "Angelic, aren't they?" commented Hannah. Harrison nodded affirmatively and listened to the harmonic chiming that permeated the square. Hannah and Harrison found themselves drifting with the bells. They chimed a peaceful song that slowly melted away one's troubles even if for a fleeting moment.

The melodic chimes ended their serene song as Harrison's and Hannah's eyes met once again. Harrison broke the silence and asked, "Are you visiting Rome?" "Actually I'm working," Hannah replied. "I'm a journalist for the *Washington Sun*. I was sent to Rome on special assignment to cover the Pope's…" Hannah stopped suddenly and chose to modify her response in hopes of showing some sensitivity to the holy man's friend. "I'm writing a documentary about Josetta's papal reign and his impact on Roman Catholics, Catholicism and Christians around the world. I started the assignment

11

about six months ago before the Pope became ill. You said you just visited the Pontiff? How is he?" "Off the record?" retorted Harrison. "Off the record," Hannah echoed. "Not well, I'm afraid" said Harrison. He continued, "But he is a strong man, a man who has weathered many crises throughout the years I've known him—even before he was elected to the Holy See. He won't die until he is ready for death."

Hannah nodded as if underscoring Harrison's comment. She asked, "Are you in Rome to visit an old friend or does something else bring you to Italy?" Harrison was cautious in his reply: "I'm on assignment just like you." 'Just like you' he thought to himself. Harrison could hardly believe what he was saying. "I work for the U.S. government," he stated and decided not to convey his special duties for the President of the United States. After all, he did not trust Hannah; for that matter, he seldom trusted anybody except those he has known over the years and who were part of his inner circle. Harrison concluded that not confiding in others was the primary reason why he was still living today. Beautiful or not, he was not about to go against his training and judgment.

Hannah interrupted his inner thoughts and asked, "What do you do for the government?" "I'm a negotiator, sort of a troubleshooter if you will," replied Harrison with somewhat of a grim look on his face. He hoped that she would let it go at that to avoid covering up for national security issues and what not. Untrue to journalistic prying, Hannah accepted the response and did not force the issue. She simply said, "Interesting." Perhaps Hannah already surmised the situation and was being prudent. 'Perhaps,' Harrison thought to himself.

Yet, her lack of interest interested him. He asked, "Would you care to join me for lunch?" "Yes, very much, thank you," replied Hannah without substantial thought.

"I know a small place that is within walking distance from

here," said Harrison. "Casa di Pasta," he offered while putting his hand out to motion her down the steps. Casa di Pasta was one of Harrison's favorite dining establishments, one that he visited often in his many taps to romantic Roma. It was conveniently close to the Vatican and featured a variety of Italian cuisine.

Chapter 3

The Holy Man and the Man of the Gun

Hannah and Harrison began walking the short distance to the restaurant. There was a brief silence interrupted by Harrison, "Have you worked long for the *Washington Sun?"* Before Hannah could respond, what sounded like gunshots rang out in their direction. Harrison instinctively cradled Hannah and crouched for cover in the doorway of a nearby building as a car sped by them with its wheels squealing. Puffs of white smoke were left in the wake of the car as evidence that the tires temporarily raced faster than the vehicle itself. Harrison stood cautiously and attempted a glimpse at the speeding vehicle, but was unable to determine the license plate number. Even without such identification, he had a very good idea of the origin of the gunfire.

Hannah cried out, "What's going on, Harrison?" Harrison helped Hannah from the ground. He pushed her there rather roughly as demanded by the urgency of the situation. "Are you all right?" asked Harrison. "Just a scraped knee, I think" replied Hannah. She continued, "What was that all about? Was that...was that a gunshot?" Harrison thought momentarily of diffusing the situation with some half-truths, but he has grown increasingly weary of building relationships on hidden and twisted facts.

"Yes, they were Hannah" stated Harrison as calmly as he could. "But why?" asked Hannah in such a way as to imply, 'Why you?' knowing full well that she has no known enemies in Italy—at least not of the ilk that would hunt her down and kill her. Harrison took a deep breath and said calmly once again, "Sometimes my assignments for the President attract, shall we say, some undesirable, seedy characters. They would like nothing other than to see the President's negotiating efforts fail if not at least interrupted. I'm sorry that you got involved in my little war. Perhaps we'd better take a rain check for lunch under the circumstances." "Nonsense" replied Hannah in her best journalistic firm and assertive tone. "You invited me to lunch and you're not going to get out of it that easy," Hannah smiled. Harrison smiled back and approved of her moxie. He liked risk-taking in a woman, an appealing woman at that. Harrison asked mockingly, "So, you're not afraid?" "Of course I'm afraid," Hannah retorted. "I don't usually get shot at when I'm in the company of a man, even a handsome man."

Harrison accepted the compliment without a remark and countered, "It's your life." He swung out his right hand and motioned Hannah to finish their short walk to the Casa di Pasta. However, this time, Harrison was hyper-vigilant as he took in a panoramic view of their surroundings. Nothing seemed out of the ordinary although he knew that appearances could be deceiving. Harrison and Hannah continued walking ahead more cautiously than before. Harrison observed that even Hannah was looking around much more than before the brief barrage of bullets.

The couple, strangers to each other, arrived at Casa di Pasta without further incident and entered the cozy, dimly lit restaurant. It was busy as always, but Paolo Peddu, the owner of Casa di Pasta, recognized Harrison immediately. Paolo moved sharply through the gathering hungry crowd. He stepped lively toward the newly met couple and said excitedly, "Ciao, Mr. Rossetti. How wonderful to see you again!" "Ciao," Harrison returned. "I would like you to meet Miss Littleton." Paolo smiled as he turned toward Hannah and politely said, "Ciao." He turned back toward Harrison, "Your usual table, Mr. Rossetti." "Si, grazie" replied Harrison. Paolo motioned Harrison and his guest to a discreet table in the corner of the restaurant. He gave his special guests two menus and left momentarily.

There was a short silence between the strangers broken by Hannah. "What do you recommend?" she inquired looking up and down her menu. "The pasta is all good here because of their special sauce. It was a family recipe that Paolo received from his great grandmother—subtle and not too spicy. So, just order your favorite pasta and I promise you won't be disappointed." With that, Hannah and Harrison returned to their review of their menus and the mouth-watering entrees before them.

Paolo returned with the house salad and several loaves of hot Italian bread. 'What a handsome couple,' he said to himself and asked, "Are you ready to order, madam?" "Yes, I think I will have the cannelloni" Paolo smiled, "Si" and turned to Harrison. "Your usual sir?" "Si, grazie" replied Harrison. Paolo took their menus and left their table.

"Your usual?" Hannah smiled with some irony in her voice. "Is that another secret or can you tell me 'your usual'?" "Meat ravioli," came Harrison's 'what else' kind of reply. Harrison's thoughts drifted away from their conversation even with the striking distraction before him. He had a really good idea who was behind the spray of bullets. Harrison's digression did not go unnoticed by Hannah. "Spia?" she said coyly. Harrison's hair literally stood on end as he was shocked back to the reality of the present. He looked at Hannah and for one of the very few times in his life he was at a loss for words. The couple silently gazed at each other as Harrison's shocked expression did not wane. A flash of Josetta's image past by in memory as the name *Spia* was uttered so blatantly.

"I'll ask you not to refer to me in that manner again,"

Harrison said defensively and with ire. His facial expression betrayed the feelings he had not intended to expose to Hannah. Harrison was dismayed at himself for failing to control his emotions upon hearing the term of endearment coming from anybody except from his holy friend, Josetta. Yet, he was uncertain as to why it disturbed him so. He made no immediate sense of his reaction, which in itself told him he was analyzing the events too superficially. Perhaps that was it—thinking and analyzing—odd problem solving tools for trying to illuminate an emotional response. Harrison was only vaguely aware of Hannah's distress in crossing a line that she had not known was drawn. She wanted to say something, perhaps that she was sorry; however, she dared not to at the moment given the consternation displayed by the complex man sitting across the table from her. Harrison continued his inner review of his…his what? His embarrassment of hearing *Spia* spoken out of the context of his relationship with Josetta…his anger because indeed that characterized much of what he was…his sadness due to memories of his holy friend flooded his mind…his secrecy for that which was always a part of him…his what? 'Damn it,' thought Harrison. Josetta again passed in his memory ensued by a quiet smile. Harrison's egocentric thoughts were consuming him. He glanced upward and observed what appeared to be concern and hurt on Hannah's face. "I'm sorry," Harrison said as he shook his head not knowing further what to say. How could he tell Hannah why *Spia* upset him so when he was confused himself over the hold that it had on him…or was he simply ignoring the obvious?

Harrison again looked at Hannah. There appeared to be more concern than hurt in her expression now. She reached out her hand and gently placed it on Harrison's arm. The gentle touch was reassuring to him and he nodded his thankfulness to her. "We don't need to talk about that now," said Hannah in a tender voice. Again, Harrison was at a loss for words and nodded. He thought to himself that there was no sense in trying to explain to this charming, sensitive woman who had moxie what he did not understand himself.

They quietly finished their salad aware of each other yet not violating each other's personal and emotional space. Hannah knew that what she had said had struck a nerve, a deep nerve. It was not important to her now why that was. She sensed that she would find out some day what lay below the surface of this intricate man.

Paolo returned to the table with their main course. Hannah politely complimented the owner on the taste of his house salad. 'A fine blend of seasonings' she thought. Harrison reinforced the sentiment and said, "As always, Paolo." "Grazie," uttered the proud man before leaving the table. Hannah and Harrison began eating their main course. "This is wonderful," Hannah said excitedly after consuming several mouthfuls. Harrison agreed and commented, "You know, for all the times that I've been here, the rich taste of the sauce never changes."

"How long have you known Paolo?" Hannah asked. "Almost as long as I've known the Pontiff," was Harrison's reply. He continued, "Actually, Josetta introduced me to Paolo and the Casa di Pasta about—well, I guess it would be about twelve years ago. Josetta was a priest from one of Italy's local regions at St. Maria Goretti parish. I was on special assignment at the time and much younger. Communism was a more severe threat back then than it is now. The covert operation in which I participated took an unsuspecting turn. We were betrayed and my colleague was killed. I was severely wounded. I wasn't sure where I was going or who to trust when I came upon this small church. "St. Maria Goretti?"

18

Hannah interjected. "Yes," replied Harrison. "And the man that helped you was Joseph Josetta?" surmised Hannah. "Yes, except that was not his name at the time. His birth name was Josepha Modesta...Father Josepha Modesta. He was, and still is, a fearless man of God. Josetta helped me and he was well aware that he put his own life very much at risk. He sheltered me in his church and sent one of his parishioners to find the local doctor. Meanwhile, Josetta did what he could to clean my wounds and stem the tide of infection. He told me that this was nothing new for him as he often observed his father provide similar acts of benevolence in war-torn Italy during World War II."

"I bet the Pontiff has helped you out of trouble many times since then," smiled Hannah. "Trouble, always" mused Harrison thinking of his holy friend. "Well, obviously you pulled through since you are here," noted Hannah. "I pulled through only because Josetta risked his life for mine—a stranger to him. The one who betrayed our operation got word that the local doctor was summoned to the church to treat 'gun wounds.' He had a very good hunch that I was the wounded man."

"This Judas came to the church?" asked Hannah realizing that she played on the identified betrayer of Jesus. "Not only did he come to the church, he came even before the doctor arrived. Josetta was treating me in the small vestibule of the church. What struck me at the time was Josetta's street smartness. You'd think a man in his line of work would be 'brain smart' and 'street stupid.' Josetta knew that I was still in danger and the fact that I escaped was a mistake that would not be overlooked. Once he dressed my wounds as best as he could, he took me through a hidden stairway under one of the pews. The crude stairs led downward under the church to burial vaults for the local priests and nuns. This burial place was not public knowledge. Josetta believed I would be safest there. He asked me to remain quiet and that he would return once the doctor had arrived. Josetta feared the worse and indicated he'd do his best to wash away the blood stains on the church floor and on himself."

Hannah's interest intensified as she peered deeper into Harrison's eyes. He continued his story: "I could hear muzzled sounds coming from above and echoing in the silent vacuum. In the solitude, the cold dampness of the burial grounds began permeating my aching body. The pain of my wounds surfaced as my adrenalin slowed following the care provided by Josetta. He patched me up the best he could, but the tide of blood continued oozing from my wounds."

Harrison stopped momentarily and winced as if he again was feeling the pain of long ago as it occurred then. Hannah leaned forward and gently stroked his hand. Harrison sighed at the touch of the beautiful woman. He continued, "I did not realize everything that was unfolding above me or how grave was the situation. What I tell you now was what emerged based on what Josetta told me and what I experienced." Harrison's attention was drawn briefly to the tender stimulation at the hands of Hannah. He regained his focus and continued, "Josetta had just completed washing away the bloodstains on himself and the church floor when two strangers entered the sanctuary. They did not approach the padre at first, but they began walking up and down the aisle glancing between the rustic pews. The bulges in their jackets did not go unnoticed by Josetta. He knew that they did not come to his church to pray, but rather they came looking for their prey."

Harrison's recounting was interrupted by Paolo who observed much food still on their plates: "The food... You don't like?" Hannah and Harrison said together, "The food is wonderful. Grande!" "Ah, grazie" said the restaurateur. In a desire to justify why she still had much food on her plate, Hannah offered, "Harrison was just telling me about the time he first met Pope Josetta." "Josetta," said Paolo softly and with respect. He then made the sign of the cross by touching his right hand to his forehead, to his chest, to his left shoulder and then to his right shoulder. Paolo pulled a crucifix from inside his shirt; one blessed by Josetta, and kissed it reverently.

Upon paying his respect to the Pontiff, Paolo said to Harrison, "You owe much to Josetta—he gets you out of trouble, yes?" "Out of trouble, always" mused Harrison for the third time today. Paolo looked inquisitively at his old friend. Harrison waved his hand as if to say 'never mind' and then said, "Si, Paolo, Josetta has done much for me." Harrison's remarks brought an approving and knowing smile to the owner's face. At that, Paolo said, "Mi scusi" and left the couple's table.

Hannah was anxious for Harrison to continue his life story. "So?" she asked innocently. There was a pause before Harrison retorted, "So what?" Hannah simply stared at Harrison and he got the message. Harrison took a deep breath and commented, "Maybe we should take a moment to finish our food before it all becomes cold." A furrow developed on Hannah's forehead as she gazed intently at Harrison. She said in a loud voice, "Food! Food! How can you think of food at a time like this?" "Because I'm hungry" was the storyteller's honest reply.

Hannah did not appear as amused as he did to his response, honest or not. Harrison decided that it was best to comply and recalled, "The men in the church were growing impatient, as they did not find me. They began opening what doors they could in the church. Josetta was concerned that they might find the hidden stairway under the pews. At grave personal risk, he decided to approach the gunmen. As Josetta

approached one of the men, the stranger put his hand inside his jacket swelling the size of the already prominent bulge. The holy priest introduced
himself to the gunman and asked if he could be of service. At first, the stranger said nothing and continued his search. Josetta persisted in questioning the man and asked..." Harrison's recanting was interrupted once again by Paolo who handed him a message. Harrison thanked the owner who withdrew and then quickly scanned the message given to him. Hannah observed a tense expression on her companion's face and asked, "Is there something wrong?" There was a pause as Harrison thought for a moment as he stared away from Hannah. He turned toward her and said abruptly, "I have to go now. I'm sorry about lunch. We will have to finish our story later." Hannah asked hurriedly, "Where can I get a hold of you?" He shook his head 'no' and said, "You can't. However, tell me where you are staying and I will contact you when I can." Hannah appeared disappointed wondering if she would actually ever hear from Harrison again. "I'm staying at the Albergo Sull'acqua." Harrison nodded and called for the owner. Paolo appeared and Harrison requested, "Please take care of my friend, Hannah." He gave Paolo fifty dollars in Italian lire, told Hannah that he would talk to her later and left the restaurant. Hannah sighed as she sat alone at the table. Unbeknown to her, it would be one of many times that she would find herself alone as 'urgent business' called Harrison away. She gazed at the exquisitely tasting food on her plate, moving pieces nonchalantly with her fork. "Well," she said aloud to no one, "No sense in letting this fine cuisine go to waste." As if receiving confirmation of her thoughts from nobody in particular, Hannah picked up Harrison's plate of meat ravioli and gently moved the succulent pasta onto her plate. 'Who said you can't mix pastas?' she thought

rhetorically.   Hannah devoured the food on her plate less delicately than if Harrison were still present. It was almost too much for her, but she managed to consume most of what remained on her, er, their plate.

Chapter 4

You're Mine Tonight

"Roma! Roma!" hailed the train conductor. The announcement jarred Hannah away from the past and back to the present. It took her several seconds to realize where she was and where she was going. Hannah glanced at her watch and noted happily that the train arrived on time in Rome. It also dawned on her that Harrison never did finish telling the story about how he first met Josetta. 'Well, we'll see about that!' she thought to herself and tried to feel miffed without much success. Harrison told Hannah that he would try to meet her at Saint Peter's Station. Hannah was becoming all too familiar with Harrison's inability to consistently comply with his schedule. She did not like it, but she was learning how to tolerate it—not accept his inconsistencies mind you, but tolerate them nonetheless.

The train pulled into Saint Peter's Station on schedule. Hannah peered through her window seat to the crowd of people who gathered to welcome the rail passengers and board the train for other destinations. Her eyes darted for their full range of movement as she strained to see her beloved Harrison. Disappointment crept inside her, as her eyes detected nobody recognizable. Hannah sighed, grabbed her belongings and bit her lower lip. As she stepped off the train, she heard a charming and familiar voice that brought a smile to her face. "Didn't think I'd make it, did you now?" taunted Harrison. "On the contrary, I knew you'd be here," said Hannah although her long face just moments ago masked her true sentiments. She dropped her belongings and reached out to give Harrison a sustained bear hug. Harrison returned the firm embrace and said, "Missed me, huh?" "Actually, I've been too busy fitting my wedding dress to miss you too much," replied Hannah as she continued her nuzzling. The expression on her face and the enduring embrace, however, belied her words. Hannah did miss Harrison. She always missed him. She never knew if the last time she saw him...if the last time she touched him...if the last time she heard him...would indeed be the last time.

Hannah regretfully disengaged herself from Harrison and peered intently into his eyes at arms length. Harrison decided quickly that whatever that facial expression meant, he took a remorseful offense and asked apologetically, "I know that look and for whatever I did, for what I'm doing now or for what I'm about to do, I am truly sorry." 'There,' thought Harrison to himself, 'that should cover just about everything.' Meanwhile, Hannah was pleased with herself in her training of Harrison. She snapped, "You didn't finish it!" Harrison looked bewildered and asked with genuine naiveté, "Didn't finish what?" He added quickly, "And please don't tell me that if I don't know what you are talking about, you're not going to tell me!" Hannah was just as quick to stop the smile that was forming on her face and said, "You didn't finish your story about the first time you met Pope Joseph Josetta!" Harrison shook his head in amazement and quipped, "Hannah, I began telling you that story about four months ago when we first met—over lunch at Casa di Pasta." Harrison shook his head and said with some irony in his voice, "For God's sake, it just dawned on you at this moment?" Hannah replied, "No, silly! I was thinking about how we first met on the train ride from Carrara."

Harrison smiled, kissed Hannah firmly and said genuinely, "You are indeed a gem!"

"Well?" said Hannah neither persuaded by Harrison's manner nor maneuver. "You want me to finish it right now?"

asked Harrison rather astonished. "Yes," replied Hannah. "Right here in the middle of the train station?" Harrison asked incredibly. "Yes," insisted Hannah. "I have a better idea," Harrison noted. "Josetta wants to meet you principally because he does not believe that anyone in this world would or could put up with me, let alone love, marry and live with me twenty-four hours a day. It just so happens that we have an audience with Pope Josetta tomorrow. You can ask His Holiness to finish the rest of the story." Hannah gleamed at the news only to be interrupted by Harrison, "Ah, but he wants to meet you as my betrothed, not as a journalist. He worries that there won't be anybody around to take care of me after his death." This was more than acceptable to Hannah in light of having the honor to meet this great, holy man of God.

Having reached a pleasant compromise, Hannah and Harrison left the train station. He hailed a cab and requested that the driver take them to his suite at the *Fontana Spruzza* hotel. "Si," replied the driver. However, before he drove off, Hannah interjected, "No, honey. I want to so some shopping before we go to the hotel." Harrison nodded and requested that the driver go instead to the *Piazza de Spagna*.

The cab sped away from the station. The *Piazza de Spagna* is the heart of Rome's most fashionable shopping area. Everyone, because of the Spanish steps ascending grandly from the Piazza, recognizes it. It was a sunny day in Rome making the drive a pleasant one for the senses. "Now what do you need to shop for, my dear?" asked Harrison. "Oh, you know, wedding stuff," was her general reply. Harrison continued, "Remember, we have reservations for dinner at the *Commedia Bastona* this evening. The Italian-American comedian Monk Melloni is on stage tonight. He was a former priest and now a comedian—go figure!" "What is it with you and these priests?" Hannah joked. "They're my guardian angels," was Harrison's childlike reply.

The cab arrived at the *Piazza de Spagna*. Hannah and Harrison stepped out of the cab and found themselves at the bottom of the Spanish steps leading to the Piazza. There were a number of native residents and tourists perched on the steps watching street musicians, vendors and other sightseers. The multitude of young lovers did not escape Harrison's eye as he mumbled to himself and thought, "Amore!" "Watch it, lover boy! You belong to me," cautioned Hannah. "I wouldn't have it any other way," Harrison replied judiciously.

Hannah and Harrison window-shopped for a good part of the afternoon at the fashionable boutiques. They blended in the surroundings much like the natives of Rome which was aided by Harrison's command of the Italian language. Harrison did not question Hannah's purchases or the lire that flowed out of his pocket much like the water out of Rome's fountains. Money was not an issue for this special occasion.

Much to Harrison's satisfaction, Hannah finally completed her shopping. The couple hailed a cab and headed for the *Fontana Spruzza* hotel. The trip to the hotel was a short one. Harrison paid and tipped the driver. He gathered Hannah's purchases, no mere feat for the human male, and followed her into the lobby of the hotel. Harrison set down the packages and walked up to the clerk. He asked for the keys to room 1310. "Certainly, Mr. Rossetti" was the clerk's reply. A porter gathered the purchases and the couple took the elevator to the 13th floor. Hannah remarked, "I guess you are not particularly superstitious," as she walked out of the elevator. Harrison smiled at Hannah, but did not counter with a response.

The porter opened the door and the couple entered the room. Hannah nodded her approval of Harrison's choice of suites. The porter secured the packages and left the room after receiving a generous tip from Harrison. He brought his fiancée's packages and suitcases into the bedroom and placed them on the king size bed. Hannah began sorting her belongings and purchases, placing them in their proper place.

Hannah turned to Harrison and asked, "What time tomorrow morning are we scheduled to see the Pontiff?" "Well, if nothing out of the ordinary occurs, at eleven o'clock," was his tempered reply. Harrison continued, "We have about an hour to freshen up before dinner." Hannah walked over to Harrison and kissed him passionately as she embraced him. She said seductively, "We may need more than an hour..." The two lovers floated onto the bed as Harrison muttered, "Indeed."

Harrison and Hannah arrived at the *Commedia Bastona* about an hour late for their reservation. They had sufficient time for a light meal before the comedian, Monk Melloni, was scheduled to come on stage. Hannah and Harrison finished their wine and meal just as the lights lowered. They ordered espresso as Joseph walked on stage.

"Buona sera e benvenuto a bella Roma!" Harrison translated for Hannah, as needed: "Good evening and welcome to beautiful Rome. My name is Monk Melloni. I'm a native of Perguia, but spent many of my early years growing up in America. I'm also single. In fact, I've been single for quite awhile. I know this because I use to dream about women. Then I began dreaming about women eating food. Now, I just dream about food!" Monk paused as the crowd laughed and applauded.

"For those of you who haven't guessed, I'm Italian. We Italian men tend to be excessive in what we do. When we're dating, we send lots of flowers; we hug and kiss a lot; we pinch a lot; we pinch a lot; we pinch a lot..." repeated Monk as he made a pinching motion with his fingers on his right hand. The comedian continued, "And we're excessive when we end a relationship too 'cause you're likely to wake up with a horse's head in your bed...or even worse, my cousin Guido!" The audience laughed as Monk paused.

"We don't even treat our dead with respect. Italians bury their dead with their butts sticking up out of the ground. That way when we visit the grave, we have some place to park our bikes!" The audience laughed again and applauded.

"As an Italian growing-up in America, we pretty much lived by the same rules and sayings that guided other families—we just said them a little bit differently. When the American parents tried to teach their children to always be prepared, they said, 'Don't get caught with your pants down.' My parents taught me the same thing except they said, 'No canna live in Venice with no gondola!" Monk continued after some laughter from the crowd, "And when American parents told their children to 'always wear clean underwear in case of an accident and you have to go to the hospital,' my parents taught us the same thing except they said, 'No canna live in Venice with no gondola!" More laughter was heard from the audience. "And when American parents told their children to 'always look before they leap,' my parents said, 'everybody,' (Monk peered into the crowd and held out his hands) 'No canna live in Venice with no gondola!" The audience laughed and applauded.

"Like most Italians, I grew up in a Catholic family. We have many beliefs and one of them is that our guardian angel is always with us. In fact, in elementary school, the good nuns always reminded us to sit far to the left and leave room for our guardian angel that always sat on our right side. You knew this was true each time you looked in any classroom. What you saw was one or more Catholic students tumbling to the floor because they moved too far and fell out of their chairs!" Some light laughter rose from the audience.

Monk continued, "I love my parents, but talk about neurosis on parade! Stress around them is quite relative. Over the years, I've developed this three-night visiting rule. I can't visit for more than three consecutive nights. If I do, I run out of patience; I run out of energy; and I run out of Imodium—I just run out all over the place!" Harrison, Hannah and the crowd erupted in laughter.

"You know, I've been single for so long that I decided to join a singles group here in Rome. I often think back about the time I spent in a Catholic seminary. Now, I find myself in a singles group!" Laughter rose from the audience. "Had I known I was going to live a celibate life anyway, I think I would have stayed in the priesthood!" The audience laughed and applauded.

"Seminarians or not, we were typical teenagers. I remember once we were attending a Good Friday service at the local convent. Within this cloister of nuns, the good sisters took the vow of silence. Imagine any woman taking the vow of silence!" The comment drew cheers from the male audience and jeers from the women. Monk continued, "The nuns did not interact with the outside world. They were not on line; there was no Internet. The convent used this rotating wooden tube as a conveyance for material. A simple pull of the rope rang a bell signaling that the material was ready. This was quite efficient unless the hearing-impaired nun was on duty that day. You could ring that terrible bell 'til hell froze over' and it wouldn't matter." The crowd laughed. "My friend and I argued whether or not he could fit inside the tube. After much serious debate between the two of us, he decided to take the direct approach and jumped right into the cylindrical transporter. As my friend crouched in the tube to prove he could fit, I impulsively pulled the rope. I don't know why I did it. It just seemed like the natural thing to do." Laughter erupted from the crowd. Monk continued, "The bell rang and the cylinder began rotating. My friend, who was about to pick up some bad habits, disappeared into the swallowing jowls of the convent. And he was gone in an instant. I imagined, like in a bad science fiction episode where the transporters went amuck, he would return as a melted molten mess of massive mucous membranes! I began firing off 'Our Fathers' and 'Hail Mary's' like it was my last anointing and Satan was right on my tail. Then, in desperation, the only thing I could think of saying was, 'Beam him back, Scotty!" The audience laughed.

Monk paused and then said, "After several long minutes, the tube rotated back slowly. My friend gradually appeared, his atoms arranged seemingly in all the right places, and nothing looked obviously wrong. I asked him, "What happened? What did you see?" Even though he was in a trance-like state, he managed to mutter, "No canna live in Venice with no Gondola!"

Monk paused briefly and said, "Thank you all for coming tonight. Thank you very much." The audience applauded loudly to show their appreciation. Hannah and Harrison applauded with them and followed the crowd out into the romantic Roma evening.

Harrison and Hannah returned to their hotel. They barely walked inside their room when Hannah kissed Harrison in a long embrace. The moment was very intense as they quickly undressed each other. They fell into bed and continued their embrace. Love with Harrison has always been satisfying both physically and emotionally...and tonight was no exception. Their high state of arousal minimized the need for much foreplay. Hannah and Harrison reach their orgasmic peaks and were entwined in a lover's embrace.

Chapter 5

Software Down

It was nearly three o'clock in the morning when a barely audible buzz was heard from the phone. The lovers were still intertwined in their embrace. Harrison freed himself as gently as he could so as not to awaken Hannah. He reached for the phone and half-jokingly hoped it was a wrong number. Harrison was as alert as anybody could be when awakened abruptly during the early morning hours.

Harrison switched on the nightstand light and picked up the phone. He managed to mumble, "Hello." "We have a special-coded message for Hardware" was the terse reply. Hardware was Harrison's designation assigned specifically to him by President Ashton. Harrison said abruptly, "One moment" and gathered paper and pen to transcribe the message. He returned to the phone and uttered, "Ready." Harrison listened intently to the message as he translated its true meaning. A look of horror transformed his groggy facial expression as he decoded the incoming dispatch.

Harrison hung up the phone slowly without looking at the bridge base for the receiver. He stared at the deciphered message as if he had surely made an error in his transcription. Harrison read the message aloud as if hearing it would provide credibility to its content: "Whereabouts of Software unknown. Report home immediately." Software was the designation that President Ashton assigned for herself.

Harrison stared intently at the message, as he stood motionless in the silence. He closed his eyes only to have them reopen to the same insane reality. He phoned the Rome airport and asked for his private hangar number. Harrison requested that his private jet be readied for a flight to the United States and that he would be there within the hour to file his flight plan.

Harrison gazed at his fiancée who was sleeping angelically before him. He knew he would be unable to meet with Josetta tomorrow as scheduled. Harrison gently nudged Hannah, but she did not awaken. He shook her softly once again and called out her name. Hannah stirred, but once again she did not awaken. Harrison shook Hannah again while shouting loudly, "Hannah! Hannah!" This time Hannah awoke slowly and focused her vision on her intended. "Harrison?" she called out. Hannah asked unsurely, "Harrison. What's the matter?" Harrison did not immediately answer her realizing that she was not fully conscious. Hannah sat up at the side of the bed. She stared at Harrison, but she did not say anything. He looked as if his life energy was drained from his face. Harrison spoke finally, "I've been ordered to return to Washington, D.C. on the next flight." He offered nothing more. Hannah had a queried look on her face, but did not request anything further from him. Harrison spoke, "You know I can't tell you why, but it is urgent." Hannah got up from the bed, wiped the sleep from her eyes and kissed Harrison. She went to the closet and retrieved several suitcases. She packed Harrison's clothes as he washed and dressed.

Numerous scenarios and their contingencies raced through Harrison's mind since he received the flash message. In all the years of service with the U.S. government, there never had been a severed link between the President and those sworn to protect the temporary occupant of the oval office. 'How could Software disappear without a trace?' thought Harrison. Brushing aside the political realities of the office for the moment, he wondered how Elizabeth Ashton—the woman, wife and mother—was faring. Harrison was aware of his growing sadness for Software, but he knew that he must try to remain focused.

Harrison knew that the security staff already took steps even before he received the coded message. Vice-president Neff Jameson, codename Scanner, was first notified of the President's disappearance. Modem, codename for President Ashton's husband, Richard Ashton, was advised. The chiefs of staff and heads of the Security Council were informed. These steps were typically taken all things being equal. 'But,' thought Harrison, 'Are all things equal with the disappearance of the first woman President of the United States?'

Harrison's thoughts were interrupted by Hannah's question, "How long do you think you will be gone?" She knew the reply without asking the question. "It's impossible to say," was Harrison's expected response. "What should I do about our scheduled appointment with His Holiness tomorrow?" asked Hannah. "Josetta," Harrison said silently bowing and shaking his head. Josetta was looking forward to meeting Hannah probably just as much if not more so than Hannah meeting him. Harrison always looked forward to his visits with Josetta. He especially awaited tomorrow's visit with great anticipation. Harrison so much wanted his holy friend to meet the woman who was to take care of him for the rest of his life. Harrison looked at Hannah with some anguish and uttered slowly, "I'm afraid I'm not going to be able to visit Josetta with you." There was a brief pause as Harrison registered the disappointment in Hannah's face. Harrison asked, "How do you feel about visiting the Pontiff without me?"

Hannah responded without delay, "I think you know it would mean much more to me…well, to all of us if we could all visit together." Harrison shook his head in agreement. He reiterated, "But I will not be here tomorrow. I may not be back for a long time." "Is it that serious?" inquired Hannah. "Yes, I'm afraid so," was the grave reply.

The comment brought the communiqué about Software back into focus. Harrison finished dressing and called the hotel clerk. He requested a cab in ten minutes to take him to the airport. Harrison turned to Hannah and said, "Why not think about it? The visit is not scheduled until eleven o'clock tomorrow morning. Just be sure to cancel the appointment with the Holy Office if you decide not to go. But I know you, Hannah. Give my regards and love to Josetta."

With that, Harrison embraced and kissed Hannah. As he began pulling away, she brought him closer. Hannah wanted to keep his arms around her for as long as she could. She did not know when she would see him again or *if* she would see him ever again. Harrison understood Hannah's body language and held her tightly against him. Now they were both reluctant to let each other go. "Oh, Harrison" cried Hannah in breaking their silence. She knew that from what little he told her and not keeping his scheduled visit with his holy friend that the situation was indeed grave.

Time was working against the lovers. Harrison slowly pulled away from the embrace that united them, an embrace that gave him a sense of peace and caring. Hannah regrettably let him go as they kissed once more. "I'll call you when I can, but don't expect to hear from me anytime soon or often," said Harrison. Hannah gently stroked the face of her beloved as she spoke in a trembling voice, "I'll be thinking about you…" "You mean worrying about me," Harrison interrupted. "That too," said Hannah exposing a glimpse of a smile. With another kiss, the couple parted and Harrison left the room.

The tears that Hannah proudly held in check streamed freely down her face. She walked slowly toward the bed and slid back under the covers. Hannah turned off the light at her bedside. She knew that the darkness produced by her action was a feigned attempt at engaging sleep. Hannah's mind was racing with concerns for her Harrison. There was no way for Hannah not to worry when she was not with him. Although Hannah needed her rest, sleep would take a backseat not only tonight, but also perhaps many nights.

Chapter 6

Target 'Target One'

Harrison arrived at the Rome airport less than two hours after receiving the message that reported the disappearance of Software. Not knowing President Ashton's whereabouts was disturbing in and of itself without having any knowledge of the circumstances of her disappearance. Harrison paid the cab driver and walked toward the hangar that shrouded Target One, his private jet. He filed his flight plan to Washington, D.C. and reviewed his plans for scheduled refueling.

With everything in apparent order, Harrison boarded Target One and entered the cockpit. He belted himself into the pilot's seat and began his routine instrument check for the flight. As Harrison stepped through the checklist, the scent of Hannah on his clothes made his mind drift to thoughts of her and their embrace of not long ago. Distracted by the image, Harrison took a deep breath, cleared his mind and focused on his flight preparations.

With the checklist complete, Harrison rolled Target One out of the hangar and began taxiing toward the runway. He radioed the tower his intentions, "Roma Airport, this is Target One, over." After a slight pause, the tower replied, "Go ahead Target One." "Target One ready to taxi," transmitted Harrison. "Target One, you are clear for takeoff on runway 318," authorized the tower. "Roger,". replied Harrison. He accelerated the jet and listened as the engines grinded from a low hum to a high pitch scream. Harrison steered Target One in the direction of runway 318. He glanced skyward at the distant horizon. The darkness was retreating as dawn broke over Italy. Harrison turned the corner onto runway 318. He stopped at the edge of the runway and scanned his instrument panel one last time for any anomalies, but he was alerted to none.

Harrison radioed the tower for final clearance. "Hold for incoming flight," was the traffic controller's warning. "Roger control," radioed Harrison. Except for the droll scream of the engines, silence shrouded the cockpit. As the time of the hold by the tower grew, so did Harrison's impatience. He was anxious to become airborne for it was in the air that he planned to contact Mentor. Harrison received his orders from and was responsible to Mentor. There was no paper trail for Mentor or the organization that Harrison pledged his allegiance. The line from Mentor to the President had no branches; neither did the line from Mentor to Hardware. Harrison's reflections were interrupted by Roma control, "Target One, you are clear for take off. Have a pleasant flight. Ciao." "Thank you. Target One out."

The scream of the engines increased in pitch as Harrison accelerated and guided the jet down the runway. The rumble of the runway gave way to the smoothness of flight as the jet lifted off the runway. Harrison continued his glide path until Target One reached 10,000 feet in accordance with his flight plan. He engaged the autopilot and unbuckled himself from the pilot's seat. Harrison glanced at the instrument panel and scanned the many devices to determine that their readings were within normal parameters. Having satisfied himself of their performance, he walked out of the cockpit and into a small office adjacent to the cockpit.

The size of the office belied the power of the electronics, weapons and other equipment it contained. Harrison pushed one of several buttons on his desk that lowered a panel on the wall. The opening revealed sensitive communications equipment adapted with scrambling devices and peripherals such as a fax machine, video conferencing monitors, and satellite tracking instruments.

Harrison sat in front of the communications array and donned a set of earphones. He placed the transmitter in scramble mode and broadcasted freely, "Hardware to Mentor. Hardware to Mentor. Over." Static filled his ears, as no reply was forthcoming. Harrison repeated his broadcast and waited. Within a minute came the reply, "Hardware, stand by for Mentor." Static again filled the silence...a long silence. The anticipation heightened Harrison's senses as the adrenalin surged within him.

"Hardware, this is Mentor, came the long awaited voice. Harrison responded immediately, "Mentor, this is Hardware, go ahead." "Harrison, quickly, what's your altitude?" "Target One is at 10,000 feet" was the pilot's terse reply. Harrison continued, "Why do you..." but Mentor interrupted him. "Not sure, listen carefully. Scout, who was stationed in California and Eagle, who was based in Texas were ordered to fly here by me shortly after you received your message in Rome. Both their planes disappeared off radar at 8,000 feet." "Sabotage?" queried Harrison. "Much too coincidental to suspect otherwise," was his superior's reply. Mentor continued, "We have cleanup teams headed for their last known radar position, but that will take considerable time. Suspect either a time bomb or one trigger by altitude once it is armed. We can't take any chances, Harrison. I need you on this one. Suggest you canvass Target One and maintain present altitude. Do not, I repeat, do not go below 8,000 feet."

Harrison's adrenalin flowed freely once again. "Understood Mentor, was his reply. "Where is Software?" asked Harrison. "Likelihood that security has been compromised. Will discuss all circumstances surrounding Software upon your arrival," replied the executive. The comforting voice continued, "Be careful, Harrison. Use your sixth sense and even that seventh sense of yours. Come home safe." "Will do Mentor. Hardware out." With that, Harrison closed the communications panel and returned to Target One's cockpit.

Harrison entered the cockpit and stared immediately at his altimeter. He sighed with some relief as it continued to read 10,000 feet. Harrison gazed at the other indicators to rule out even the slightest hit of tampering or sabotage. He checked the autopilot's heading, speed and altitude one more time. He also inspected his fuel level. This was not a time to make a mental error. 'Must keep above 8,000 feet,' he reminded himself. Harrison decided to search the jet methodically and started at the rear of the plane. He grabbed a flashlight, left the cockpit and headed toward the back of Target One. Harrison hoped that if there was an explosive device aboard that it was inside the jet and not mounted on the external fuselage. That would be very bad news indeed. Harrison also reminded himself that the explosive device could be time-detonated and not impacted by the jet's altitude.

Harrison began his search by opening every panel above the seats, including the overhead storage compartments. He shined the narrow intensive beam of light into every nook and cranny visible to the naked eye. Harrison looked for any sign of an explosive device, especially extra wires mounted along the fuselage. He was quite familiar with Target One as he helped perform maintenance on her for the past five years.

The longer that Harrison searched the queasier his feeling. 'It should be the other way around' he thought to himself. 'What if I missed something?' echoed in his mind. His thoughts turned to more personal feelings. 'Never see Hannah again? And Pope Josetta and President Ashton?' Harrison returned to his search and focused intently on finding something before his search's end. Time seemed to pass quickly for Harrison. 'Too fast' he believed as he knew that time was not on his side. Harrison reached the front of the jet in his search, but found nothing above the seats. He turned around and looked back to where he had been. 'Could I have missed something?' Harrison shrugged that possibility. He knelt down and bent over as he flashed the narrow beam of light under the first row of seats. He reached under each seat with his free hand in an attempt to uncover something that felt out of place. Harrison cautiously carried out this same search pattern for the remaining five rows of seats. As he finished exploring the last row of seats, he shook his head in disbelief that he had not found any explosive device or hint of sabotage.

Harrison next opened the floor panels near the middle row of seats that led to the small cargo hold under the belly of the jet. He pushed back cautiously each panel, feeling around the edges and underneath for anything out of the ordinary. Harrison then leaned forward causing his head to disappear below floor level. His light scanned the cargo area and revealed nothing but cobwebs. Harrison tried to remember the last time he stored equipment in the cargo hold.

Harrison backed out of the opening of the cargo hold. He secured the panels to the opening on the floor and replaced the section of carpeting that covered the panel doors. Harrison entered the cockpit of the jet once more to check on the status of the autopilot and other instruments. He was again relieved to find that Target One was maintaining 10,000 feet and heading toward the eastern continental seaboard of the United States.

Feeling satisfied with Target One's autopilot performance, Harrison left the cockpit and walked into the small office where several hours earlier he learned the fate of his colleagues...his former colleagues, Scout and Eagle. 'His former colleagues' he thought reluctantly. He pondered momentarily whether or not he would suffer a similar fate. Harrison began his search of the office by removing the panels that hid various electronic components. He examined carefully the electronic gear paying close attention to the motherboards, wiring and cabling. Harrison pushed aside wires and removed components as he searched for any sort of detonating device. 'At this pace,' he thought to himself, 'the search will take considerable time.' He then mumbled in irony, 'I hope I've got the time.'

Harrison continued the cumbersome task of checking for any abnormality to his equipment. His search thus far yielded nothing except that his office was overrun with dust mites. Harrison was beginning to think that Target One was not violated and that he was safe. Or was it just a false sense of security that replaced his diminished adrenalin?

Harrison completed the search of his private jet in less than three hours. If there was an explosive device, it was not on board. It was unsettling to Harrison that the device may be mounted to the outer hull of his jet. Will he disappear with Target One as the turbojet descended below 8,000 feet? Harrison gave some thought of inspecting Target One a second time, but decided that his initial search was a thorough one.

Harrison sat at his desk and prepared a fax for Mentor: "Exhaustive search of Target One negative. Proceeding according to plan. Will land at alternative site. Say again, will land at alternative site. Will need transport." Harrison decided not to throw caution to the wind if internal security was indeed compromised. Typically, he would fly into Washington Dulles International Airport in Chantilly, Virginia, but there was no sense in showing his colors if Target One survived the descent. Harrison inserted the note and pushed several buttons that automated the transmission process. The fax machine rang out with its familiar electronic signature. The note was scrambled as a matter of routine and sent to Mentor.

Harrison returned to the cockpit. He was about six hours away from the continental United States. He planned to start his descent while still over the Atlantic. If Target One exploded at or below 8,000 feet, he did not want to endanger the innocent people below by dropping a rain of torn and twisted metal on them.

Harrison folded his arms and laid back as far as he could into the pilot's seat. He did not dare close his eyes, but he needed some mental rest. Harrison's thoughts drifted to Hannah as they always did in his semi-relaxed state. He looked at his watch and realized

that it was almost ten o'clock in the morning in Rome. If Hannah decided to keep their scheduled visit with Josetta, his fiancée and holy friend would meet for the first time in one hour.

Chapter 7

The Holy Man and the Sinner

Hannah sat in front of the mirror trying to achieve the proper appearance respectful of the office of the Holy See. She has met and interviewed a number of dignitaries during her career as a journalist, but none holds a match to the audience with the Pontiff. Hannah decided to keep their scheduled appointment with Josetta even though Harrison was unable to be with her. She so wanted to see the two men together who on the surface seemed to be such a mismatch of purpose and ideals. Besides, Hannah knew full well that she would spend a great deal of her time thinking about Harrison and the risks that he was taking for his country.

Hannah called the front desk and asked that a cab be ready in thirty minutes. She stood near a full-length mirror and made final adjustments to her appearance. Hannah glanced up and down the length of the mirror and was satisfied with her image. She walked over by the desk and sat down. Hannah opened each desk drawer in turn until she came across some hotel stationery. She knew that Harrison might not be able to contact her anytime soon and decided to write him a letter. Hannah desired minimally that Harrison knew she was thinking of him. She thought for a moment with the pen hovering over the stationery. She began writing as she became satisfied with her thoughts. Hannah wrote:

"Dear Darling,
    I know that you are busy and engaged with your mission. I just wanted you to know how much I care about you. Time away from you passes slowly. I

decided to meet with your holy friend, Josetta. I'm sure he'll have some interesting things to tell me about you [that which Hannah was certain]. At the least maybe he will finish your story! I will give him your love. I look forward to seeing you again. My thoughts are with you.

Love, your H."

Hannah addressed the letter as Harrison had instructed her with a simple post office box number somewhere in Washington, D.C. She was not sure where in Washington the letter terminated, but she was certain that Harrison would receive it when the conditions were 'right.' Hannah grabbed her purse and held onto the letter. She took the hotel elevator down to the lobby. The hotel clerk greeted her and said, "Your cab is ready, Miss Littleton." Hannah replied, "Thank you. Please post this letter for me." The clerk took the letter from Hannah. She walked out the door where a cab was waiting for her. The cab driver stood by the door and opened it for her as she approached. Hannah slipped inside the rear seat of the cab. The driver closed the door and walked around the back of the cab to the driver's side. He sat in the driver's seat, turned around toward Hannah and asked, "Where to, Miss?" "Vatican City," was his passenger's reply. The driver turned facing toward the front and put the cab in gear. He drove away from the hotel and headed for Vatican City all the while glancing intermittently in the mirror at his beautiful passenger.

The drive was a pleasant one in the late morning. They arrived at the Vatican in less than thirty minutes. Hannah paid the driver and passed the Swiss Papal Guards as she entered the Holy See. She walked up to a frocked priest sitting at a desk and introduced herself, "Good morning, Father. My name is Hannah Littleton. My fiancé, Harrison Rossetti, and I have an audience with the Pontiff at eleven o'clock this morning. However, Mr. Rossetti was unable to keep the appointment." The good Father smiled at Hannah and opened a ledger on the desk. He scanned the names and appointment times with his finger looking for Harrison's familiar name. The priest came upon the names of Harrison and Hannah and said, "Yes, Miss Littleton. Your visit has been confirmed. Pope Josetta is ill although seems in better spirits today. He always looks forward to a visit from Mr. Rossetti. He will be disappointed that Mr. Rossetti was unable to attend this morning. I'm sure, however, that he will be happy to meet with you. Please have a seat and we will call for you when the Pontiff is ready." The priest motioned to a row of chairs across from the desk. Hannah thanked the holy man and took a seat as indicated.

As Hannah waited, she occupied herself by looking at the various paintings and carvings on the wall. That the Vatican had one of the best art collections was well known and from what little that Hannah observed from her vantage point, such a claim was not an unwarranted one. Behind Hannah was the *Lord's Prayer* written beautifully in Italian. She read the words to herself:

'Nostro Padre, che arte in cielo, ha santificato è il Suo nome il Suo regno viene, Suo sarà fatto, Su terra come è in cielo. Ci dia questo giorno il nostro pane quotidiano E perdona noi le nostre trasgressioni come perdoniamo quelli che va oltre i limiti del lecito contro noi E piombo noi non in tentazione, ma consegna noi da cattivo. Amen.'

Hannah's thoughts suddenly turned to Harrison. 'The human mind was so amazing; someone or something can be so far away and yet so nearby in one's mind' she thought to herself. She took a moment to pray for her beloved's safe return to her.

Hannah's prayer was interrupted by a short, thin cleric.

"You must be Miss Littleton," said the priest. He reached out his hand and introduced himself, "I am Father Alan Pusniche. Harrison did not exaggerate his claims about you." Hannah was somewhat taken back at the clergyman's familiarity, but managed to reach for the cleric's hand and shake it firmly. "You know my fiancé?" she managed to ask with some humility. "Oh, yes" said the priest. "Mr. Rossetti has visited the Holy Father for many years and is quite familiar to those of us in the Holy Office. Is Harrison not with you?" "No," Hannah replied conveying disappointment. "He received an urgent call early this morning and is flying back to the States as we speak." "It's always urgent for your Harrison" commented Father Pusniche. Hannah was unsure as to the tone of the comment, but agreed, "Yes, it seems to be." The priest motioned Hannah to follow him as he walked ahead of her.

Hannah and the priest walked down a long passageway that led to a door protected by a Swiss Papal guard. Neither the sentry nor the priest spoke, but the guard stepped aside as they approached. Father Pusniche opened the door and Hannah found herself in the outer office of the Pope's private quarters. The priest motioned Hannah to sit at one of the office chairs and said, "If you will sit here, I will check if the Holy Father is ready to receive you." With that, the cleric disappeared behind a second door.

The papal office was not what Hannah had expected. It appeared stark in contrast to the ornamental trappings of the Vatican proper. The office reflected the life of a simple, humble man. A wooden crucifix hung on the wall above the door. A picture of Jesus wearing a crown of thorns adorned another wall. The papal desk appeared to be that of highly polished walnut. Three stacks of paper were neatly arranged on the top of the desk along with the usual office supplies. There was an overstuffed chair behind the desk that appeared out-of-place, perhaps used temporarily by the Pontiff since the onset of his illness. Hannah wondered how often Harrison sat in this very office awaiting his holy friend.

Within 15 minutes, Father Pusniche returned to the outer office. He smiled at Hannah and then he asked her to follow him. The priest walked through the archway of the inner door with Hannah immediately behind him. They entered a narrow passageway that was dimly lit. The walls were bare and peeling in several places. Hannah was surprised at the distance traveled down the corridor. They finally reached the end of the passageway and proceeded through another archway. Hannah found herself in a small waiting room that contained three chairs and nothing more. Father Pusniche requested that she sit one more time as he entered the Pontiff's bedroom. Hannah smiled at the priest and complied with his request.

Hannah sat for a brief minute and was then motioned by Father Pusniche who stood at the doorway. She walked through the door as requested. As Hannah entered the room, the priest smiled, bowed toward the Pontiff and quietly left the room.

Hannah was mesmerized as she first gazed on the Holy Father. He was sitting up in his canopy bed with a broad smile on his face. His complexion was pale and he seemed tired. She walked the few steps to the side of his bed and sat in a chair used apparently by his guests. Josetta spoke first, "Buona mattina [good morning]. Welcome to Vatican City, Miss Littleton." "Good morning, your excellency. Please call me Hannah" was the woman's simple request. The Pontiff shook his hand and said, "And you, please call me Josetta." Hannah shook her head affirmatively as the Pontiff continued, "I'm sorry that *Spia* is not with you. How is Harrison?" Hannah was somewhat taken aback at the holy man's use of *Spia*, but she was beginning to understand why Harrison preferred that she herself did not identify him in that way.

The genuine warmth in Josetta's voice reflected the intensity of their friendship. "Harrison is fine. He so much wanted to be here today and asked me to be sure to convey his respect and best wishes to you. He received an urgent message from Washington early this morning and flew out immediately." Hannah's face could not hide her disappointment and concern for Harrison. Her expression also did not go unnoticed by Josetta. He attempted to comfort and assure Hannah, *"Spia* is highly trained and can take care of himself, Hannah. You may have to get use to this worrying about Harrison given his occupation." Hannah appreciated the holy man's concern for her whom he just met for the very first time. She was also comforted by the passion in his voice. Josetta continued, "It will take a special woman to care for him and adjust to his lifestyle…a woman with, what did *Spia* say, a woman with moxie? He told me that you are that woman, yes?" Hannah smiled as she remembered her first encounter with Harrison. She replied with confidence, "Yes, I am that woman." Josetta smiled and nodded in approval at her conviction.

"Tell me about yourself," the holy man said although he knew much about Hannah already as she was one of Harrison's favorite topics and certainly a healthy diversion from the rest of his lifestyle. "Well," Hannah replied, "I was born in Boston, Massachusetts in the United States. My father was editor-in-chief of a Boston newspaper before he retired. My mother was a housewife and took care of my two older brothers and me. Although my brothers did not, I guess I got the newsprint bug early. The newspaper fascinated me. My dad read parts of the paper to me each evening. I seldom asked questions about the content of the articles, but always wanted to know how the writers went about drafting their stories." Josetta was vitalized by the passion in Hannah's voice. She continued, "I studied journalism at Harvard. I was hired as a journalist by the *Washington Sun* five years ago and now cover special assignments." "Like the death of a Pope?" interrupted Josetta with an uneasy smile. "Harrison and I pray for your recovery and hope you have many years. You've been quite progressive, you know." "Progressive?" uttered Josetta with disdain. "There's that word again," he muttered with a push of his hand.

Hannah asked, "Harrison told you how we met?" "Yes," said the Pontiff with a broad smile. "I guess I'm somewhat responsible since he met you after a...shall we say a dejected visit with me?" reflected the holy man. "Then maybe you will finish the story about how you met my Harrison?" begged Hannah. "Did *Spia* not say anything about our early partnership in crime?" queried Josetta. "Partnership in crime?" the betrothed lady asked in turn. Josetta stared at Hannah, but did not say anything. She clarified, "Yes, in a manner of speaking, he did; however, my dear Harrison did not finish the story and apparently left out more than I suspected. Harrison thought that perhaps you might give me a first hand account." Hannah paused and then continued, "He told me that he was on a mission in Italy that had gone badly. He was wounded and found his way to your church in Carrara. Harrison stated that you bandaged his wounds as best as you could given the severity of his injuries. He told me that you hid him in the burial vault below your church. Harrison said that two gunmen came looking for him in the church and you confronted them...And that's where our dear friend Mr. Rossetti left me hanging, your Excellency" said Hannah with slight annoyance. "Ah, yes" commented Josetta with concern. He continued, "I can see why he would stop there." "You mean my fiancé intentionally ended the story at that very point?" asked Hannah more in irritation than annoyance.

"Perhaps…Perhaps my dear friend was trying to protect me and what I had to do that day 17 years ago." Josetta's voice grew hoarse and he coughed to clear his throat. He thought back 17 years ago and the images of that day flooded his mind as if the events occurred yesterday. "Forgive me," he said humbly. Hannah smiled as if to say, 'Never you mind.' The holy man proceeded, "As *Spia* told you, two gunmen entered my church. They were rather rude men and shall we say not at all patient?" Josetta paused briefly as his statement echoed. He continued, "One of the gunmen was a lean, tall man who had a scar on the right side of his nose. The other thug was more menacing, a big fellow with murderous eyes and several tattoos on his arms. He also had two scars on his face that were larger and more visible than the other gunmen."

Josetta rested for a moment, cleared his throat once again and continued. "Mi scusi. I knew that if they found the doorway to the burial vault below the church where Harrison was hidden, he would not survive the confrontation. I too would be…how do you Americans say, 'loose ends' and expendable. It was obvious that these men were not here for negotiation. They were out for blood."

Josetta rested momentarily and then proceeded, "When the gunmen first entered the church, they did not have their guns drawn. However, it was clear from the bulges in their dress that they were very well armed. The gunmen did not approach me at first. They busied themselves looking around the church by opening doors and checking between the congregational pews." The Pontiffs rendition of the events of his first meeting with Harrison was again interrupted by coughing and clearing his throat. "I am sorry" he offered. "Maybe you should rest and I can come back another time" Hannah suggested. "And leave you hanging again like our beloved Harrison?" said

Josetta emphatically. "Besides, I don't know how much time I have." The comment saddened Hannah, but she did her best to conceal it.

Josetta managed a slight smile and proceeded, "The gunmen were nearing the end of their search. They had scrutinized the obvious. I knew that they would soon be disgruntled by their efforts and search the less obvious. I decided to approach them in hopes of defusing the situation or at the very least steer them away from the church. I greeted the tall, less threatening gunman who simply stared at me. After introducing myself, I asked if I could be of service. Again, the gunman stared at me and uttered nothing. Our one-sided conversation, however, did not go unnoticed by the other assassin."

Josetta stopped to rid himself of the rasp in his voice. His cough lingered this time. Hannah asked if she could get him anything to which he nodded 'no'. The holy man continued, "As the second gunman approached, I again introduced myself and smiled uneasily. He took out a large caliber handgun from inside his jacket and struck me hard on the side of my face. I collapsed to one knee, not a position for which I'm unfamiliar by the way, and held the side of my face which ached severely from the blow." As the holy man spoke, Hannah noticed a scar on the left side of his face. Josetta continued, "The tall gunman did not move or react in any way. He apparently had witnessed such viciousness before from his colleague. The other gunman who struck me walked forward and aimed his gun inches from my head. At that moment, I knew I was dead. Whether or not I betrayed *Spia,* their brutality certainly suggested that I would be sacrificed. Theirs were not the kind of enterprise known for leaving loose ends."

Josetta patted his chest as he coughed once again. "Mi scusi. This persistent cough is most irritating...," he said as he paused and waved his hand. "I was too frightened to be scared," said the holy man in truth with a hesitant smile. Hannah listened intently and easily understood how others gathered strength from this humble man. Josetta continued, "The man holding a gun in one hand and my life in the other said tersely to me, 'You are hiding a man, a wounded man. You will turn him over to me if you value your life!' He then cocked his gun. I enjoyed and valued life, of course, but my soul was at peace with God and prepared always for death."

Josetta stopped and reached for a glass of water from the bedside table. Hannah rose immediately, picked up the glass and handed it to him. Josetta took several sips from the glass and returned it to Hannah. He contemplated for a moment what he told Hannah thus far and spoke slowly. "I asked the gunman to help me up off my knee. I knew that if I were to gain the upper advantage, it was going to be at that very moment. The other gunman still had his hands down with no weapon in view. As the mercenary with the gun reached out with his free hand to assist me, I jerked his hand quickly. He stumbled to the ground, in shock I imagine, losing his gun in the process. Whether by fate or an act of God, the gun skidded toward me. I was not a stranger to firearms as my father often took me hunting as a 'bambino'—a little boy."

Josetta began coughing once more. Hannah rose from her chair and gave the Pontiff his glass of water. The holy man took several swallows of the liquid and returned the glass to Hannah. Hannah sat down as Josetta cleared his throat and continued, "I only had seconds to beg for God's mercy and forgiveness as I grabbed the gun. The thin, tall assassin who a moment ago was unarmed had reached for his weapon. I said aloud, 'Mother of God please forgive me.' I fired once dropping the man to the church floor. He laid still and he appeared no longer a threat. I then turned my attention to the other gunman who was no longer on the floor. He reached under his jacket presumably for another weapon. I fired again, but the weapon did not discharge. Several more pulls of the trigger yielded nothing but my disbelief and fear. The assassin pulled out a large knife and lunged toward me. I attempted to move out of the path of the man and his weapon, but was unable to do so. The cold steel of the knife forced itself into my left upper chest. The gunman dislodged the knife and was prepared to stab me again. As I lay on my back, I knew I would not survive a second assault. I again asked for God's forgiveness and to accept my soul in His Kingdom. The assassin smiled smugly and I remember his words to this day: 'You should have surrendered him. Now you will die for your misplaced loyalty.' As the gunman reached back with his knife to end my life, semiautomatic gunfire rang out. The mercenary fell backward to the ground in a hail of bullets. He lay motionless as the knife that would have ended my life dropped slowly out of his hand. I managed with some effort to turn around toward the direction of the gunfire. Our friend Harrison was moving toward me."

Hannah's eyes moistened as she better understood Josetta's friendship with her Harrison. She comprehended clearly now the bond that existed between the holy man and the sinner. They saved the lives of each other risking their own. Yet, Hannah was aware of Josetta's guilt of serving as the reluctant instigator of violence and death. It must be intolerable for a man of God ordained to protect life, to uplift life and to celebrate life to take it away even under such extraordinary circumstances. Josetta's personal demon was an ongoing struggle of conscience in his life.

Hannah stood and moved toward Josetta. She reached out to him. Their hands joined and they held each other firmly. Hannah spoke, "You need your rest, Holy Father. I cannot tell you how much meeting you has meant to me. I understand why Harrison speaks so fondly and genuinely about you. Thank you for reliving a painful part of your past just for me." Josetta waived his hand as he often did before he spoke and said, *"Spia* and I have shared much over the years. And now he brings me you. You are much prettier on the eyes than your fiancé—be sure to tell Harrison I said so." Josetta and Hannah both managed a smile. Hannah spoke, "I will tell him. Meanwhile, you get your rest. I want to meet again when Harrison and I can visit together with you. Your friendship means so much to him." "And you? You can take care of my *Spia* knowing what you know and don't know about him?" said Josetta coyly. They both understood what was said and left unsaid. Hannah replied, "We will all take care of each other." Josetta afforded a hearty laugh, one of few laughs in the past months, and countered, "You should be a diplomat!" The two growing friends managed a laugh again. Hannah knelt at Josetta's bedside and spoke, "May the strength of God be with you." Josetta nodded as he watched Hannah rise and disappear from his sight. He lay back in his bed, coughing once again. Josetta closed his eyes in hopes of securing some needed sleep. He drifted to sleep not knowing if he would awaken again in the physical world, not knowing if he would share in the friendship of Harrison and Hannah.

Hannah attempted to control the tears swelling in her eyes as she walked down the narrow passageway. As she walked out the corridor, Father Pusniche stood on the other side. Hannah thanked him for his kindness. She could hardly control the wetness in her eyes and quickly walked out of the Vatican. Hannah cried quietly but openly as the noon sun shined directly overhead. Except for the tears, it was a beautiful day in Roma.

Chapter 8

Going Down

The uncertain journey from Italy to Washington, D.C. was nearing its end. 'Hopefully, that will not be prophetic' Harrison thought to himself. He sat motionlessly in the cockpit as the autopilot sustained the aircraft's navigation, speed and altitude. Target One has maintained 10,000 feet since its departure from Roma Airport. A thorough search of the private jet revealed no explosive devices—well, at least no explosives on board. Harrison bit his lower lip as he once again considered the possibility of an external detonation. He could not keep the fate of his colleagues from disrupting his thoughts. Would Harrison suffer a similar fate as did Scout and Eagle at 8,000 feet?

Harrison grabbed his flight map as thoughts of Hannah drifted into his mind as they often did during the course of the flight. He assumed that her visit with Josetta had ended by now. Harrison hoped that his holy friend was lying comfortably. He wondered if Josetta finished telling Hannah the events surrounding their first meeting. Sadness came over Harrison much like storm clouds spoiling a sunny, summer day. It distressed him that he was not able to meet with Hannah and Josetta. He prayed that Josetta would still be alive and sufficiently well to receive them once the objectives of his mission were resolved. On the other hand, perhaps it was Harrison's life that was in jeopardy.

'My mission' Harrison yelled loudly in anger as he threw his flight map to the floor. 'I might die even before my mission takes off!' Harrison pondered, 'Where was President Ashton? Was she still alive? Why was she kidnapped? What plan had Mentor designed to resolve the situation?' The questions rattled through Harrison's mind, but no answers were provided even superficial ones. Of course, if Harrison did not survive the descent to the airport, neither the questions nor their answers would be particularly meaningful to him.

Hannah's image once again sailed into Harrison's mind. He was amazed that he had survived without Hannah for so many years and yet…and yet he could not remain focused for several hours outside of her presence. Harrison thought that if his fate should mimic that of his colleagues, he would never see Hannah again. She knew that his missions were sometimes very dangerous, but she was unaware fortunately of the recent deaths of his colleagues.

The moment of releasing the autopilot and beginning the descent to 8,000 feet was fast approaching. Harrison walked out of the cockpit and sat behind the desk in his small office. He wanted Hannah to know that his last thoughts were of her, if indeed they were his final thoughts. Harrison removed a sheet of stationery out of his desk. He gathered his thoughts and began writing:

"My Dear Hannah,

I will soon land in Washington and receive my assignment. I regret that you are not with me. You are always in my thoughts. Your presence in my life has created a void when you are not here. I miss your soothing voice, smiling face and gentle touch. The moments pass so differently when we're apart, my love. Your radiance compliments the beauty found in nature and natural things are fortified by your presence. Without you, my love, the beauty of the rising and setting sun is diminished. The twinkling of stars in the night sky is tarnished. I am more whole with you than without you. I miss you terribly. Be assured that I will contact you as often as the mission permits. Take care, my love.

Your H."

Harrison glanced at the message before placing his labor of love in the fax machine. He quickly sketched a cover page with instructions as to where the fax should be redirected. Harrison then pushed the coded buttons to send his letter to its destination. The machine whirled and his innermost thoughts were transported across the vast sky. Harrison checked that the ending procedure flashed on the facsimile indicated that his letter was processed successfully.

Harrison left the office and entered the cockpit of Target One. He immediately scanned the instrument panel as he sat down in the pilot's seat. The plane's current position indicated that he was about one hour outside of the alternative Washington, D.C. airport. It was time to release the autopilot and return Target One's controls to his capable hands.

Harrison took hold of the autopilot switch and let his hand rest for a moment. Adrenalin was building quickly as he mused to himself, 'Well, are you a man or a mouse?' Harrison rubbed his cheeks with his free hand and let his fingers glide downward across his chin. He took a deep, slow breath and radioed the Washington D.C.-2 airport. "D.C.-2, this is Target One. D.C.-2, this is Target One, over." Static filled the blue sky as he awaited a reply. A moment passed before Harrison heard from the tower. "Target One, this is D.C.-2, over." "D.C.-2," Harrison radioed, "Request permission for a gradual descent to 8,000 feet." The transmitter was again void of human voices and static filled the air. The tower then interrupted the static. "Target One, you are clear for a gradual descent to eight-zero-zero-zero. Change your heading to course 365 and contact the tower when level at 8,000." "Roger, D.C.-2" confirmed Harrison. "Good luck, Hardware," added the tower. Harrison knew that the use of his code name was a sign of respect to him and in memory of his two comrades who failed to make it home.

Harrison was calm outside, but his body was tingling with inner tension. He again placed his hand on the autopilot switch where it had been moments ago. Target One and he were at an impasse once more where neither could ignore the other. The man and his plane were at a fork in the road where all paths led in only one direction—down.

Harrison grabbed hold of the steering as he switched off the autopilot. The jet dipped slightly as he held the steering firmly. Harrison scanned the many dials and gauges of the instrument panel to look for any warning signs of danger. He pushed forward on the steering and the jet began its slow descent. Harrison gazed at the altimeter—9,500 feet. He searched the gauges again and noted nothing suspicious. Harrison looked back at the altimeter—9,000 feet. He swallowed voluntarily and leveled Target One at 9,000 feet.

Harrison's mind raced as he reexamined his search of Target One. This was not the time to make a mistake, even a minor one. He knew Target One forward and backward. If there was something hid on this plane, it could not have escaped him. Harrison did not have time to research the jet. He was running low on fuel. If an explosive did not tear him apart in midair, an empty fuel tank would accomplish the same as he slammed into the ocean.

Harrison shook his head to clear his thoughts. He was certain that he did not overlook anything on board. Still, outside was another matter. Harrison again pulled forward slightly on the steering and Target One responded by gliding downward. He searched the instrument panel repeatedly, evaluating parameters as he read them. Nothing was out of order, so far.

Harrison checked the altimeter—8, 500 feet. The cockpit was quiet beyond the whine of the engines. 'So far so good,' he thought to himself. He looked again—8, 400 feet. Unexpectedly, a high pitch-warning buzzard broke the eerie silence. Harrison scanned quickly the panel in front of him. The buzzard drew his attention to an illuminated gauge. "Oh, damn," he exclaimed. The warning light was indicating fire in his left engine. Harrison glanced in the direction of the engine. He saw some smoke and a flash of fire. He reacted instinctively and pulled the extinguisher switch for the left engine. Harrison had little time to think, but he wondered whether a detonation device had been planted in the engine—or was this simply an unbelievably horrible coincidence? Harrison struggled to maintain an even flight level. He decided to cut the left engine in hopes of restarting it once the fire and smoke subsided. He flipped another switch and terminated the flow of jet fuel to the damaged engine. As he fought for control of his jet, Harrison transmitted an SOS, "Mayday! Mayday! D.C.-2. This is Target One. One engine on fire and down. Struggling to maintain 8-3-0-0 feet. Heading 3-2-7 about 20 minutes outside of D.C.-2. Do you read?" Harrison did not wait long before repeating his message: "Mayday! Mayday! D.C.-2. This is Target One. One engine on fire and down. Struggling to maintain 8-3-0-0 feet. Heading 3-2-7 about forty-five minutes outside of D.C.-2. Do you read?"

Harrison did not have to repeat his SOS a third time. "Target One, this is D.C.-2." There was a pause from the tower and then a familiar voice transmitted. "Hardware, this is Mentor. What's your status, Harrison?" "It's good to hear your voice, Mentor" said Harrison. "Things are not good up here. I've shut down my left engine fire-warning indicator.

Struggling to maintain altitude and course with one engine. Uncertain whether an explosive device is planted or a technical problem. Do not know how long I can maintain level flight, over."

"Harrison, I've already lost two agents—two friends. I don't want to lose a third," was Mentor's reply. "Can you restart your engine? Over." Harrison struggled with the vibration of Target One as he worked at maintaining his altitude. He glanced at the altimeter and read 8, 250 feet. What if the engine fire was simply coincidental and an explosive device was armed to detonate at 8,000 feet? Harrison shook his head and focused on the crisis at hand. If he did not maintain control, the resulting accident would be just as fatal as any bomb purposely planted to end his life.

The sweat rolled down Harrison's face as he gripped firmly Target One's steering. He knew there was a chance at survival if he could restart the engine. Harrison glanced to his left and no longer observed any smoke or fire trailing from the engine. He wondered how much damage had occurred and whether the integrity of the engine had survived the insult. With these thoughts racing through his mind, Harrison finally replied to Mentor; "Don't know the extent of damage. No smoke or fire observed in left engine...now approaching 8-2-0-0 feet." Harrison managed a brief smile as he radioed, "Which door, Mentor, the lady or the tiger?" Mentor did not respond although he grasped Harrison's meaning. As Target One approached 8,000 feet, whether the engine restarted or not, an explosive device would seal Harrison's fate.

Mentor broke the silence between the two men: "So, what's it going to be, Hardware?" Harrison being a student of efficiency decided to descend below 8,000 feet. He reasoned that there was no use in struggling to restart Target One's engine only to be blown to bits seconds later. Although

Mentor knew Harrison well enough to deduce the answer, Hardware spoke tersely, "Will descend to 7,500 feet before attempting restart." After a moment of silence, he spoke more softly and grappled with the words, "Greg...I faxed a note to my special box. It's to Hannah. Be sure that she gets it, won't you?" This time there was no pause between to the men. "Send it yourself when you get here," was Mentor's quick reply. He continued, "Harrison, I have scrambled helicopters for support and rescue. Good luck and see you soon." "Roger," was Harrison's brisk reply.

Harrison restored the microphone to its slated slot. He checked the instrument panel for any variance in parameters and noted none except those relative to the stalled engine. He glanced at the altimeter once more and read 8-1-5-0 feet. The sweat from his brow seeped like water streaming unchecked from a broken tap. In a few moments Harrison would know his fate—at least a part of it. If there was no detonation device, fate once again would have the opportunity to play its hand. The engine would have to restart if Harrison was to land the jet safely. The odds were not in Hardware's favor, but they would certainly improve if Target One survived the descent below 8,000 feet.

Harrison closed his eyes momentarily and envisioned Hannah. He wanted a sharp image of her and as that image unfolded he got that and more. Tears swelled in Harrison's eyes as the loveliness of Hannah crystallized in his mind. He wanted desperately to be out of danger—to be with her. He wanted to tell her, right now, how much he loved her.

Harrison blinked the tears away from his eyes and reality shrouded him. He gazed at the altimeter and read a somewhat blurred 8-1-0-0. Harrison stared straight ahead and observed for the first time the bright sun and clear blue sky. He glanced at the instrument panel one final time before pushing forward on the steering. Target One responded to the mechanical command and dipped its nose. As Harrison struggled to maintain control over the damaged jet, he stared intently at the altimeter. Target One was descending...8-0-7-5 feet...8-0-5-0 feet...8-0-2-5 feet. Harrison gripped the steering firmly as he approached 8,000 feet. Target One continued to descend and now was at 8,010 feet. The failed engine was silent. Its healthy twin screamed as the jet proceeded with its descent working overtime to provide the power necessary to keep Target One airborne.

Harrison lightly pushed forward on the steering and kept a watchful eye on the altimeter—8010 feet...8009 feet...8008 feet...8007 feet...8006 feet...8005 feet... 8004 feet...8003 feet...8002 feet...8001 feet. Harrison squinted his eyes and grasped tighter the steering as he now read 8000 feet. He leveled out at 8000 feet to ponder his fate; yet, there was still no other choice but down.

Harrison focused once again on the altimeter readings and pushed the steering forward—7-9-5-0 feet...7-9-0-0 feet...7-8-5-0 feet...7-8-0-0 feet...7-7-5-0 feet...7-7-0-0 feet. No visible changes occurred during the course of his flight and more important, no explosion. Harrison took a deep breath and felt some reduction in tension. He was unwilling to relax in order to keep the sharp edge necessary to sustain him during the unfolding crisis. Harrison decided not to radio Mentor. He knew D.C.-2 was tracking him on radar and were aware of his altitude. Harrison suspected that Mentor was breathing a little easier as well. The first crisis appeared over unless an explosive device was armed for a different altitude or by time. Harrison was not going to allow the possibilities to fog his thinking. He would need all his cunning and training as he attempted to restart Target One and keep a level flight.

Harrison flipped open the switch that he closed previously

to choke off jet fuel to the downed engine. He hoped that the fuel was surging through its normal path in preparation of providing sustained nourishment. Target One was losing altitude. Harrison glanced at the altimeter and noted a flight altitude of 7,500 feet. 'It's now or never,' Harrison thought to himself.

On the ground, Mentor was relieved that Hardware was maintaining 7,500 feet and that Target One was apparently intact. The question of demolition or not appeared to be answered. Harrison was indeed fortunate. Mentor was in the position of having to replace two irreplaceable colleagues. He did not want to replace a third. As much as he wanted to contact Harrison, Mentor resisted the temptation knowing that Harrison would soon face his second challenge—restarting Target One's left engine.

Up in the sky, Harrison closed his eyes briefly. His eyes opened as quickly as they closed. Harrison glanced at the altimeter, which was now at 7,000 feet. He checked the fuel gauge and noted that the amount of petroleum indicated was barely sufficient to land at D.C.-2—he hoped. As the healthy engine whined, Harrison flipped the switched to restart the left engine. At first, he heard nothing and noted no change. Harrison switched off the engine and then tried once again. He glanced at the altimeter and read 6-0-0-0 feet. He forced the switch hard as if the extra pressure would make a difference. He yelled aloud, "Come on! Do it, damn it!" Another glance of the altimeter indicated that his altitude was now at 5,000 feet.

Mentor continued to monitor the altitude of Target One on the ground. He asked the radar traffic controller of Harrison's status and was told, "5,000 feet and descending fast, sir." Mentor requested that he be informed of Target One's descent for every 200 feet. The air traffic controller nodded his understanding of the order. Within several minutes, Mentor heard "4,800 feet sir and still descending." Mentor stared skyward as if Target One would appear intact above him. His thoughts were interrupted once again by an updated report, "4,600 feet sir and dropping." Mentor banged his fist against the ledge before him and said inaudibly, "Damn you, Harrison!" His right fist remained closed tightly as if he was contemplating repeating the action. "Sir, 4,400 feet and still descending" was the familiar recount. The air traffic controller looked at Mentor with concern and perhaps was simply mirroring the distress on Mentor's face. Mentor nodded his head slightly as if to confirm the traffic controller's suspicions. Within moments, "4,200 feet sir" echoed in the enclosed control tower. Mentor wanted to displace some of the tension developing within him. He began pacing the tower placing his hands behind his back. The more he paced, the less it seemed to help overall. Several minutes later he heard, "Now at 4,000 feet and still descending sir." Mentor's pace quickened. He knew that Target One would disappear off the radar in a few minutes at its rate of descent. Mentor closed his eyes as if he desired some inner peace. His grasp for inner strength was interrupted by another progress report, "3,800 feet, sir." Again the air traffic controller stared at Mentor, but turned around to focus on the monitor that was projecting Target One's plunge to earth.

Mentor continued his swift pace up and down the tower's corridor. He ached as he heard progressively plummeting reports on Target One..."3,600 feet...3,400 feet, sir...3,200 feet and falling, sir...3-0-0-0 feet, sir." It became clear to Mentor that Hardware was meeting with little success at restarting Target One's engine. Perhaps what the missing explosives did not accomplish, the left engine of Target One would and seal the fate of its sole passenger.

Target One was racing toward terra earth. Harrison continued the pressure on the engine switch. He looked at his altimeter and read 2,900 feet. Harrison checked the fuel flow to the engines and the gauges betrayed nothing out of the ordinary. What was clear, however, was that his fuel was dangerously low. Harrison stopped engaging the engine switch. He checked the altitude once again and noted that Target One was now at 2,800 feet.

At D.C.-2, the air traffic controller echoed Harrison's flight level as he had repetitively done so since Target One's descent. Mentor knew that they would soon lose radar contact, as the private jet would be below radar signals. In the end, they would know nothing on the ground unless Harrison radioed them or they found the remains of Target One. As Mentor considered the possibilities, the controller interrupted his thoughts, "Sorry, sir. He's off radar now. Nothing more we can do from here." At those words, Mentor headed his way out of the control tower. A helicopter was waiting on the ground to take him to the last known radar contact. From there, a trajectory given Target One's rate of descent would be used to identify the jet's most probable and perhaps fatal position.

Harrison glanced at the altimeter as he turned the engine switch again. He was now at 2,000 feet. Unexpectedly, the once silent engine began a slow whine and its turbo began its revolutions. Target One continued its involuntary descent and was now at 1,500 feet. The whirl of the engine became stronger. The stability of Target One was improving. Harrison was feeling relieved as he managed to level out Target One at 1,200 feet. With the accomplishment of level flight, Harrison body flushed out the tension that just moments before invaded his every cell. His pilot seat was wet from the nervous sweat that oozed from every gland of his body.

Mentor was making his way toward his helicopter. He saw

from a distance that its blades were revolving and idling, ready for take off. Mentor reached the copter in moments and stepped up to enter its inner hull. He motioned to the pilot with a "thumbs up" indicating his readiness for flight. The pilot nodded and the blades of the copter increased their whirl and whined. As the pilot began his ascent, Mentor received a radio message from the tower. The radar controller said with excitement, "Chopper One, there is an incoming message from Target One. Will transfer him to you on frequency 142.5." Mentor radioed back, "Roger, Tower. Will pick up on frequency 142.5." The pilot turned the radio dial to the designated frequency. Mentor was relieved to hear the undeniable voice of Harrison: "D.C.-2, this is Target One. Please acknowledge. D.C.-2, this is Target One, over."

Mentor could not disguise the excitement in his voice as he transmitted, "Harrison, don't you ever do that to me again! Do you hear me?" Harrison smiled broadly at the welcomed voice of Mentor. He radioed, "I'll gladly change places with you next time, Greg!" The colleagues and friends both laughed— something neither were able to do over the past several hours. They both wanted to jump in victory, but their circumstances did not permit them to do so.

Harrison transmitted, "Requesting permission to land at D.C.-2, over." The D.C.-2 control tower responded, "Permission granted, Target One. Come to heading 357 and use runway 222. Please acknowledge." Harrison radioed, "Acknowledged D.C.-2. Coming to heading 357 and will use runway 222. Will see you in about one hour, Mentor." "Roger, Hardware" transmitted Mentor. He added, "Welcome home!"

Harrison smiled and replaced the microphone. He checked his fuel gauge. It would be thin, but he believed there was sufficient fuel to land at D.C.-2. 'I certainly hope so,' he thought to himself. Mentor no doubt recalled the copters that were ordered to search for Target One's wreckage.

Within moments, D.C.-2 and runway 222 were in sight. Harrison made the final adjustments to Target One's glide path. He eased its nose downward and neared terra firma. Target One was centered over runway 222. Harrison pushed forward on the steering causing the tires to make contact with the pavement below him. Target One bounced and vibrated before its wheels made sustained contact with the runway. Harrison took a deep breath and slowly released it from his lungs. He throttled back on the engines to slow Target One and the jet gradually slowed. As the jet began to crawl, Harrison turned off the runway to a side path at the right. The path led to a special hangar where Target One would receive a thorough maintenance and diagnostic work-up.

As Harrison approached the hangar, the wide doors were opened and he was signaled to enter the shelter. He followed the directions given to him by the grounds person. Harrison slowly guided Target One to its resting place and throttled off the engines. He released his seat belt and stood to leave the cockpit. Harrison steadied himself as his "sky legs" made him wobble in his walk. He opened the jet's outer door and stepped out onto the mobile metal stairway that was placed in position. Harrison turned suddenly and patted Target One on her hull.

Harrison walked off the final step and both feet were now planted firmly on the ground. He turned around to take a look at Target One, perhaps to thank her for safely returning him. As Harrison walked away from the hangar, Mentor came running toward him. The two men grabbed each other firmly as they paused momentarily. They made eye contact, but remained silent. Mentor broke the silence, "Glad to see you, Harrison. You know, I don't need any more gray hairs than I already have." "Gray hairs," Harrison mused, "You're lucky to have any hair at all!" The physical and emotionally drained men smiled.   As they walked out of the hangar, special explosive and engineering teams passed them.   Harrison guessed that Mentor ordered that Target One be scrutinized inside and out to rule out the cause of the engine fire and perhaps a failed explosive charge on her outer hull.

Chapter 9

Double Take

Mentor, whose real identity was very guarded and known only to the President and the special agents he controlled, walked with Harrison into a waiting limousine by the air traffic control tower of D.C.-2 airport. Mentor nodded at the driver whom Harrison suspected knew their destination for he did not reply or utter a word. Harrison stared at Mentor who was staring back at him. "It's really good to see you in one piece, Harrison" beamed Mentor. "Not as happy as I am to see you Greg," replied Harrison. He very seldom addressed Mentor in the familiar, but he believed that the circumstances and the genuine warmth of their relationship justified its intimate use.

Harrison continued, "I regret the loss of agents Scout and Eagle. They were good agents and family men. I feel sorry for their families." "Yes, that they truly were" said Mentor. He continued, "They were not expendable. Their children had a right to grow up with fathers. It will be difficult to replace them after so many years. If not for the Grace of God and Hannah, I'm afraid that you too would be counted among them." Harrison neither grasped Mentor's subtle meaning nor responded verbally, but could not disguise the inquisitive look on his face. Moments later he asked simply, "Hannah?" "Yes, Hannah," insisted Mentor. If you were in the States as were Scout and Eagle, I have no doubt that Target One and you would have met a similar fate. Apparently, whoever was behind the sabotage literally did not have the time to reach your destination out of the country." "Well, you know I can always count on Hannah to save me from myself was Harrison's meager attempt at levity to lighten up a morbid

70

scenario.

Glancing out of the limousine's window, Harrison noted that they were headed into the heart of D.C. He asked somewhat hesitantly, "Where do we go from here?" "There is a special meeting scheduled for six o'clock this evening at the White House" replied Mentor. He continued, "We were ready to proceed with the meeting with or without you since we were uncertain about the outcome of your flight." "How comforting," mused Harrison. Mentor smiled in return and said, "We will drop you off at your place so that you can rest and refresh yourself. Be sure to dress formally. I suppose that you may want to contact somebody special, but I advise against it." "Oh?" was Harrison's simple inquire. "It is clear that whoever knew that Scout and Eagle worked directly under the President and murdered them, undoubtedly know that you do as well and would like to seal a similar fate for you. Contacting Hannah now could jeopardize your safety as well as hers." Harrison turned away and faced forward. The words spoken by Mentor were undoubtedly true. Harrison turned back toward Mentor and said with some sarcasm; "I bow to your superior thinking as usual" for he indeed did desire to contact Hannah.

Both men smiled and remained silent for several minutes, each lost in their own thoughts. Harrison soon broke the quiet by asking, "Any word about Software?" Mentor did not respond immediately and when he did reply, he chose his words deliberately: "Everything we know about President Ashton and what you need to know will be discussed this evening." This time it was Mentor who turned away from his agent. Harrison was both confused and concerned. It was unusual for Mentor not to relate something about a case, even some speculation; yet, he understood the seriousness of the situation in that it centered on not only the disappearance of the

President of the United States, but the first woman President of America.

The limousine slowed and pulled out of the mainstream of traffic. They were in front of Harrison's apartment. The limo came to a stop as Mentor turned toward his number one agent and said, "Harrison, this is the most serious crisis that we have faced during my tenure in D.C. Having lost several responsible and well-trained agents, I'm not willing to sacrifice another. Watch your backside. Whoever was behind all this obviously wanted to dismantle our organization in order to minimize the effectiveness and quickness of our response. I won't let that happen!" Mentor paused briefly and purposefully made direct eye contact with Harrison before continuing, "Hardware, you are ordered not to question anything at the staffing. The goal of the meeting is to dispense information. You will be briefed more fully later. You will not question anything you see or hear. Do we understand each other?" Harrison was unfamiliar with the tone of Mentor's voice, but has never had reason to question Mentor's directives. The two men shared a strong professional relationship for many years. Harrison had no delusion about who was in charge. As if to assure Mentor of his allegiance, Harrison affirmed, "You know I've never doubted your leadership, Greg, and as always, you have my complete support." In an attempt to inject some humor into the situation, Harrison added, "I'll just be a fly on the wall." Mentor smiled and nodded. The two men firmly shook hands and Harrison stepped out the limousine. The car pulled away from the curb and Harrison entered his apartment building.

Harrison walked up several flights of stairs to his apartment. He looked carefully at the apartment door and observed no foreign markings. Harrison unlocked the door and walked directly to his left as he entered his apartment. As he approached the alarm panel, he noted that the pattern of lights indicated no intrusion. Harrison scanned the apartment and observed nothing out of place to the human eye. He walked carefully through the rest of his apartment, but noted nothing out of the ordinary. Harrison entered his bedroom and stooped over to remove a section of carpeting. He next removed a panel concealed underneath the carpet, which revealed a secondary, independent alarm system. Harrison checked the settings to ensure that they agreed with the primary system. He again observed no deviation from that which was expected. Harrison closed the panel and replaced the section of carpeting so that it once again blended with its surroundings.

Harrison took a deep breath and sat on the edge of his bed. On an impulse, he wanted to call Hannah simply to say "hello" and express his love. However, he knew that Mentor was correct. What could be said in a brief conversation did not outweigh the risks of being exposed and putting Hannah in harms way. In any event, Hannah would receive his earlier fax and that he knew would have to suffice for the moment.

Harrison glanced at his watch. It was already mid-afternoon. He had three hours before he was expected to show his presence at the White House. Harrison decided to unwind and relax in the hot tub. He undressed and stepped down into the warmth of the hot tub. Harrison relaxed as the whirling hot water helped soothe his aching muscles. It was the first time that he realized his tiredness and the stress created by today's crisis. Harrison remained in this relaxing state for about an hour. He then stepped out of the hot tub and headed for the shower. He turned the faucet that released a stream of steam. His outstretched hand interrupted the stream as he adjusted the temperature of the water. Satisfied to the touch, Harrison slipped in the shower. He lowered his head and stood silently as the hot water massaged the back of his neck. As the water temperature grew colder, Harrison knew that he overstayed his welcome in the shower. He turned off the water and grabbed the nearby towel. Harrison stepped out of the shower as he dried himself. He slipped into bed and set the alarm to awaken him in one and one-half hours. Harrison fell asleep quickly for a needed rest.

It seemed to Harrison that he just put his head to the pillow when the alarm blared and woke him. He rose out of bed and stumbled to the bathroom. After a quick shave and comb of his hair, he dressed in a pressed dark blue suit and matching tie. Harrison's attention in the mirror was drawn to the blinking light of his answering machine that rested on his bedside nightstand. The electronic device identified that it was holding eleven calls. Although Harrison did not have time to retrieve the messages, he knew there was a high probability that at least one of the eleven messages was from Hannah. Harrison walked over to the night table and tapped the retrieval button. After halfway listening to eight messages from friends and business contacts, the ninth caller was unmistakable: "Hi, honey! Miss you. My bed is always cold without you. Yours better be too! [laughter] The days are very long without you. Oh, I met with Pope Josetta. What a wonderful and perceptive man he is. He sends you his regards and hopes to see us together soon." The message went silent for a moment. "Please keep safe, my H. Love you very much." Harrison tapped the stop button, as he was no longer interested in the remaining messages. He sat down on the bed and stared momentarily across the room.

Harrison glanced at his watch and noted that time was quickly passing. He finished dressing and took a final look in the mirror as he adjusted his tie. He appeared presentable by his own standards and walked out of the bedroom. Harrison entered the kitchen and headed toward the refrigerator in hopes of satisfying his twinge of hunger. He opened the fridge door and peered inside. Besides the inevitable green mold characteristic in the home of single men, nothing seemed edible except for a container of fruit on the bottom yogurt. 'Oh, good,' Harrison thought to himself. 'Cherry. My favorite.' He reached inside and removed the plastic container. Harrison glanced at the clock once again only to note that time continued to tick away. This was not a conference for which Harrison planned to be late. He hurriedly gulped the pleasant-tasting yogurt. He tossed the empty container into the wastebasket using his top professional basketball player form and skill.

On his way out, Harrison stopped at the security panel and reset the intricate alarm. He walked out the door and hurried down several flights of stairway. He walked outside the apartment building and hailed a cab. The drive to the White House was less than 20 minutes away. A cabby saw the waving of a hand and left the mainstream of traffic. Harrison entered the cab as it pulled to the side of the curb. "To the White House, please" remarked Harrison. The driver lifted his eyebrow and replied, "Yes, sir!" The driver drove back into the mainstream of traffic and sped toward the heart of D.C.

Harrison pondered the whereabouts of President Ashton and why Mentor did not offer the slightest hint of the circumstances surrounding her disappearance. He closed his eyes and tried to rest for a few minutes more. The beauty of Hannah eased into his consciousness. Her haunting image in the inner windmills of his mind always brought an engaging smile to his face. Harrison realized that he nodded off when he was awakened by the cab driver's gentle shaking. "Sir. Sir! We're at the White House, sir." The voice registered slowly and Harrison wiped his eyes. He stepped out the cab and paid his fare. He also gave a generous tip for the driver's trouble. Harrison walked up to the first of several guard sites that would clear his way into the White House. He produced his identity card at the guard's request. The guard appeared satisfied that the photo and physical characteristics matched the man standing before him. "You are clear to enter, Mr. Rossetti" said the guard. The identity card was returned to Harrison as he walked through the outer checkpoint. He entered a side entrance of the White House and approached a second guard. Harrison again produced his identity card and was cleared through the secondary checkpoint.

Harrison approached one of several White House elevators. The lift operator smiled and asked, "What floor, sir?" Harrison smiled in return and requested, "Third floor, please." The operator pressed the mechanical buttons and the elevator lifted upward. Within moments, Harrison stepped off onto the third floor. He headed toward the deliberation room down the long hallway. He entered the conference room and sat at his designated seat identified by the customary nameplates placed on the conference table. Harrison glanced around the room and noted that no security council members were present, only a handful of selected government agents. Harrison nodded in response to his colleagues that made eye contact with him. He observed that four top seats remained unclaimed. The President's chair at the head of the table was empty as Harrison expected. Three other seats remained empty: Mentor and those of his two fallen colleagues whose fate he himself escaped earlier in the day. He checked his watch and noted that time had passed for the start of the meeting. A late starting time was unusual for conferences headed by Mentor in the absence of the President. As he waited, Harrison reminded himself of Mentor's warning to not question anything that he saw or heard at the meeting. It was a peculiar request for Mentor who often sought and welcomed his input and expertise. It bothered him somewhat that he did not know what was behind Mentor's unique appeal.

Harrison noted a quieting in the room as Mentor made his appearance. The man with a heavy weight on his shoulders nodded to the men and women gathered in the room. Mentor made eye contact with Hardware and gazed unflinching at his colleague and friend. Harrison saw a disturbance in his supervisor's eyes, something rarely seen given the asserted personality of the man.

Mentor sat at his designated seat next to the empty chair of the President. He did not speak. Mentor gazed straight ahead perhaps deliberately avoiding any eye contact with his agents. As time ticked away, an eerie silence clouded the room. One literally could hear a pin drop. Harrison's anticipation grew as he hoped to gain information about the circumstances surrounding the disappearance of Software. He also wondered what his role might be in investigating the President's whereabouts and helping to bring to justice those involved in her kidnapping.

Ten more minutes passed since Mentor entered the conference room. The creaking of the conference room door unexpectedly broke the eerie silence. Harrison wondered who was entering the room, but before he completed his thought, his colleagues began standing around him. Harrison also stood although he was unaware why until he turned around to see who entered the room. To Harrison's confusion and perhaps more to his disbelief, he made eye contact with the President of the United States, Elizabeth Ashton.

Chapter 10

Confusion Would Be an Improvement!

Harrison shook his head as if the mere act in and of itself would visually clear the image before him. President Ashton was reported as 'disappeared,' assumed kidnapped. Yet, unless Harrison's eyes deceived him, the President was neither seized nor detained. His attention turned to Mentor as the President made her way to the seat at the head of the conference table.

The confusion on Harrison's face was apparent to Mentor. For his part, Harrison stared intensely at his superior with the facade that undoubtedly did not hide a thousand questions. Yet, he knew that no questions would be entertained and no answers forthcoming—at least for the moment. Harrison continued to stare at Mentor as he attempted to fight an underlying sense of friendly betrayal that was ripening in the pit of his stomach. Mentor sat motionlessly as he returned his stare to Hardware perhaps fighting his own sense of betrayal. 'How could Mentor not tell me that the President was alive and well?' thought Harrison. 'He must have had his reasons' entertained Harrison absorbed in self-thought...'or perhaps Mentor was caught off guard just like I was' he reasoned. Harrison soon developed a sense of uncomfortableness with his feelings. He knew Mentor for a long time, too long to be knowingly misled.

Mentor had guessed correctly his friend's uncertainty to the unfolding events. He knew that Hardware felt betrayed that he was not informed fully of the situation, particularly following the briefing between the two men just a few hours ago. Mentor concluded correctly that Harrison was quite shocked to be in the presence of the President whose whereabouts were supposedly unknown.

Both men turned their gaze from each other to President Ashton as she called the meeting to order. The wooden gavel echoed sharply as it struck the surface of the highly polished walnut conference table. The hum around the table diminished as the President again used her gavel to call the meeting to order. Then, silence shrouded the deliberation room.

President Ashton began the meeting somberly and said, "Good evening." A quiet chorus of "good evenings" echoed from around the room. The President continued tersely, "I won't waste your time. Domestic attacks against our government have increased markedly over the past five years displacing priority concerns about the risk of foreign insertions. Much like our war on drugs, our campaign to curb domestic terrorism is falling short of its objectives. We cannot continue our present course and survive as a democratic government. It is time to review our current objectives..." President Ashton paused and scanned the steely eyes of her agents. She then said affirmatively, "No, it is time to scrap our failed approach at counteracting domestic terrorism..." she paused briefly..."and implement a bold plan that seeks to reach a compromise with some of the more tenable ideals of our country's 'dissidents.'"

Eyebrows raised and facial impressions winced around the conference room. A low murmur could be heard. Harrison glanced toward Mentor perhaps seeking his superior's affirmation of what President Ashton was proposing. Mentor returned no such acknowledgment and turned his gaze away. Harrison was left to his own thoughts. 'Was the President suggesting that the government capitulate with domestic terrorists?'

Harrison's thoughts returned to President Ashton as her gavel smacked against the conference table three times. Then she said in mockery, "Good. I can see we are all in agreement." The President eyed carefully each of the individuals gathered at the table perhaps making some attempt at assessing the impact of her words. She particularly paused at Mentor and Hardware as if these two men could somehow make or break her yet unspoken plan.

In an effort to bolster reassurance, President Ashton clarified, "I don't mean that we 'give in' to domestic terrorism. Yet, it's clear that we cannot continue our present course without some compromise. We are not only losing the battle, but we are about to lose the war as well. The cost of homegrown terrorism has increased steadily by 10 percent each year in the past five years. Such a cost to people, property and financial resources are now unacceptable!" President Ashton paused. She banged the table with her left fist and reiterated simultaneously, "Unacceptable!" President Ashton shook as the emotions of her guileless stance literally drained from her face for everybody to witness. She paused briefly once again and said more softly, almost in a whisper, "Unacceptable!"

All agents' eyes were focused on the President. What transferred to this moment did little to clarify the confusion experienced by Harrison. His gaze shifted once again to Mentor, but there was no recognition this time. Harrison turned his attention back to the President who began outlining her plan for 'compromise' with extreme factions and homegrown terrorism.

President Ashton asserted, "The incidents at Waco, Ruby Ridge, Lizton Fields, Oklahoma Federal Building, Elmore Fams, Shepard Hills, Cumberland Elms..." The President paused and shook her head in disgust before she continued, "So many others that have impacted upon not only their intended yet innocent victims, but all peoples of these United States of America. I will not let this shameful chapter in our history continue and cast its dark shadow over my administration. We can no longer afford to turn a deaf ear to people who have grown weary of the integrity and effectiveness of our government. Our inability to hear beyond the rhetoric of dissidents has paralyzed us and limited our response to a singular retaliatory stance. And where has this stance gotten us?"

President Ashton paused and scrutinized each agent once again to assess her impact on the audience before her. She focused on Mentor more so than any other agent in the room. Such attention did not go unnoticed by Harrison. He wondered whether Mentor was aware of the content of the President's speech even before she spoke. If so, why was Harrison left out in the cold? He has known Mentor for a long time, long enough to know that Mentor would have difficulty supporting any plan that might undermine the government of the United States and allow extreme factions to gain a vital foothold in America.

Harrison's attention returned once more to President Ashton as she continued her view on placating domestic terrorism: "What I'm proposing is a ten-step plan which I will specify for you now." The President paused briefly to sip some water from her glass. The agents at the conference also took a similar opportunity by filling their glasses. As the sounds of clanking glassware diminished, President Ashton started detailing her ten-point plan to assimilate domestic terrorism into American politics:

"Step one: Review prison cases and release those dissident terrorists in federal prison whose crimes do not include direct acts of violence against the people of the United States;

Step two: Provide financial compensation to these individuals for time loss on the job and emotional reparation;

Step three: Discontinue federal wiretaps on suspected terrorists where there is no direct, concrete evidence of intention to commit a crime despite a positive past history of such crimes;

Step four: Direct the FBI and IRS to no longer use their strong arms in investigating individuals just because their views differ from our government's stance;

Step five: Develop a moderated committee whose membership includes people appointed because of their distinct dissident views to provide input to governmental activities, funding and law;

Step six: Arrange that such a committee is solely responsible and reportable to the President;

Step seven: Allow for equal access time in all broadcasting media, particularly during federal, state and local elections;

Step eight: Provide guidelines and sensitivity training to all branches of law enforcement in their exchanges with our country's dissident terrorists;

Step nine: Provide guidelines to local governments on how to develop and maintain open forums so that varying viewpoints can be heard, documented and implemented; and lastly,

Step ten: Reinitiate efforts to support vigorously the right of law-abiding American citizens to carry arms as provided in our Constitution."

As the President finished outlining her platform, the silence was deafening in the room. One could not only hear a pin drop, but a feather as well. Agents in the room stole glances at each other, but said nothing. What the President proposed was shaking hands with extreme factions at a time when domestic terrorism was not only on the rise, but flaunting their powers to strike arguably anywhere and at any time. A pervasive shock shrouded the conference room. Nothing would be said unless Mentor spoke out; however, he apparently had nothing to say or was ordered to maintain silence.

President Ashton shoveled her papers at the lectern and spoke once again: "I know that you'll need time to study and consider what I've proposed this evening. A detailed report on the ten steps that I have outlined will be delivered shortly to your offices. I will expect a proposal from each of you within next several days on how your respective sections will assimilate my ten steps. Thank you. That is all."

At that, President Ashton left the conference room. Upon her departure, the silence of the room gave way to a low murmur. Harrison peered directly across the table at Mentor. For a moment, the two colleagues, the two friends, just stared at one another. Harrison was unwilling to believe that Mentor would lend his support to President Ashton's platform. He also was uncertain as to why Mentor did not raise one single question during the briefing, why Mentor did not query the President on a single step of her unprecedented proposal.

The buzz in the conference room lessened as the agents began filtering out the door. Harrison glanced at Mentor who remained seated at the conference table. He remained seated as well as all but two other agents left the room. Harrison was about to speak, but Mentor held up his finger symbolically asking him not to talk. Mentor glanced at the two agents who were still in the conference room. They were in an indisputable discussion about the details of the President's briefing.

One of the agents glimpsed Mentor from the corner of his eye. It was not difficult to interpret Mentor's facial expression of impatience. The agent quickly tapped his colleague on the shoulder. He motioned him to follow him out of the conference room door and within seconds, the meeting room fell to silence.

Harrison, who witnessed the recent exit of his colleagues, turned his attention toward Mentor. The two men were face-to-face once again. This time, however, Harrison was determined to get some answers—some truthful answers. He peered into Mentor's eyes and shook his head. Harrison spoke first. He disarmed their formal association by addressing their personal relationship: "Greg, I don't understand what is going on! I can't believe that you're going to support the President in this endeavor." A twinge came across Harrison's face as his declaration bordered on insubordination if not treason.

Mentor did not respond immediately. His left hand supported his chin as his fingers tapped continuously over his mouth. It was as if Mentor was stalling for time in order to formulate his words. In reality and unknown to Harrison, Mentor knew exactly what he was going to say to his colleague and friend. It was difficult for him not to disclose the covert information that he possessed, especially to Hardware. Yet, circumstances dictated the utmost secrecy. Mentor knew that the smallest of leaks would certainly doom any plan to counteract the sinister plot unfolding before them. Not even friendship or apparent betrayal of their association could be measured against what he knew to be true.

Harrison, for his part, was being very patient. As much as he wanted information and to understand the circumstances before him, he learned over the years not to push Mentor. Harrison was well aware of the heavy responsibilities shouldered by Mentor. Although Harrison's curiosity was eating away at him, Mentor would speak when it was prudent to do so. He waited for Mentor's clarification of the unfolding events.

Mentor removed his hand that was supporting his chin and finally spoke: "Well, what do you think Hardware?" Harrison was rather stumped at the question. In fact, he did not expect a question at all. What he expected were some answers from Mentor, information that apparently was not immediately forthcoming. However, he knew that since Mentor addressed him in his coded vernacular, he expected a formal response. So, what indeed did Harrison think? Hardware scratched his head and spoke deliberately as his chose his words cautiously: "On the surface, sir, it seems that President Ashton wants our country's dissident terrorists to develop a strong foothold in American politics."

Harrison wanted to say more—much more. Yet, he thought better of questioning Mentor and simply said what he had thought during the course of the President's presentation. Harrison could not imagine that Mentor had formulated a different conclusion, or at least, he did not want to consider such a possibility. He made direct eye contact with Mentor to ascertain whether they were indeed in sync. Mentor then said rather matter-of-factly, too calmly for that matter, "You're essentially correct, Hardware." He added, "And that is exactly where we will concentrate our efforts—in support of President Ashton's proposal."

Harrison said nothing, but his confused expression and disbelief at the words spoken were certainly written across his face; and as such could not have escaped Mentor's awareness. The two men stared at each other, a social skill that was happening all too frequently since his return from Rome. Mentor broke the silence and directed, "Meet me at Station Zero at twenty three hundred hours." Mentor spoke nothing more. He left his seat as Hardware respectfully acknowledged, "Yes, sir." Harrison was now alone in the conference room as his superior exited. The clarification he was hoping for did not occur. What Harrison understood was that the situation had

increased in seriousness and danger for Mentor to evoke a
rendezvous at Station Zero.

Chapter 11

A Lady in Waiting

Although it was late night in Washington, D.C., in Roma dawn was approaching. Hannah had a restless sleep and thought better than to argue with the breaking dawn. She faced away from the center of the bed, but smiled as she turned around to greet Harrison only to realize that he was not there. Hannah's smile disappeared quickly as her hazy thoughts began to organize themselves and were no longer able to block out reality's intrusion. She remembered that her fiancé was ordered away early the previous morning. Hannah's tranquility was replaced by growing trepidation. She knew that the urgency by which her Harrison left Rome was an indication of the risk and danger he faced in the unfolding crisis—a crisis whose nature and intensity were unknown to her.

Hannah seemed paralyzed, as she lay in bed unable to move. She pondered where Harrison was at this very moment in time. She also wondered if he was thinking of her as she thought of him. Hannah, however, was secure in her relationship with Harrison. She shook her head to clear her thoughts and threw back the blue satin covers. Hannah turned over once again and stepped out of her comfortable, warm bed. She headed toward the bath to take a shower. Hannah reached through the curtain and turned on the water. The stream splashed against her hand as she adjusted the mix to her desired temperature. Hannah thought, 'That feels great' and stepped into the shower. The hot water and steam were relaxing, almost like a sensual sauna. Hannah's mind began drifting as the water tapped its musical dance on her soft, wet skin.

Hannah's thoughts wandered into the not-so-distant future and her wedding day. In the midst, she saw her Harrison waiting down the long bridal pathway to the altar. She smiled as she envisioned Pope Josetta standing near Harrison waiting to celebrate the sacrament of Matrimony. Hannah could not identify the usher standing next to Harrison. She knew him only as 'Greg,' the gentleman that her fiancé talked about frequently. Hannah knew that 'Greg' worked with her beloved, but did not know his capacity or exact relationship to Harrison. She mused that much about her H. seemed so hush-hush.

A sudden cold change in the water temperature jerked Hannah back to present day reality. The future faded quickly even though it was really never present. Hannah continued her shower and thought of her agenda for the day. She first was going to check on the health status of Pope Josetta and file her column with the *Washington Sun* in Washington. She hoped that she might have a brief, unscheduled visit with the Pope although she knew that the odds were less than those of getting struck by lightening. Then it would be off for some afternoon shopping at the *Piazza de Spagna* in the heart of Rome's most fashionable shopping district. Hannah was determined to find a gift for her fiancé, the man who had everything!

A woman shopping for a man is a much different experience than a man shopping for a woman, Hannah thought. Indeed! They may pretend, but men do not enjoy shopping—real shopping that is—not going into a single store and coming out 10 minutes later with a single purchase. Such an activity is neither shopping nor even a reasonable facsimile thereof. You cannot expedite shopping. You cannot find the perfect gift on the first try and if you do, it is not the perfect gift. Women know that—men take it for granted! 'Oh well,' thought Hannah, 'Viva la difference!'

Hannah finished toweling her soft skin dry. She picked out her wardrobe for the day and dressed hurriedly. It was a conservative dress as her first stop this morning would be the Vatican. There was a briefing schedule for nine o'clock this morning to update journalists on the Pope Josetta's medical condition. Hannah smiled softly as she recalled her recent visit with Harrison's friend and patriarch of the Roman Catholic Church. It was unfortunate that she had not known Josetta earlier in his reign when his physical health was less debilitating and he was full of vigor.

As Hannah finished dressing, there was a knock at her door. She walked quickly out of the bedroom and opened the hotel door. It was room service with her breakfast that she had ordered last evening. Hannah motioned in the direction of the dining table and the waiter began emptying the tray of its food contents. He asked if there was anything else she needed. There was not and Hannah opened her purse to tip the kind man. The waiter thanked her and left her hotel suite.

Hannah returned to the bedroom and completed her morning ritual of adorning makeup. She glanced at the clock and quickened her pace as time was slipping away as it always seemed to do. Hannah finished dressing, left her bedroom and sat at the breakfast table. She spread cherry jam on her toast and poured milk over her cereal. The coffee was still hot to the touch as she poured herself a steaming cup. As Hannah sipped her coffee, she buzzed the front desk and asked for a taxi in half an hour.

Hannah finished the last of her toast and cereal and headed back to the bedroom. She glanced at the clock and noted the passing of time. She finished the last of her primping and headed out the door. Hannah nodded to the hotel clerk who returned her recognition with a smile. She walked out of the hotel's main entrance and was greeted by the doorman who hailed her taxi. In moments, Hannah was on her way to Vatican City. As the taxi drove away from the hotel, a black sedan drove up behind her taxi and kept a discreet distance. The sedan turned, as did the taxi. Either the sedan's occupant was shadowing Hannah or they too were on their way to the Vatican.

The trip to the Vatican was picturesque. Hannah so admired the Italian countryside. The sedan continued its prowling at a judicious distance. Hannah hoped to find Pope Josetta feeling better. Perhaps His Holiness may desire an unscheduled visit from a friend. She would ask. It would not hurt to ask.

Hannah arrived at the Vatican with several minutes to spare. She paid the cab driver and walked up the stairs of the Vatican. The black sedan stopped to the side of the road. The lone gentleman seemed satisfied with waiting at the curb across from the Vatican. Hannah presented her credentials and headed to the press briefing room. Fr. Edgar Soergel was scheduled to present the briefing as it had been since its inception. Fr. Soergel had been at Josetta's side for many years, including ten years before he rose to the papacy.

The conference room was teaming with print, radio and television journalists. Hannah nodded her greetings to her familiar colleagues and friends. There was a buzz in the room common to such occasions. Hannah glimpsed the Rev. Soergel from the corner of her eye and made her way toward him. She nodded at the holy priest as their eyes met. "How good to see you again, Miss Littleton," said the holy man. "And you, Father," replied Hannah. "Have you enjoyed your stay in Rome?" asked the prelate. "Yes, very much" noted Hannah and then added with a broken smile, "Although my fiancé had to leave unexpectedly." "I'm sorry" was the padre's sincere concern.

Edward Galluzzi

Hannah had not thought of Harrison since early this morning. She wished that he could not only be here with her, but also with his holy friend, Josetta. Hannah asked, "How is His Holiness?" "I wish I could say that His Holiness was doing better" was the grave response. "I will begin the briefing soon" he continued. "Perhaps the Pontiff might want a visitor today?" Hannah asked hopefully. "You?" inquired the priest. Hannah nodded and the holy man broke into a smile. "Yes, he may indeed want a special visitor today. I will let you know shortly after the briefing." "Thank you," Hannah replied warmly. Fr. Soergel nodded once more and made his way to the conference room podium.

The commotion among the journalists dimmed as they became aware of the prelate's stance at the podium. The dim murmur soon shifted to silence. Fr. Soergel cleared his throat and welcomed the journalists to the briefing in his rich, baritone voice: "Good morning. On behalf of the Vatican, I thank you for attending this briefing, your sincere interest in the health and well being of His Holiness, and your prayers. As you are aware, Pope Josetta has been ill now for nearly six months. During the course of his illness, the Pontiff has celebrated his 75th birthday. He has had his good days and bad days—some terrible days. Although Pope Josetta's physical strength has fluctuated accordingly, his emotional and spiritual strength nevertheless has remained intense. We are always concerned about respiratory problems and its complications. In particular, respiratory acidosis has recurred this week and physicians have labored to reduce the level of pulmonary carbon dioxide. We have reported to you before that His Holiness has suffered from headaches and drowsiness. The doctors have treated him with enriched oxygen and, thus far, his condition has not progressed to a stupor or coma, as is the course with many patients with chronic respiratory failure.

91

The Pope has not required mechanically assisted ventilation, which we take as a good sign. He is alert generally, resting comfortably and retaining sufficient nutrients in his daily food intake as not to require ongoing IVs. His Holiness continues to make papal decisions and, as far as he is able, conduct papal business as patriarch of the Roman Catholic Church with the support of the *Curia.* "

Fr. Soergel paused as he took off his glasses and wiped his brow. He returned his glasses to their familiar station and continued, "It is our hope that His Holiness will increase in his strength and vigor. We are thankful to the people of the world for their thoughts, prayers and many wishes that they have sent to the Holy Father. Thank you for your attendance and interest in Pope Josetta. Good Morning."

Fr. Soergel left the podium and greeted the journalists as he made his way out of the conference room. Hannah and the prelate's paths crossed once again. "Ah, Miss Littleton" said the holy man. He continued, "If you would please wait in the outer office, I will see if the Holy Father feels up to having a visitor." "Thank you," replied Hannah. She greeted her friends and colleagues as she made her way to the outer office. Fr. Soergel disappeared through another door into the inner sanctum of the Vatican.

Hannah finally made her way to the outer office and sat awaiting word from Fr. Soergel. Another 20 minutes passed before he appeared with his head bowed. He looked at Hannah and said, "I'm sorry, this is not becoming one of the Holy Father's 'good' days. He is coughing hard and is complaining of a headache. We summoned his physician. Perhaps another day." Hannah acknowledged the priest with an understanding nod and thanked him before heading toward the exit of the Vatican.

Hannah walked out into a bright, sunny day in Rome.

Unable to see Josetta, she decided to do some serious shopping—the intensive shopping of which she was quite capable. Hannah walked toward the area to hail a cab and was soon greeted by its driver.

She entered the cab and requested her destination: *"Piazza de Spagna."* The driver pulled away slowly from the Vatican and merged with the traffic. The black sedan that had waited patiently across from the holy place resumed its discreet stalking of Hannah. For her part, Hannah was neither aware of its presence nor able to appraise its risks.

Chapter 12

Station Zero

It was twenty three hundred hours and Harrison found himself at Station Zero. Each agent had a Station Zero—a unique place known only to Mentor and his respective agent. It became necessary over the years to identify secured safety houses given the marked advancement and capabilities of electronic eavesdropping technology, not to mention the assassination of numerous agents. Tonight, Harrison hoped to gain clarification about the events that transpired since he left Rome.

Harrison used his electronic key that not only matched physically the key lock tumblers, but also was encoded with a unique electronic signature to provide additional security. He entered the doorway and realized that he had only thirty seconds to disarm the motion, sound and touch sensors that permeated the home. Harrison extended his left hand and flipped the wall switch that illuminated the passageway. A dim light bathed the room in almost moonlight luminance. Yet, it was sufficient light for Harrison to navigate through the entry room without bumping into the furniture and other objects. He encountered a row of switches and flipped them as well. Other rooms of Station Zero were illuminated in the moonlight glow. Harrison headed quickly toward the security panels to disarm the protective features of the home, but found that Station Zero's security system had already been disabled.

Harrison released his gun from its holster and headed for the main meeting room. As he entered the room, he was startled by a lone figure sitting in a chair. Harrison instinctively aimed his gun directly at the figure. "Don't shoot, Hardware" said a soft voice. The voice was unmistakably that of Mentor. Harrison returned his gun to its holster and stretched out his hand to greet Mentor. "Good evening, sir," Harrison said. He continued with a wry smile, "I should have known you'd be punctual."

Mentor returned the warm handshake and greeting. He spoke tiredly, "Hello, Harrison. I apologize for all the 'cloak and dagger,' but as you will soon discover, it has become unfortunately quite a necessity." "No apology necessary, sir" was Harrison's reassuring reply. Greg looked weary and drained. It was clear that the day's events inundated his supervisor and friend.

Mentor removed a single sheet of paper from a file and laid it slowly in front of Hardware. He motioned for Harrison to review the sheet. Harrison reached out and picked up the single sheet of paper. He began reading its contents to himself and realized readily that it was President Ashton's ten point plan to assimilate domestic terrorism into American politics:

"Step one: Review prison cases and release those dissident terrorists in federal prison whose crimes do not include direct acts of violence against the people of the United States;

Step two: Provide financial compensation to these individuals for time loss on the job and emotional reparation;

Step three: Discontinue federal wiretaps on suspected terrorists where there is no direct, concrete evidence of intention to commit a crime despite a positive past history of such crimes;

Step four: Direct the FBI and IRS to no longer use their strong arms in investigating individuals just because their views differ from our government's stance;

Step five: Develop a moderated committee whose membership includes people appointed because of their distinct dissident   views to provide input to governmental activities, funding and law;

Step six: Arrange that such a committee is solely responsible and reportable to the President;

Step seven: Allow for equal access time in all broadcasting media, particularly during federal, state and local elections;

Step eight: Provide guidelines and sensitivity training to all branches of law enforcement in their exchanges with our country's dissident terrorists;

Step nine: Provide guidelines to local governments on how to develop and maintain open forums so that varying viewpoints can be heard, documented and implemented; and lastly,

Step ten: Reinitiate efforts to support vigorously the right of law-abiding American citizens to carry arms as provided in our Constitution."

Upon Harrison's review of President Ashton's words, he looked up at Mentor. Neither spoke a word for a moment as if neither wanted to empty the contents of their minds. It was clear that Harrison would not speak first as he ascertained that he would put himself politically and legally at risk if he indeed shared his thoughts. He was determined to wait out his supervisor on this one and reflected that this was the only prudent approach. It was not a good time for his custom impulsivity and to jump right in as it were. Yes, indeed, Harrison would wait out Mentor no matter how long it took.

As it happened, Harrison did not have to wait long. Mentor knew that it was not Hardware's place to say what had to be said. Mentor seemed to muster some courage, to delve deep within himself, and broke the silence that permeated the two men: "My friend, our country is in peril for resuming a conflict that ended 140 years ago—a civil war." Harrison heard the words, but the shock of their content cushioned the inhumanity of their true meaning. Hardware's gaze was frozen on Mentor as he continued to speak: "Our country will not survive another civil war, not with today's technology and weaponry—nor will our enemies stand by and allow such a conflict to take its course without intervention based on their own greed and desire to deeply influence if not overthrow the government of the United States. Such a conflict would indeed be an opportunity they politically could not pass up. The stakes are too high and the rewards too great. President Ashton's plan to assimilate domestic terrorism will be the end of us."

Mentor paused to permit Harrison a moment to digest the genuine and unmistakable meaning of his words. Hardware was at best astonished at the specificity of Mentor's explanation. He did not disagree with his superior, but they both knew that such words were treasonous no matter their source. Both gentlemen had to proceed with extreme caution. Treason in the United States at this level of government was more likely punishable by execution than imprisonment for life without parole—neither sentence appealed to Harrison.

Harrison had not yet recovered from the insensibility caused by his superior words when Mentor spoke again: "I believe that the explanation for President Ashton's stance is that she is not President Elizabeth Ashton!" 'Forget the treachery,' thought Harrison; now, he was concerned about his dear friend's mental stability. Before Hardware could counter, Mentor echoed his thoughts: "I know you must think I'm a madman, but you need to hear me out."

Harrison could only nod in agreement as Mentor pitched his defense: "Yesterday, before I contacted you in Rome, Modem asked to meet with me." Harrison recalled that the codename for President Ashton's husband, Richard Ashton, was Modem. He returned his attention to his superior explanation. "We met away from the White House. Modem expressed his concern; well, more like his disbelief, that his wife who returned from a weekend-long political fund-raising convention in Montana was not his wife." Mentor paused for a moment to allow for the incredulous words that he spoke to register with Hardware. For Harrison's part, he reminded himself that Mentor has always been a credible source of information and he had no reason to question him now, no matter how dubious sounding the data. He peered into the eyes of his superior as he offered the evidence to support his allegation: "Modem does not deny the bodily identification of his wife—she looks physically in every detail and aspect as Elizabeth Ashton—even down to her scar. The President has a one and one-quarter inch scar on her left buttocks that she received from an accident when she fell out of a tree as a young child. Nobody would doubt that they were in the presence of Elizabeth Ashton merely by her physical appearance." Mentor had Hardware's complete attention and focus as he continued, "What Modem came to realize and subsequently began to question were the apparent gaps in his wife's knowledge about their lives and, as a matter of discretion, let's say more intimate aspects of their relationship." As Mentor's words trailed from his lips, Harrison began to formulate his own thoughts on the prospects: 'brainwashed; an identical twin; a double; possibly surgically altered or…he shook his head and mused slightly as he thought of an extreme possibility, a clone?'

Mentor has known Hardware for a long time, including his thinking process. As he 'watched' the gears turn in Harrison's mind, he remarked, "I can almost guess what you're thinking. I also know you may be right. Your assignment, Harrison, is to investigate with extreme discretion the possibilities of this phenomenon. We need to know if she is a brainwashed or indoctrinated Elizabeth Ashton…or whether she has been altered or swapped. We cannot tip our hat on this one, Harrison." Mentor reiterated slowly and forcefully, "You must be discreet and judicious in your investigation. We have the advantage, slight at it may be, as long as whoever orchestrated this contemptible act on the Presidency believes he, or she, has succeeded in the deception."

Harrison thought for a moment and formulated carefully his reply to Mentor: "Greg, this is like a plot out of a novel or movie. I've never known you to be an alarmist, but you got me a little scared. What you are saying and advocating borders on treachery—and to investigate a sitting President without her knowledge or the complicity of congress was unheard of. Other than President Ashton's husband, are we the only two people who suspect what you just described?" Mentor read the disbelief in Hardware's voice and saw it in his face. He returned, "No, I informed Scanner of Modem's concerns about his wife." Harrison recalled that Scanner was the vice-president, Neff Jameson. He again listened to the words of his superior: "As a matter of accountability and checks and balances, I agreed to keep Scanner fully informed of our activities and findings. He is aware of the delicacy of the assignment on which we are embarking. I assured him that we would do everything within our power to protect the office of the Presidency. The vice-president will disavow any knowledge of our plans and actions if there becomes a need to do so. In essence, Harrison, we are on our own and out on a limb…a very short limb. I cannot promise you that we will come through unscathed, or for that matter, still alive and employed in the service of the United States. I cannot order you to take this assignment. Your acceptance of this mission is strictly on a voluntary basis with no penalties, neither personally from me nor professionally from our government, for refusing the assignment."

Harrison did not hesitate in considering his options and knew that Mentor was already aware of his decision. He addressed his superior: "Sir, I've never refused an assignment from you or your predecessor and I don't intend to start now." Mentor was afforded a brief smile as he nodded his head in acknowledgment. Harrison then asked, "What do we know and where do we start?" Mentor retrieved President Ashton's itemized solution to counteract domestic terrorism from Hardware and responded, "This document suggests the involvement of right wing extremists and factions. It seems more than a coincidence that Modem initially suspected something incongruent following her trip from Montana. Software attended the conference in Montana's capital city of Helena. However, our intelligence reports indicate that most extremist activities have taken place around the city of Sarhea, particularly in the range area, which is near the base of the Rocky Mountains. I believe that it is there where we should concentrate our initial investigative efforts."

Harrison nodded affirmatively and asked, "Has Target One been cleared?" Mentor replied, "Yes. I contacted the base before I left to meet with you here. There was no bomb or any kind of detonation device found inside or outside your personal jet. Your left engine was repaired. It is clear, now, that being out of the country did indeed save you from the terrible fate of agents Scout and Eagle. Whoever is involved in this conspiracy simply did not have the time to search you down and sabotage Target One. Your jet has been under guard since it was cleared and deemed safe for flight."

Harrison interrupted, "Did our investigation uncover any leads, any leads at all?" "Findings are only preliminary at best and minimal at this time," said Mentor. He continued, "Our explosive experts did rule out pilot error and an act of nature.

The one part of tangible evidence that we have is one piece of what is believed to be a detonation device found at one of the crash sites. It is my understanding that a partial code number was lifted from the fragment. The wreckage of both planes was collected." Mentor paused and looked at his watch. He then continued, "They are in transport as we speak to our center in Virginia."

Mentor paused before asking with genuine concern in his voice, "What about Hannah? Do you think she is out of harm's way?" Harrison discerned the sincerity in his friend's voice and responded, "Thanks for your concern, Greg. I know Hannah is at risk because of her relationship with me. I'm not leaving anything to chance. Do you remember Jacob Jarley?" Mentor searched his memory briefly and then a smile emerged on his face. "Jacob Jarley," Mentor said deliberately. "Old 'Scrooge?" he asked as his smile broke into a reserved laugh. Their ex-colleague had dawned the codename 'Scrooge' in that his birth name resembled that of the character from the Charles Dickens' novel, "Scrooge," written at the time of great poverty in England. Harrison spoke, "I've hired him to follow and keep an eye out for Hannah. He is very professional, very discreet—and very expensive!" Hardware and Mentor managed a smile between them. Mentor interrupted, "Hannah is indeed in good hands. That should really ease your mind." Harrison nodded in agreement.

Mentor's expression grew urgent as he spoke, "Harrison, when can you leave?" Noting the urgency in his superior's voice, Harrison replied, "I can leave now. I was able to sleep for several hours before our meeting here. I just need to pack a few things at the apartment and…" His words were interrupted by Mentor: "We've taken the liberty of packing your suitcases and other essentials, including the usual weaponry, explosives and communication gear. They are already aboard Target One.

Harrison, we have to be careful on this one. The individuals or organizations behind this treachery already have proven they will stop at nothing—even murder. Your communication pack contains your contact schedule with me. I expect you to follow it. I can't afford to lose any more hair and the hair that I have left is still turning gray."

The two friends smiled. Mentor continued, "You will find a map in the case file marked 'Double Trouble.' There is an Air Force base at Great Falls, Montana which is about 350 miles south from the town of Sarhea. You will find the coordinates on your map. I apologize in advance that I cannot give you any backup on this case, but under the circumstances, I'm not sure who to trust and do not want to endanger any more lives." Harrison said nothing, but nodded in agreement.

Mentor stood for the first time. He walked toward Hardware with an outstretched hand. "Be careful, Harrison, and God's speed." Harrison said nothing, but reached for his friend's outstretched hand. He knew the extremist would stop at nothing. Harrison was aware of the risks involved and knew he may not see his friend again. He may not see Hannah again. Harrison firmly shook the hand of Mentor and then his superior was off into the darkness.

Harrison flipped the switches of the main conference room as he exited. Station Zero returned to its dim, moonlight luminescence. Harrison walked down the hallway and managed to navigate toward the back entry room without bumping into the furniture and other objects. He headed once again to the security panels to enable the protective features of the Station Zero. Harrison punched in the digital code and armed the security system. He realized that he had only thirty seconds before the motion, sound and touch sensors would betray him. Harrison exited quickly from the home and used his electronic key once again to secure Station Zero. He began the long walk to his car which he parked at some distance to help maintain the site's secrecy.

Chapter 13

The Hunter and the Hunted

Harrison glanced at his radiated watch and noted that the hour was approaching 1:00 a.m. Time had sped ahead as it often does for Harrison. He took several steps and stopped suddenly. Harrison thought he had heard something, perhaps seen something, but he was not sure. Given what has transpired, there was not much of which he was still certain. He quickly scanned the area and noted that nothing appeared out of place. A wisp of fear awakened his adrenalin and as always gave him the edge he needed for increased alertness and survival. Harrison wondered if perhaps the terrorists had finally caught up with him...or was it just an alley cat on the prowl for excitement? He stood motionless and strained his senses as far as humanly possible. Again, nothing alerted his senses beyond the din of the night. Nothing appeared out of place. Yet, it was usually at such moments when he was most apprehensive. Harrison took several more steps away from Station Zero and disappeared into the cover afforded by the night sky. A darkened figure stepped out from the side of Station Zero and into the faint moonlight. The solitary figure remained motionless in the same spot that Harrison himself stood. The figure turned and glanced smugly toward Station Zero as if it betrayed its secrets. The figure turned once again and disappeared down the same path of darkness taken by Hardware.

Harrison walked slowly but steadily to his car. His vision, compromised by the darkness, only served to heighten his other senses. Harrison was bothered by something, perhaps more of a nagging annoyance than anything specific. He had no doubt that he was marked by whoever murdered his colleagues. Harrison would heed Mentor's warning to watch his backside. His nagging feeling was becoming more of a nuisance. Harrison decided that he could no longer ignore his gut. It told him what it often told him: 'Wait and see.'

Harrison spotted some dense bushes up ahead and decided to make his 'wait and see' stance there. He shoved the bush tentatively to determine whether he would be pushed in return. Feeling no sharp pain, Harrison found his way into the thick and crouched. He reached behind his back and drew out his gun. The position in which he found himself was uncomfortable but tolerable. Harrison purposely breathed slowly and quietly in order to sensitize his hearing. A brush of a leaf, snap of a small twig or crackle of a rock was all that was required to betray his unforeseen prey. Harrison remained crouched as he strained to pickup any sign, any sign at all that he was being followed. He faced straight ahead into the moonlit darkness waiting for his unforeseen prey.

As minutes passed, no one intruded on the stillness. Perhaps, Harrison thought, perhaps his 'nagging feeling' this time was in error—just the jitters given the nature of his present assignment. Harrison, however, decided to wait. As time pushed ahead, his focus waned as Hannah's image crept into his thoughts. Harrison smiled to himself as a pane of anxiety overtook him. He worried about his intended even though his trusted colleague 'Scrooge' was watching after her. Harrison glanced at the illuminated dial of his watch and noted it was now 2:00 a.m. How Harrison wished he was lying beside Hannah, holding her in his arms, kissing her full lips and feeling her sensual warm body against his.

As Harrison became increasingly preoccupied with thoughts of Hannah, the stir of gravel refocused his attention to the imminent situation. He leaned forward straining his senses once more. Harrison pulled his gun toward him and withdrew its safety. He froze as he took slow, silent breaths. Harrison's adrenalin flowed openly now as he prepared to attack—much like a lion ready to pounce on its unsuspecting prey. He was confident that he had the upper hand in the pending conflict. He survived many other such battles, more or less!

Harrison did not have to wait long. He grabbed his gun now with both hands and steadied his aim toward an advancing figure in the dark. The figure walked slowly, then stopped. The figure appeared to sense the need for caution as the stranger gazed from side-to-side. For his part, Harrison stayed still, frozen in time and not wanting to risk losing his upper hand. The figure seemed satisfied with its superficial surveillance and continued approaching. Harrison reviewed his options. He was certain that this was not simply an innocent stranger wandering around in the night. Harrison wanted the element of surprise on his side even though he realized that any trained agent learns to expect the unexpected. A brief moment of surprise was all that was needed, however, to make the difference. Timing was indeed everything.

Harrison told himself to wait. He needed to be patient. Harrison grasped his gun firmly and aimed it toward the advancing stranger. He put his finger on the trigger for the first time and squeezed lightly. The unidentified person continued approaching Harrison. He adjusted his aim as the stranger verged upon him and began to rise from his crouching position. Harrison told himself to wait a few more seconds, just a few more seconds.

The stranger continued walking slowly toward Harrison, but then stopped suddenly. The unidentified person reached in a pocket and withdrew an object that glimmered in the moonlight. Believing that the element of surprise was no longer in his corner, Harrison jumped from his crouching stance and yelled firmly, "Stop where you are!" He observed that the stranger appeared more menacing up close. "Drop it!" demanded Harrison. The stranger stopped, but did not let go of the object. Harrison screamed once more with anger, "I said drop it!"

Upon hearing Harrison's second demand, the stranger slowly let the object drop to the ground. The stranger's hands rose up in the air without a single word from Harrison. Harrison let his left hand fall from his gun, but kept his gun trained on the stranger. He slowly approached his unknown assailant and told himself to use extreme caution. Perhaps this was the person who assassinated his colleagues.

As Harrison drew closer, the stranger's face achieved definition. He suddenly realized that the stranger was a woman. That realization caused Harrison to lower slightly his gun and like on cue, the female stranger karate kicked the gun out of his hand in one swift move. She had stolen the element of surprise from Harrison and a skirmish ensued. The woman lunged at Harrison and the two went collapsing to the ground. They rolled back and forth shifting top positions as they both fought for the upper hand. However, neither antagonist achieved control and the rumble continued. The movement across the ground drew the rolling couple toward one of the two guns that was dropkicked unceremoniously to the dirt. The stranger was first to reach the proximity of the gun. She stretched one hand toward it, but the gun was inches away from her grasp. She attempted to roll Harrison in the direction of the armament when he as well spied the weapon. The conflict heated, as the stakes were now higher. They were not only struggling with each other, but both were attempting to grasp the weapon that would give one of them the upper hand and perhaps death to the other.

Harrison and his assailant continued to struggle as their

personal battle intensified. He did his best at trying to gain control over his formidable opponent, but he was having little success. She was on top of him now. A sharp pain rose suddenly across his face as the stranger's fist found its mark. Dazed briefly, another jab landed on his face as the stranger continued to pummel him. Harrison knew that he must stop her before he drifted into unconsciousness. Aching from the serial blows, Harrison picked his moment and blocked the punch that was again headed toward his face using his left hand. Having stopped her momentum, he struck a blow with his right hand to her chest. The stranger keeled over and Harrison jabbed at her face with another punch. This time, she fell backwards and off of him. Harrison knew the opportunity afforded him would be brief. He turned around touching the dirt as he moved in an attempt to make contact with one of the two weapons.

Harrison felt around frantically as the stranger began to regain her composure. Out of the corner of his eye, he saw one of the weapons. As Harrison crawled toward the gun, the female stranger who had collapsed upon him blocked his approach. Her velocity and momentum pushed him to the ground once again. Harrison struggled to change positions with her when the stranger withdrew a knife from inside her jacket. He noticed it quickly as it glimmered in the moonlight. Harrison stretched out his right hand and firmly grasped the stranger's arm that yielded the knife. It was push-against-shove as the two sleuths attempted to exert their respective skills and strengths—essentially putting the knife in a tug-of-war.

The fight over the weapon was essentially a draw. Harrison knew that he had to get her off-balance and began to shove her sideways as he pushed against her arm. The stranger fell to the side and he rolled with her to secure his grasp on her arm. Her hand was close to the ground now and Harrison saw his opportunity. He repetitively smacked her hand on the dirt and by the fourth swat, the weapon fell loose and to the ground. Harrison pushed away the female stranger and grabbed for the knife. He gained his balance and turned directly to face his opponent with the knife extended toward her. The woman stood slowly and set her stance bracing for an attack. However, Harrison did not attack. He wanted the stranger alive in hopes of gaining information that would shorten his search for the people who kidnapped the President.

Harrison took a moment to catch his breath and then spoke even though his words were interrupted by irregular heavy breathing: "Come at me again and you're dead!" The stranger did not move. Harrison glanced around quickly hoping to see one of the guns glimmering in the moonlight. He spotted a weapon and move toward it as he kept his eye on his attacker. Harrison bent down and quickly picked up the gun. He tossed the knife aside and walked in the direction of the attacker, aiming his gun steadily toward her. For her part, the attacker did not move.

Harrison stopped and spoke once again, "Who are you and why were you trying to kill me?" The woman gazed at him with eyes of steel and said nothing. Harrison was growing impatient and pulled back the trigger. He said more forcefully, "Tell me why you were following me!" His attacker finally spoke. "I was not following you. You came at me like a robber or rapist and I reacted in my defense. I didn't know who you were and I still don't know who you are." He countered, "You don't think I'd believe that anybody, let alone a woman, would be walking by herself in this sparsely populated area in these early morning hours?" The woman responded sarcastically, "You don't believe a woman can find her way around in the dark?" and added, "Do you mind if I put my arms down, they're getting tired." Harrison said quickly, "No, keep them up where I can see them."

The stranger did as ordered and kept her hands up in the air. Harrison was growing impatient and asked again, "Why were you following me? Murdering two agents is not enough for you?" The woman did not change her expression or blink an eye at Harrison's accusation. If she indeed was a murderer, she was unwilling to betray her hand merely through questioning. Harrison decided that he would get no where with her here and needed to take her to Mentor for interrogation. Harrison ordered, "I haven't the time for this. Turn around and start walking." At first, the woman did not move. As if expecting somebody, her eyes shifted left and then right; or perhaps she was looking for alternatives to her predicament. Harrison wanted to waste no more time and angrily yelled, "Move!" At this, the stranger did as commanded and turned around. She started walking back toward Station Zero. Harrison walked behind her with his gun pointed and set for trouble. He maintained a discreet difference as he recalled embarrassingly that he lost his gun to her outstretched leg. He would not let this happen a second time—at least not a second time in the same day!

Harrison and the stranger walked slowly back to Station Zero. He kept his discrete distance and watched carefully for any treacherous moves. Harrison hoped that he could get back to Station Zero without further incident. There was too much at stake now. If the lady had information to give, Harrison would be eager to listen. Any plan to manipulate the Presidency was necessarily complex and any clues would be extremely helpful. Upon reflection, Harrison believed that coming across this woman was indeed a stroke of luck. Could she provide sufficient information to focus more readily his investigation and eliminate following questionable evidence?

Harrison and the stranger continued their walk to Station Zero. Without explanation or reason, the female agent collapsed and fell to the ground. Harrison took no chances and aimed his gun directly to her head. He spoke with ire in his voice, "Get up or I'll blow your damn head off!" The downed woman neither moved nor said anything. Harrison repeated his warning, but the forewarning was not heeded. The woman remained still with no movement observed. Harrison kept his gun aimed at the stranger's head as he carefully rolled over her body. Her arms and legs were limp as he turned her body toward him. Harrison carefully checked her pulse from the carotid artery near the base of her neck. He felt no pulse. 'How could this be?' thought Harrison. It was clear that she took something, perhaps some kind of poison. How or when the poison was administered Harrison did not know.

Harrison sat staring at the dead woman for a moment. He put down his gun and grabbed the woman's arms. Harrison dragged the woman into some thick brush and covered her with what he could find on the ground. He walked out of the brush and turned around toward the position of her body. Satisfied that he could not see anything, Harrison continued his trek to his car. He was angry with himself for not searching her thoroughly although justified his omission in that she would have attacked him under a search. Harrison simply shook his head at a lost opportunity and a lost life. Yet, this was now a problem for Mentor.

Twenty minutes passed before Harrison reached his car. He stopped short of the vehicle and surveyed the area for anything out of place. After several minutes of caution, Harrison was satisfied that the area was clear and walked toward his car. He used his electronic safety remote to unlock it and sat in the front seat. Harrison immediately locked the doors and picked up the phone. He dialed and after several minutes heard a familiar voice. Harrison was identified by the carrier signal and Mentor said, "Hardware, I didn't expect to hear from you so soon. Is anything the matter?" "Plenty" was Harrison's short reply. "Are you all right, Harrison?" "Yes, Greg" was his response. Harrison added, "However, you'll find a female body, approximately 35 years of age, in the woods directly south of Station Zero." Harrison continued, "Please arrange to have her picked up. It would not be good for a local resident to accidentally come across the body in the morning."

Mentor agreed and acknowledged that he would take care of the matter. He then asked his agent, "Any idea who she was?" "Not really," replied Harrison. "You know," said Mentor, "she could have followed me to Station Zero. Did you kill her, Harrison?" "No, I did not. She nearly killed me. I was walking her back to Station Zero to contact you to have her interrogated when she collapsed in front of me." "Poisoned?" asked Mentor. "Most likely," replied Harrison. He continued, "If she took it in my presence, though, she camouflaged her move perfectly. I saw nothing that telegraphed such a move. As callous as these people seem to be, I would not be surprised if she took or was administered the poison without her knowledge hours before her assignment." "Suicide?" asked Mentor in disbelief. "Well, suicide or she was murdered at the hands of her own comrades to guarantee her silence," suggested Harrison. There was a pause as the two men speculated independently about the dead woman. Mentor said to his agent in a cautious voice, "Be careful, Harrison. If she was indeed a part of the conspiracy, your position might be compromised." Harrison interrupted, "It would be appreciated if you could send me as much information as you can on her." "I will," replied Mentor. He continued, "However, we can't go through the normal lab procedures on this one. It may take a little more time, as I cannot afford to expose our mission to the White House. We may not know anything about her until after the mission is over." "I understand," was Harrison's reply. "I am headed to the hangar and Target One. I will contact you after reaching the mission target." "Good luck, Harrison—and be extremely careful" spoke Mentor with genuineness in his voice. "Thanks Greg and out." With the communication terminated, Harrison sped away and drove to reunite himself with Target One.

Chapter 14

The Calm Before the Storm

Harrison drove at a high rate of speed to the hangar protecting Target One. He wondered how the female stranger picked up his trail especially since he was quite careful in his approach. Or was she indeed shadowing Mentor as he indicated? Harrison stared straight ahead as he sped to the undisclosed airport. He knew that time was critical and the element of surprise might have eluded him. Harrison was disgusted at his susceptibility to a direct encounter with the domestic terrorist. He prided himself in his skills and cunning, only to be reminded of his mortality every now and then. Yet, it was his sharpness that kept him alive when the seduction of death beckoned so often at his door.

Harrison continued down the public road for another mile before turning left onto a dirt road. Dust swirled behind him as he continued dangerously at a high rate of speed. Harrison justified the risk as he traveled the road often and knew it well. He drove for several miles before coming to a clearing. One could not see the camouflaged hangars, but they were there. Harrison drove to the location disclosed to him by Mentor where he expected to find Target One. He slowed as the hangar became visible to the naked eye and stopped at a side entrance. A guard who flashed a light at him met Harrison. He asked for Harrison's identification which was produced and carefully scanned. The guard nodded and Harrison entered the hangar. He shielded his eyes as the brightness inside the hangar was in stark contrast to the outside darkness. Target One was in view with several guards protecting it. Harrison again presented his credentials to show one of the guards. The guard verified the credentials and welcomed Harrison.

Harrison immediately boarded Target One, as time was critical. He reviewed his flight map for his destination—Montana. The course appeared straightforward. Harrison folded the chart and headed for the cockpit. He placed the charted map in clear view to refer to during the flight. Harrison sat down as he began reviewing his checklist for takeoff. He scanned carefully each item before putting the clipboard in a secure place. Harrison buckled himself into the pilot's seat and looked out the front window of the cockpit awaiting the signal to start engines. He did not have to wait long as the ground crewman twirled his hand. Harrison flipped a switch that started his right engine. He then flipped another switch adjacent to the first one and his refitted left engine energized. Harrison revved the engines and released the gear. Target One inched forward and slowly disembarked from its protective hangar. Harrison guided the sleek jet toward the runway. He contacted the tower requesting clearance for takeoff. The control tower verified Target One and gave Harrison authorization for departure. Harrison glanced at the critical gauges one more time and increased engine power. Target One sped down the runway. At the moment of critical speed, Harrison pulled the steering and Target One began its rapid ascent. It was not long before man and plane were at the scheduled cruising altitude of 10,000 feet. Harrison checked the altimeter and speedometer. Satisfied with Target One's heading and performance, he switched on the autopilot. Harrison left the cockpit area and walked into his office. Target One was on a steady course for the closest government airport to Sarhea, Montana. In this case, the airport was Malmstrom Air Force Base in Great Falls, Montana. It was agreed beforehand with Mentor that radio silence would be adhered to strictly and broken by either man only if the information to be shared warranted a severe breach.

As Harrison reflected upon this morning's events, he hoped that the silence would be interrupted by Mentor with information about his female assailant. He knew that his assignment might be jeopardized, or as Mentor implicated, his assailant was shadowing Mentor himself. Was it clever guesswork or did the currently "seated" President Ashton realize that Mentor and his agents were a formidable force, a force that had to be liquidated if her plan of legitimizing dissident terrorists was to materialize? What even was more alarming was that the control of information and disinformation by the Presidency might go undetected by other government officials and the people of the United States. By the time that the American people realized the true threat of the domestic terrorists, it would be too late much like other tragic events in American history: Japan's attack of Pearl Harbor; Germany's "final solution"; the era of McCarthyism; the Challenger shuttle; the disinformation over tobacco...The blinded naiveté of the American people to believe in a person, agency or product occurs at times even when evidence to the contrary exists.

Harrison reflected that supremacy and extremist movements in history were never in the final analysis positive influences on the American society. Had not Modem questioned emphatically the authenticity of his wife, Harrison would consider it treasonous to defy the President's authority and work actively with Mentor at exposing her in this conspiracy. And what role did this President Ashton play? A pawn controlled by others or perhaps more lethal and in command?

Harrison did not have the opportunity to ponder further the sinister nature of the seated President Ashton, or her alter ego, or her surgical twin, or her clone, or her...For at the moment,

Edward Galluzzi

he was tossed around the fuselage of Target One like atomic atoms in a particle chamber. Harrison's first thought was that of severe air turbulence. He struggled to maintain his stability as he walked toward the cockpit. Harrison entered the cockpit and was thrown roughly into the pilot's seat. He was able to right himself and buckle his seat belt.

Harrison scanned the instrument panel and then gazed out the window. Daylight was dawning, but he saw nothing tangible in front of him. 'Clear air turbulence' he thought to himself. Harrison released the autopilot and then struggled to maintain control of Target One as it bounced through the airwaves. He did not want to travel to Montana on the back of a wild stallion as it were. Harrison altered the jet's altitude and course. The turbulence soon faded. Harrison was able eventually to return to Target One's original course and speed. He was now only several hours away from Malmstrom A.F.B. in Great Falls, Montana.

Harrison left the cockpit and returned to his office. He began to review the information given to him by Mentor that detailed the operations of the conservative extremists in America. As he read through the material, his fax machine interrupted his thoughts. The cover page indicated that it was from Mentor and Harrison speculated that it was information about his female assailant. He hoped that any facts uncovered would help him in his infiltration in Montana. Harrison needed to reclaim the advantage after his earlier encounter this morning.

Two pages exited the fax machine. Harrison read the transcription aloud as if others were on the plane with him: "Hardware—please do not acknowledge the reception of this message. Known details on the assailant are as follows...

117

Name: Clona Lane Hawthorne
Alias: Lane Montana; Clona Jane; Hawthorne Lane
Last Known Address: 1406 Con Way, Sarhea, Montana
Age: 37
Ethnic Background: Caucasian
Marital Status: Single
Arrest History: None; but she was investigated in 1997 for suspicion of murder and intent to cause bodily harm *via* an explosive device; suspicion of conspiracy in abortion bombings; all evidence circumstantial and cases never brought to court."

This information provided by Mentor confirmed that he was correct in his suspicions and that his final destination of Sarhea, Montana would be a good starting point in his investigation. Harrison checked his watch and allowing for Target One's course and speed, his ETA in Montana was ten o'clock. He desired to sleep, but the thought left him as quickly as it entered his mind. He must remain alert and prepared for anything, including another assault. After all, this Clona Hawthorne was not alone in her actions against the American government. Sleep would come shortly. Harrison was scheduled to land at Malmstrom A.F.B. near Great Falls, which was in west central Montana. Great Falls was about three hours away from Sarhea by car. Harrison planned to sleep for the part of the day in Great Falls and travel under the protection of darkness to his final destination, Sarhea.

It was 9:45 a.m. and Target One was approaching Great Falls, Montana. After the sudden air turbulence, nothing out of the ordinary occurred for the remainder of the trip. Harrison had returned to the cockpit and released the autopilot. The jet's controls were rendered back to him. Harrison made the necessary course correction for his final flight path to the airport just outside of Great Falls.

Harrison contacted the control tower: "Target One to Malmstrom A.F.B. Target One to Malmstrom tower." He paused and listened to static for several moments. Then came the expected reply: "Target One, this is Malmstrom A.F.B. in Great Falls, Montana. Go ahead." "This is Target One. Requesting landing clearance and course correction." "Come to course 260 and you are clear to land on runway 290. Winds are out of the west at 10 miles per hour and gusting to 15. You are about 30 miles out. No other traffic. Control out." "Roger, control" was Harrison's sign off.

Harrison corrected his course as requested, but was too far for visual contact. He continued to cruise on the heading 260. Harrison reviewed his plans once he landed at the airport. He would lay low in a motel under the alias of Donald Marshall! until evening. At that time, he planned to rent an all-terrain vehicle for the three-hour drive to Sarhea. Harrison estimated that he would arrive in Sarhea around 9:00 p.m. At that point, the comforts of home would no longer apply. Harrison would switch to outback survival mode. As a stranger in such a small town as Sarhea, he would not go unnoticed. He would have time to organize his survival gear in his motel room as well as get some long needed rest and sleep.

Harrison glanced forward. The air force base was now coming into view. With the quiet whine of the jet engines and the scenic panoramic view, Harrison thought of Hannah. He decided to compose a fax to his intended, as there was little chance of surveillance detecting the transmission from Target One. In any case, the fax would be scrambled and sent to headquarters for routing.

Harrison enabled the autopilot once again, but remained in the cockpit due to his closeness to the airport. He grabbed some nearby writing material and began his letter to Hannah:

"My Dear Hannah,

It seems like we've been apart for weeks or months; yet, it has only been a few days. I miss you! I miss every part of you. I'm safe and hope you are the same. Looking forward to seeing you once again and doing something terribly romantic. I hope Josetta is doing well. Please give him my regards if you see him. Take care, my love.

Your H."

Harrison purposely did not comment on the status of his mission not only for security reasons, but he wanted to minimize Hannah's worrying—something at which she was skillful. After all, she knew that Harrison thought of her often even though they could not communicate directly with each other.

With the autopilot engaged, Harrison left the cockpit and faxed his affections to Hannah. He returned quickly as runway 290 came into view. Harrison disengaged the autopilot and took control of Target One. He radioed the control tower once again, "Malmstrom A.F.B., this is Target One." The tower replied, "Welcome to Great Falls, Target One. You are clear to land on runway two-niner. Come to course 2-5-0 and hold. Begin descent at your discretion. Winds are out of the southwest at 12 miles per hour and gusting to 17. You are 10 miles out. No other traffic. Upon touchdown, taxi to hangar 47. Control out." "Roger, control" was Harrison's customary sign off.

At 5 miles out, Harrison began his descent to the airport. It was a sunny morning with unlimited visibility, a pilot's dream for takeoffs and landings. Harrison cut the speed of Target One and descended gradually aligning himself with the runway. He surveyed his instruments and noted no problems or alarms. The left engine performed flawlessly despite its earlier damage. Target One continued its descent as Harrison pulled the flaps and lowered the landing gear. He was flying above the beginning of the landing strip. As Target One made contact with the runway, Harrison put flaps to full and reversed the engines. Target One slowed as Harrison began taxiing to hangar 47. Hangar 47 was a large building that housed similar private jets as Target One as well as older air force jets. Harrison followed the path designated by the ground crew and slowed Target One until it was aligned with the entrance to the hangar. Harrison cut the engines and reviewed the landing checklist. He grabbed several suitcases, one of which contained surveillance equipment, and exited Target One.

As Harrison debarked, an air force security guard approached him. The soldier greeted Harrison: "Good morning, Mr. Marshalli." The air force pilot showed Harrison his credentials as well as orders given to him by Mentor to guard Target One. Harrison thanked the solider and was directed toward a waiting government automobile. He requested to be taken to the nearest car rental office. The trip took less than 15 minutes. Harrison thanked the driver, stepped out of the car and entered the rental office.

As Mr. Marshalli, Harrison rented an all terrain jeep and drove to the motel specified by Mentor. He entered the room and tipped the clerk. Harrison opened the suitcase with his surveillance equipment and retrieved an electronic meter. He scanned the room for listening devices and once satisfied, returned the meter to its place. Harrison entered the bedroom and stripped to his underwear. He rolled into bed and quickly fell asleep. It may be Harrison's last good night sleep for quite awhile.

Chapter 15

Duty of the Cardinal Camerlengo

It was mid-afternoon in Roma. Hannah was glowing even more brightly than the sun beaming down on Roma...if that was possible. The message faxed by Harrison prior to his landing at Great Falls, Montana had reached Hannah moments ago. She stopped on the doorsteps of her hotel and read the message for a third time:

"My Dear Hannah,
    It seems like we've been apart for weeks or months; yet, it has only been a few days. I miss you! I miss every part of you. I'm safe and hope you are the same. Looking forward to seeing you once again and doing something terribly romantic. I hope Josetta is doing well; please give him my regards if you see him. Take care, my love.
                                        Your H."

Hannah shook her head, her hair flowing in the breeze, and smiled again. She was unable to put her love's message away, but grasped it tightly as she walked under the warm sun. How much she wished that she could communicate back with Harrison, but she knew that it was impossible. She received comfort in the knowledge that her Harrison knew the words she would say in return. Hearing from Harrison while he was on assignment was always uplifting for Hannah. If nothing else, she knew that even though he may be in harm's way, he was safe and alive. Nothing could mar this day, nothing. Harrison was alive and thinking of her despite all the pressing events in his day.

Hannah hailed a cab and requested the destination of the Holy City. She thought she would share her joy about Harrison's letter with Pope Josetta. The city seemed "busy" for this time of day with people rather hurried. The cab arrived at Vatican City within 20 minutes. Hannah paid her fare and began walking up the steps to the Vatican. She noted that there were more papal Swiss guards protecting the Holy See than observed on earlier papal visits.

Inside the Vatican, the immediate hall was filled with people—holy men, newsmen—all sorts of people. Hannah glimpsed Father Edgar Soergel out of the corner of her eye, the holy man who was quite helpful in arranging her papal visits, and headed toward him. Father Soergel turned to see Hannah approaching and extended his hand toward her. "Hello, Father. Nice to see you again," Hannah said sincerely and happily. "And you, Miss Littleton," replied the priest.

Hannah's expression grew quizzical as she asked the man of God; "It seems so busy here today. Is something special happening?" Sadness grew over Father Soergel face as he spoke, "I'm afraid that the Pontiff slipped into a coma about an hour ago. He is not doing well and his physician is not offering much hope." The excitement of hearing from Harrison left Hannah's face and was replaced by an equally aching sadness. She spoke, "I'm sorry, Father. I just arrived to request a visit with Pope Josetta...I..." Hannah's words trailed away, awkwardly, not knowing what to say. The holy man filled the gap, "We appreciate your kindness to Josetta. His visits with Mr. Rossetti and you strengthened him and brought him immense joy. I am sorry to break the news to you in this way. I know that your fiancé cherished his friendship with the Holy Father and would like to be here himself." The reverend paused and Hannah added, "Yes, he would, he would indeed.

Harrison will take Josetta's severely deteriorating health very hard."

There was a silence between the holy person and the newsperson. Hannah broke the silence and spoke, "Mr. Rossetti's and my thoughts are with the Holy Father and with all the sacred people who have assisted and served him. His devotion to his church and his progressive approach will be a great loss to the leadership and growth of Catholic Church—and a special loss to people of all faiths around the world." "Thank you, Miss Littleton, thank you for such kind words." The priest continued, "I am sorry, but I must leave and return to my duties." "Of course, Father," replied Hannah.

The priest held Hannah's hand warmly and bowed slightly as he left. Hannah walked to the conference room where other journalists were gathered, at least those who were aware of the recent deteriorating change in the Pontiffs medical condition. One of Hannah's colleagues asked upon her entrance, "Hello, Hannah. Have you heard anything new on the medical status of the Pope?" "No," replied Hannah. She continued, "He slipped into a coma about an hour ago and his condition has remained unchanged." At those words, a cover of silence spread over the room—a room full of journalists who typically chattered freely, silenced by nothing.

Hannah broke the stillness and asked, "Is anybody here familiar with the Roman Catholic ritual surrounding the death of a pope and the election of a new pope?" The journalists turned around and looked at one another when one of them spoke: "Yes, I do." He continued, "Miss Littleton of *The Washington Sun* I believe?" "Yes, yes I am" replied Hannah feeling a trifle off guard. "I am David Beas," stated the gentleman. He added, "I've written for the *Awenire* for 30 years; the *Awenire* for those of you who may not know is the Italian national Catholic daily newspaper. In these past 30 years, I have covered several papal reigns." Hannah's attention and those of her colleagues were drawn to their associate. Mr. Beas provided background information on the College of Cardinals and described the unfolding events that would transpire should a vacancy occur in the Holy See:

"It is a longstanding tradition of the Roman Catholic Church to elevate deserving bishops and archbishops among the College of Bishops to the College of Cardinals. These cardinals are considered 'Princes of the Church' and are called upon to support the Pontiff in the governing of the Church because of their special devotion and holiness. Many of the cardinals are leaders in the Roman Curia—the Pontiffs Ministers of State. The role that the cardinals render is that of electing a new Pontiff when the See of Peter is vacant. To these cardinals and them alone belongs this honor and grave responsibility. This is true for all cardinals except those who completed their 80th year of age upon entrance into the conclave. The maximum number of these cardinals is set presently at 120."

Mr. Beas paused briefly, drank some water and then continued: "Pope Paul VI issued the 1975 edicts for the Sacred College of Cardinals to be followed during a vacancy of the Holy See and the election of the new pope. He declared that when the Apostolic See is vacant, the government of the Church is in the hands of the College of Cardinals only in regard to customary business matters that cannot be deferred, and with respect to the preparations that are necessary for the election of the new Pope. During the vacancy, the cardinals wear the characteristic red-trimmed black cassock and red sash."

Mr. Beas paused once more before continuing: "All cardinals heading the dicasteries of the Roman Curia and the Cardinal Secretary of State cease from their offices upon the death of the Pontiff. This is true for all cardinals except for the office of the Camerlengo of the Holy Roman Church, 60 of the Major Penitentiary and the Vicar General of the Diocese of Rome. When the Pontiff dies, the Cardinal Camerlengo must verify the Pope's death—traditionally by withdrawing the sheet covering the Pontiffs face and calling the Pope three times by his baptismal name without response. When he receives no response, the Camerlengo tells his assistants that *'the Pope is truly dead.'* It is the Cardinal Camerlengo's responsibility to authorize a death certificate and make the event public by notifying the Cardinal Vicar for the Diocese of Rome. The Camerlengo must seal the Pope's private apartments. He will destroy the *Ring of the Fisherman* and the papal seal by breaking off the gold rim bearing the late Pope's name. The Camerlengo then makes preparations for the papal funeral rites and the nine days of mourning, the *novemdieles.* During the papal vacancy, it is the Cardinal Camerlengo who is responsible for the government of the Church. He will direct the election of a new Pope assisted by three cardinals with three new cardinals elected every three days." Hannah interrupted her colleague and asked, "How exactly is the new Pope elected?"

Mr. Beas responded, "After fifteen-to-twenty days of general congregations and mourning for the Pope after his funeral, the Cardinal Electors enter the conclave to choose which of them will emerge as the Holy Roman Pontiff. The cardinals take an oath before entering the conclave that they will follow the rules declared by the Pope and that they will maintain absolute secrecy about the voting and ongoing deliberations. This is a stern oath in that the penalty for disclosing the proceedings is automatic excommunication."

Mr. Beas again paused for a sip of ice water, which had long since warmed. He continued, "The cardinals are seated around the wall of the Sistine Chapel and take a ballot paper on which is written: *Eligo in suumum pontificem-I elect as supreme pontiff*...The cardinals write in their choice for Pontiff, fold the ballot and proceed to approach the altar. On the altar stands a chalice with a paten on it. The cardinal holds up his ballot in clear view of his holy colleagues to show that he has voted and then places the ballot on the paten. The cardinal then slides his ballot into the chalice. The Cardinal Camerlengo and his three assistants count the votes. Each assistant reads the name aloud, writes it down on a tally sheet and the third assistant runs a needle and thread through the center of each ballot. The ballots are then burned along with any notes made during the proceedings. Election is by two-thirds plus one more vote of the counted ballots. If thirty elections have taken place without a single cardinal being elected Pope, then the cardinals may elect by simple majority."

Mr. Beas paused and sipped more water this time before continuing: "After a cardinal has received the required number of votes, the Dean of the College of Cardinals asked the elected if he accepts the election and by what name he wishes to be called as Pope. On giving his assent, the cardinal immediately becomes *Pontificus Maximus*—the Holy Roman Pontiff. The cardinals in turn pledge their obedience to His Holiness. The Pope vests himself in the white soutane and skullcap—the pontifical clericals. When a new Pope is elected, the ballots are burned with a substance to give off-white smoke; otherwise, they give off black smoke. For decades, this is how the waiting crowds and the world determine whether their new Holy Father will soon emerge from the Sistine Chapel. The Dean of College of Cardinals then steps onto the main balcony of the Vatican and declares: *'Habemus PapamV*—We have a Pope. His Holiness appears on the balcony and delivers his Apostolic Blessing to the awaiting people and the world.

Within the short time of the election of a new Pope, a formal ceremony of Inauguration takes place at which time the *woollen pallium* is bestowed on him. Traditionally, the Pope will be carried around St. Peter's Square on the *Sedia Gestatoria*—the Papal Throne—and have the Papal Tiara placed on his head."

Mr. Beas completed his informative history to his colleagues who were appreciative of the knowledge presented. At the moment that Mr. Beas was going to entertain questions, a holy man entered the conference room carrying a somber facial expression. He walked up to the podium and requested that the journalist be seated. The holy priest identified himself as Cardinal Roberto Borchertmeyer, the Cardinal Camerlengo, and announced that His Holiness, Pontiff Joseph Josetta Modesta, was dead.

Chapter 16

An Empty Farewell

Harrison slept away a good part of the bright sunny day in Montana attesting to his degree of exhaustion. While citizens of Great Falls, Montana were hustling and bustling, he was slowly drifting into consciousness after what seemed like an eternity. It took a moment for Harrison to establish his whereabouts following his slumber. He sat up sharply by the side of the bed, rubbing his eyes and face. The moment of uncertainty passed as Harrison gathered his bearings. He turned on the television to learn of this evening's weather report for his mission in Sarhea. The picture tube illuminated readily. The words uttered by the news reporter shocked Harrison as he turned in disbelief and began walking toward his bed. He sat down quite slowly as if caught in a time warp. Harrison's eyes swelled with tears and began weeping openly—a rare occurrence for the man of cold reasoning and judgment. He listened with a touch of denial as he attempted to focus on the words coming out of the picture box: "The Cardinal Camerlengo announced today at ten o'clock, Rome time, that Pope Joseph Josetta, one of the most progressive spiritual leaders of the Roman Catholic Church, slipped into a coma and died peacefully, never gaining consciousness. The Roman Pontiff..." The words were pushed out of Harrison's consciousness displaced by acute inner pain, emotional grief and devastated loss. These emotions, however, were soon replaced by anger, anger directed toward himself for not being with Josetta—not able to comfort and say "goodbye" to a noble friend. Harrison truly thought that this Man of God would recover, would be freed from his bed, would rise once again to guide and lead his people, a responsibility that he cherished with great respect, honor and vigor.

Harrison's thoughts shifted abruptly to Hannah. 'Was she with Josetta when he died? Did his holy friend have somebody to comfort him in his final moment on this man-bound earth? Was Hannah managing her own grief?' After all, Hannah had grown very close to Josetta from her brief contacts with him nurtured by the longstanding friendship with Harrison. Harrison's anger twanged again as he felt helpless to comfort Hannah and be comforted by her. Harrison had no one in Montana to turn to. He was a stranger and must remain so if he was to infiltrate the dissident terrorists to achieve any degree of success in his mission.

Harrison wiped the wetness from his eyes and slowly walked to the restroom. He stood at the sink and stared at the man in the mirror. Regrets? Harrison had more than a few. How many assignments in his service to the government have kept him away from personally significant unfolding life events—circumstances affecting his loved ones and friends; yet, unable to provide or receive some measure of comfort...and for what? Duty? Responsibility? Country? Harrison's emptiness disgusted him. He picked up a glass from the sink and angrily hurled it at the man in the mirror.

The mirror cracked on contact and the glass broke into jagged, irregular glistening pieces. Harrison ran away in repulsion and fell into bed. He clenched a pillow as if comforting or being comforted by something human. There Harrison lay and wept, crying like a little boy unable to control his emotions. It was a long time since he curled up in a fetal position, but a time that he remembered unfortunately well. Harrison's mother died when he was on a mission ten years ago. The relationships of Pope and mother were very different.

Yet, the void and emptiness were painfully the same, eating at him with no comfort in sight.

Chapter 17

All in the Family

Harrison drifted asleep only to awaken less than one hour later. Yet, it was later than he wanted and his mourning necessarily was interrupted by duty. The sun began to set as a three-hour trip was ahead of him. Harrison freshened quickly and collected his gear for the mission. He gathered the usual infrared night equipment, munitions, explosives, identifications and communication devices.

Harrison packed the supplies in his rented jeep and headed away from the motel. He was driving north out of Great Falls, Montana looking to connect with Highway 95. Highway 95 stretched northwesterly and was the nearest interstate to his final destination, Sarhea, some 350 miles away. Harrison's mind quickly began to wander. He shook his head and realized he must discipline himself by separating his emotions from the unfolding events of the day—the death of his holy friend, Josetta, and the undoubted anguish of his fiancée, Hannah, whom he could not contact, not comfort, not support—all must be put behind him. The mission to infiltrate the extremist faction and discover the whereabouts of President Elizabeth Ashton required his full attention and cunning. Harrison understood this all too well as he was discovered once and could easily be exposed again.

It was dusk now as Harrison drove northwesterly on highway 95 to his target destination. Unlike most missions, there was no time for planning and discussing options with Mentor. Mentor was a brilliant strategist who explored all possibilities in developing a campaign. He was shrewd in evaluating the risks involved with each option and confidently narrowed down the choices under discussion to two or three. Mentor explored those two or three options with his agents. Although confident in his operational planning, Mentor listened to his agents for strategy input. He had faith in his chosen agents and left the development of mission details up to their creative talents. After all, it was their lives that were endangered and on the line.

Yet, this mission was not a typical one. It involved the President of the United States directly. The role of the Presidency was difficult enough for Elizabeth Ashton without the added political burden of being the first woman President. On all counts, President Ashton demonstrated her capabilities in leadership and politics, silencing most of her critics. Harrison grew comfortable in his role of serving Elizabeth Ashton. He hoped that she was safe, but he understood all too well the brutality of people involved in extreme factions. Priority one in Harrison's mission was to uncover President Ashton's whereabouts and, if feasible, develop contingencies to rescue her either alone or in cooperation with his colleagues. As difficult as this goal was, he knew that Mentor had a more difficult responsibility in keeping the mission covert from the alias President Ashton and her coconspirators. Even a bogus President could not successfully infiltrate the oval office without the assistance of men and women of power in Washington.

Ferreting out the treasonous individuals in the scheme was not a priority for Harrison. Discovering the whereabouts of the genuine Elizabeth Ashton, alive or dead, was foremost. Unfortunately for Ashton, either alive or dead, would provide the necessary evidence to discredit the alias President. President Ashton could speak for herself and the events leading up to her capture and confinement if found alive. If dead, the evidence of her demise would discredit the fictitious President and interfere with the objectives of the extremist faction. Harrison believed that Elizabeth Ashton was still alive if for no other reason than the role of a bargaining chip should their terrorist plans go awry. However, the extremists may not realize that they have met their match in President Ashton. Of what Harrison knew of her character and position, she will not be a willing hostage in bargaining over what she views as the venerable role of the Presidency. Ashton undoubtedly would sacrifice her life in belief of her principles before endangering the office of the President of the United States.

Harrison would concentrate his efforts on uncovering the status of the President and her whereabouts. Although contact with Mentor was risky, he knew that he would make at least two such contacts: one, to determine if more detailed information was collected on Clona Hawthorne, the assailant who died at her own hands or those of her comrades rather than be interrogated by the government of the United States; and two, to confirm plans of engagement and rescue when he discovered the status of President Ashton.

Harrison continued his journey up interstate 95. He glanced at his watch and noted the time of 8:05 p.m. Darkness was encroaching from the East. It would be another hour before Harrison arrived in Sarhea. He was still formulating his plan on infiltrating whatever group lay ahead. He knew from past experiences with radical cults and extremists that they were not difficult to locate in remote rural areas in specific regions of the United States. If he exhibited sufficient interest in their assembly without arousing suspicion, he thought he might feign interest in affiliation as he sifted through information gathered by his espionage. However, the time requirement to gain their trust concerned him. It would not be possible to seek membership and attempt to develop friendships. There was no time to lay such groundwork.

Harrison's mission might be uncovered at any moment by the alias President or her coconspirators.

Harrison determined that he would locate the terrorist's organization and with the aid of listening devices, hopefully gather sufficient clues that would lead to the status and whereabouts of President Ashton. Harrison knew the risk was high and it was up to Mentor to divert suspicion from his mission. The alias President Ashton would monitor Mentor carefully as she designated him to carry out her ten point plans in assimilating the country's conservative radicals. Harrison must make sufficient contacts to gather solid intelligence and implement whatever contingencies were feasible in rescuing President Ashton.

As Harrison passed a road marker, he glanced at the sign indicating that Sarhea was twenty miles ahead. He would arrive there in about fifteen minutes. Harrison hoped to find a cabin or some other unoccupied structure to use as his safe house. In most missions, such places were scouted in advance by intelligence and identified to the agent. The rapidly unfolding events, however, did not permit such indulgence, as Harrison knew he was clearly on his own. He did not care whether the commandeered accommodation was rustic or luxurious as long as it was vacant and appeared it would remain so for a period of time. Harrison did not intend to remain there long, even if he chose to do so, for the terrorists likely patrolled the area surrounding Sarhea.

It was time for Harrison's first contact with Mentor. He hoped to gain valuable information about his assailant, findings that he expected would expedite identifying targets and leading to the whereabouts of President Ashton. Harrison slowed his rented vehicle and pulled over to the safety apron of the road. He retrieved one of his briefcases in which he packed his scrambled cellular phone. Harrison dialed the number that

Mentor secured prior to the mission. There was a lengthy pause as if the dialed number was being transferred and rolled over. Harrison knew that security was high. He listened to several rings and then a familiar voice: "Please do not identify yourself by name or location." "Yes, s—." Harrison caught himself before identifying Mentor by *sir* thereby revealing that he was his superior. "Listen carefully," said Mentor. He continued, "I have the following additional information on the individual in question. Marital status of Clona H. reported previously incorrect. Married. Suspected one of multiple wives of Jacob H." Mentor paused and rightfully so. Harrison surmised that his assailant was the wife of, or apparently one of the wives of Jacob Hawthorne, real estate entrepreneur and suspected leader of the *AAF-A (America Always First-Always)* splinter militia faction thought to operate out of rural Montana. Mentor continued the briefing: "A bonus...alias Elizabeth A— a.k.a. Marilyn H—, suspected wife of Jacob H—." There came a pause from Mentor. As if reading Harrison's mind, Mentor added: "Will advise how later. It is important that you infiltrate the faction. Try to discover the circumstances and status of our intelligence. You will have no chance otherwise to locate, perhaps rescue genuine article. Watch your step. Be cautious of Mary Lou H., also suspected wife of Jacob H. Given what we know of the others, must suspect third has a role in the plot as well. Genuine article must be pinpointed at all cost and returned to her rightful seat. Do what you have to do to resolve. Do you understand?" Harrison recognized the grave tone that Mentor adopted in formulating his question. Harrison replied, "Yes, understand fully. What if assistance is required?" The reply was quick and cold from Mentor: "None." Silence punctuated their conversation until broken by Harrison: "If genuine package located, how do I mail it?" Mentor replied, "Not previous location or route. Contact me when package is ready for mailing. Will have a post office address for both of you." Harrison countered, "If package is broken?" "Same procedure" was the response. Mentor continued, "Need to sign off. Good luck." Harrison managed a "thank you" and disengaged communication. He stared into the darkness in front of him and sighed as he pondered Mentor's intelligence.

Harrison started his jeep and slowly left the apron of the highway. He picked up speed as he returned to his northwesterly course on highway 95. As the night advanced, the road was desolate with little-to-no traffic to navigate. Harrison judged that he was about fifteen minutes away from Sarhea and the *AFA-A* militia camp. He knew from previous intelligence reports that the *AFA-A* was armed heavily and considered U.S. laws and the constabulary as both restrictive and unnecessary. The *AFA-A* membership was known to routinely commit munitions violations and disregard the laws of the land that ban paramilitary forces. Members were prone to threaten others and commit individual acts of violence, all spurred and festered by the rhetoric provided by the leadership in the movement. Common law courts and tax evasion were more the rule than not. The *AFA-A* membership perceived themselves as answerable to no authority at any level of government. Their brand of domestic terrorism was motivated by conspiracy theories, typically unsubstantiated and sinister in nature.

As Harrison reviewed what he remembered about this particular faction, he glanced at a highway marker identifying the route to Sarhea as ten miles ahead. Harrison slowed to insure that he did not miss the exit. He had no intention to enter the town of Sarhea, but knew that he must quickly find a country road, preferably an unmarked path, one that would provide him access and cover. Harrison hoped to find some unoccupied structure to designate as his temporary base of operations.

As Harrison neared the highway exit, he quickly recounted the information uncovered and shared by Mentor. He wondered if the extremists already knew about the death of Clona Hawthorne or were in recent contact with the seated President Ashton, a.k.a. Marilyn Hawthorne. A greater risk perhaps was an accidental contact with Mary Lou Hawthorne. Was this wife of Jacob Hawthorne in the area and on a mission of her own? What alias was she using? It was reasonable to conclude that Mary Lou would have adopted an alias as did the other Mrs. Hawthornes. Harrison knew that if he did gain information regarding the whereabouts of the genuine Elizabeth Ashton, he could expect no aid in extracting her from her hidden location. Such an extraction would be less complicated if she was alive and ambulatory.

The moment had arrived as Harrison found himself at the Sarhea exit. He merged to the right and headed up the inclined exit ramp. The jeep naturally slowed to a stop given the interactive forces of gravity and the incline. The sign to Sarhea pointed right and identified that the traveler had yet another twenty miles to the rural town. In the opposite direction thirty miles away was the town of Cut Bank, Montana. Harrison steered eastward toward the small town. He darted his eyes right and left in search of a path off the main road. Harrison determined that he must find such a road within the next five miles, as he did not wish to be any closer to Sarhea than fifteen miles.

A mile had passed during which time Harrison witnessed no useful paths. He continued scanning both sides of the road for an offbeat path that led hopefully to a serviceable base of operations. Harrison eyed his odometer and noted that two miles had passed. He continued his search with some anxiety as the miles ticked off. Harrison glanced at the odometer as he was approaching the third mile from the highway exit when he caught a fleeting glimpse of a dirt road. He stopped the jeep and headed in reverse. Harrison stopped the vehicle once again at the mouth of the off-road. Things that might be revealed were hidden by the darkness; however, he was able to observe that traffic on the road appeared very light. The bright glow of his headlights disclosed the presence of high grass on the dirt path. Harrison stretched his neck to its functional limits in order to determine that he was not followed or approached unexpectedly by a passerby. He dimmed his lights and now only used his orange-glowing running lights. Harrison remained still and silent, stretching his neck once again to inspect his surroundings.

Five minutes had passed and Harrison was still waiting. He looked around again before finally turning right onto the dirt path. Harrison knew that what he perceived could be deceiving and townspeople or terrorists might reside on the rural land ahead. He glanced at his odometer before proceeding down the path. As his jeep crept the distance passed slowly. The orange running lights glowed eerily as he struggled to steer the vehicle on the thin road. Ten minutes had passed as the odometer confessed that he traveled one mile. Harrison expended one mile with no side path off the road or visible structure in the darkness.

Harrison continued his slow pace and stopped quickly. He noticed a side path off the thin dirt road. From what he could see in the moonlit darkness, grass was overgrown in the path similar to the main dirt road. Harrison steered his jeep left onto the side path. The boundaries of the road were less discernible than before requiring an even slower pace. Harrison steered carefully to maintain his position on the road. He did not know if any ravines lay ahead, but did not want to begin this portion of his mission seeking a local tow truck. Harrison continued his snail's pace deeper into the rural setting. The barely visible road took him through curves and bends. Upon traveling the path for fifteen minutes, the road straightened and ended abruptly. Harrison turned off his running lights and killed the engine. He would travel the rest of the path on foot to determine if a structure lay ahead that was uninhabited and suitable for his base of operation.

Chapter 18

One Dead? One Alive? One...?

Harrison grabbed a small high beam flashlight from his brief case. The dim moonlight afforded little illumination on this cloudy night. He no more desired to careen down a ravine than his jeep. Harrison stepped out of the road path at the point where it ended abruptly. He illuminated the land in front of him and noted it lacked the boundary collar of a main road. Harrison walked cautiously, swinging the beam of light back and forth in hopes of spotting any object that afforded clues or rendered him a warning.

Harrison continued this swing pattern for thirty minutes. He came across nothing except the scurrying of rural night creatures. Then, a structure rose up in the distance although appeared uninviting in the night sky. Harrison turned off his flashlight, quickened his pace and crouched his figure to conceal himself as he traveled the path toward the building. As he neared the structure, it grew in both size and intimidation. Harrison's adrenalin surged and his senses were alerted as he had not forgotten the hostile incident near the safe house.

Harrison neared the front porch of an apparently old, abandoned rural farmhouse. For safety and survival's sake, he assumed that the structure was inhabited. Perhaps it was a baited trap in the darkness lying in wait to spring its surprise. Harrison tiptoed up to the porch and froze, quietly waiting for signs of betrayal or entrapment. Moments passed and nothing was detected. Harrison crept again, which placed him at the first step of the old structure. He stepped upward only to hear the creaking that one might expect from such a dilapidated building. Harrison froze once again waiting for a response from the structure as if the creaking noise required a reply. Yet, no rebuttal was forthcoming. Harrison continued his approach up the stairway filling the still night air with disharmony. In short manner, he found himself at the door.

Harrison glanced to either side of him as if something might jump out of the darkness. He saw the outline of windows on either side, appearing amazingly intact and unbroken. No light illuminated the insides of the building. Harrison grasped carefully the doorknob. It squeaked briefly as he attempted to rotate the handle, but it did not open. It was locked which seemed unusual to Harrison. It also suggested a warning to him that the structure or its contents were in need of protection. Harrison released the handle and move to his right, stopping in front of the window. He attempted to lift the pane, but it too was secured. He walked left and stopped in front of the other window, but its status was no different.

Harrison thought for a moment and then headed down the front stairway, filling the night sky once again with a creaking symphony. The structure looked uninhabited to Harrison at the moment. He switched his flashlight to a low narrow beam to assist him in walking to the side of the building. The side that Harrison chose revealed no doorway or window. He walked around the corner to the back of the structure. The dim illumination exposed a door and one window. The door was flush with the ground with no creaking steps to announce his entrance. Harrison grasped the handle carefully and slowly rotated the knob. Again, the door was locked. A check of the window yielded the same. Harrison shined the pale light toward the bottom of the building. He discovered a small window at ground level that indicated the presence of a cellar. Harrison bent down and shined the light in the window. He noticed a slight gap indicating that it was unlatched. Harrison gently pushed open the window and the gap widened. He pushed harder and the breach stretched further. Harrison shined the light inside and noted what seemed to be a dirt cellar, one that was used to store the fruits of harvest years ago.

Harrison's beam of light yielded no threat, only an empty cellar. He positioned himself to slide down backwards, moving carefully as to not damage the window and provide evidence that an uninvited visitor had violated its boundaries. The space was snug, but Harrison's wiry body wriggled through the window gap. He held onto the side of the window as his feet hung several feet above the cellar floor. Harrison released his grasp and he tumbled to the ground below him. Lying on the dirt floor, he shined the beam of light in all directions. He saw nothing obvious. Harrison stood and gained his balance. He shined the light once again hoping to find a stairway that led to the floor above. The cellar was larger than it appeared at first glance. Harrison walked toward a narrow opening in the wall. The wall at that point appeared to be a mixture of dirt and brick. He passed through the opening and discovered another section of the cellar. This partition, however, had a stairway that led upward to the floor above.

Harrison walked to the stairway and placed his foot on the first step expecting to hear the inevitable creak. Instead, he heard a low moan, barely audible. He soon realized that the cry was not from his weight on the step. Harrison stood paralyzed in the hope that a similar cry would reveal its source. He remained still for what seemed like a very long time and was rewarded for his patience. The low moan broke the silence once again and to Harrison's ears it was distinctly humanoid. His body pivoted toward the sound and he illuminated the cellar in front of him. Another narrow opening in the wall was revealed. Harrison walked briskly while extending his hearing. He paused at the opening and shined his light in the partition. Unlike the previous sections of the cellar, this particular partition was not void. Harrison's light exposed a number of boxes, broken furniture and other objects covered in cobwebs. Stored on the shelves on the far wall appeared to be 15-20 dusty bottles of wine. Harrison stood quietly hoping once again to achieve a fix on the lonely cry. However, moments passed and Harrison heard nothing. He stepped to the other side of the opening and stood transfixed once again. Moments passed…and nothing. Harrison wondered if the silent and eerie darkness was playing tricks on his senses or encouraging his imagination. Perhaps there was nothing to hear after all.

Harrison shook his head as if to release unwitting cobwebs from his mind. He knew what he heard and would wait patiently to hear it again. Harrison cautioned himself not to start talking to himself—just listen. He stood still once again and waited. His patience was rewarded a second time, as the low moan was now distinguishable. It sounded like an individual in pain, perhaps a woman, and was coming from behind the boxes. Harrison made his way to the boxes. There was no obvious path through or around them. Harrison selected a box and lifted it to test its weight. He was able to lift it with some straining. He positioned the flashlight to afford him sufficient illumination. Harrison worked at rearranging the boxes to open a path leading beyond them. They were stacked three high and five-to-six deep. He worked carefully unaware of their contents and unwilling to take the time now to check them. Harrison moved box after box, gradually exposing a footpath beyond them.

Harrison estimated that fifteen minutes had passed as he relocated the last box. He retrieved his flashlight and walked through the pathway that he created. Harrison found himself on the other side of the boxes. He focused his flashlight and revealed several pieces of old furniture, one of which looked like a woman's hope chest. Harrison heard no moaning during the time that he moved the boxes to create a passageway. He stood silently again as he directed his flashlight around the cellar. Harrison neither saw nor heard anything. The dirt floor and the walls revealed no other openings or doorways. He waited once again, but he heard nothing. Harrison walked over to the hope chest-like furniture. It was different in appearance in that the wood was not covered with dust and cobwebs like other objects in the cellar. Harrison realized that the furnishing was used recently.

Harrison flashed his light on the lock, but noted that it was not padded. A skeleton-like key was protruding from the lock. Harrison illuminated his surroundings once more before bending down to turn the key as if he expected something or someone to lunge at him out of the darkness—not that assailants ever pounced on him before under the cloak of darkness. Harrison focused the light beam on the key and turned it to unlock the chest. He took a deep breath and for the first time, un-holstered his gun. Harrison stood back as far as his outstretched arm permitted. His familiar adrenalin rushed as it always did in these times of heightened alertness.

Harrison lifted the top of the chest. He was breathing rapidly and his eyes widened as the image registered in his mind. In the chest lay a woman, unclothed, with her hands and feet bound by rope and a cloth gag around her mouth. Her body appeared badly bruised from head-to-toe and much dry blood was visible. The woman's eyes were closed and she exhibited no movement. Harrison wondered if the woman was dead. He bolstered his gun and focused the light on the woman's face. Harrison thought that if she was not dead, she certainly was left for dead. As he debated the issue in his mind, the woman let out a moan muffled by the gag. She was still alive although barely clinging to life.

Harrison began to aid her by undoing her mouth gag. He then unbound her hands and feet. Harrison was uncertain about moving her without knowing her condition beyond the fact that she was critical. He chose not to move her for the moment, but knew that she needed liquids for her emaciated body. Harrison was not ready to explore the floors above and remembered the bottles of wine on the wall. He retraced his steps through the pathway he created, shining the flashlight on the far wall. Harrison picked a random bottle of wine. He blew the dust off the bottle and walked back to the battered woman.

Harrison approached the hope chest and gazed at the badly beaten woman. She lay motionless except for an occasional smacking of her lips. Harrison unwrapped the cork and stuck his knife in it. He crudely removed the cork, mostly in pieces, and situated the bottle near the woman's mouth. Harrison carefully poured drops of wine on the woman's lips. Initially, she did not react to the fluid. Not having this natural reflex was not a good sign. Harrison continued to pour drops of wine on the woman's lips. He reached down and with his finger stimulated her lips by rubbing them. The woman responded to the stimulation and began licking the drops of wine. Harrison continued to pour drops of wine as the woman gathered what she could with her tongue.

As Harrison continued providing the dying woman a weak link to life, the stranger gradually opened her eyes. Harrison rubbed the woman's hands and called out softly, "Wake up, please. Wake up." She seemed to be peering directly at Harrison, but he observed only emptiness in her eyes. The woman did not acknowledge the figure that knelt beside her. Harrison gently shook the stranger's shoulders and called out once more, "Wake up, please. Wake up." The woman stirred and opened her eyes for the second time. Harrison shook her gently once again and asked, "Can you hear me?" He repeated his question much more slowly, "Can - you - hear - me?" The woman's transparent gaze became focused as she squinted her eyes and for the first time must have realized that she was not alone. Harrison smiled at the stranger and said, "That's better. You can hear me now, can't you?" The woman did not speak, but affirmatively nodded her head ever so slightly. Her eyes moved rapidly as her alertness and consciousness of her situation improved. The stranger's face exhibited pain and reflected the severity of the battering that she received. Harrison took pity on the woman and said, "You've taken quite a beating. Try not to move." After a brief pause, he asked, "Who are you?" The magnitude of the woman's anguish became apparent as she attempted to speak. Her lips moved, but no sound accompanied them. She drew her head back as if her pain intensified and shot through her face. The stranger fought to control her agony only to shake her head in silence. Tears began streaking down her face reflecting her physical pain as well as her growing awareness of her situation. Perhaps she was remembering the events leading up to her present condition.

At that moment, the stranger became aware of her state of undress. She glanced at her nakedness and averted her eyes from the kind gentleman who knelt beside her intended coffin, quickly showing her embarrassment. Harrison observed her shame and shined his light around the cellar in search of a blanket or some other fabric. He spotted what appeared to be an old sheet covering a piece of furniture. Harrison stood and held out one finger to the woman motioning her to wait. He noticed her acute panic as he was leaving and assured her that he would return quickly. Harrison hurried to retrieve the blanket, shook it violently to release what dust it held and returned to the woman. He lowered the blanket and softly covered her nakedness with the cloth. The stranger did not utter a word, but her facial expression broke into a slight smile in appreciation of Harrison's random act of kindness.

The thought that this gravely beaten woman somehow was linked to his mission did not escape Harrison. The woman was frail and critical, her wounds were likely mortal, but he needed information from her before she lapsed back into unconsciousness or death. Harrison realized sadly that he could do nothing to save the woman, but perhaps dispense justice by avenging her assailant or assailants.

Harrison renewed eye contact with the woman and asked once again, "Tell me, who are you? Why are you here?" The woman looked at the kind stranger, licked her lips several times and spoke in a broken, whispered voice, "Mary Lou. My - name - is - Mary - Lou." Disbelief came across Harrison's face which must have projected some impact on the woman. Her eyes widened and she appeared fearful as if she had said something wrong or offended the gentleman. Harrison, too, was shocked by her revelation. His facial expression shifted to one of dubious belief as his questioning conveyed more of interrogation than querying for information: "Mary Lou? Mary Lou Hawthorne?" The woman was taken aback by the gentleman's declaration. Neither the beaten woman nor the kind gentleman spoke for a moment. Finally, the wounded stranger acknowledged the man's inquiry: "Yes. I am Mary Lou Hawthorne." Harrison asked, perhaps as a reality check, "Wife of Jacob Hawthorne?" "Yes," was her weak reply as the woman closed her eyes and nodded affirmatively. She added, "Well, one of Jacob's wives."

Harrison could not believe his good fortune. Despite Mrs. Hawthorne's physical condition, he must make what he could of the opportunity afforded him. The other Mrs. Hawthorne who assailed him slipped through his fingers. He did not want this to happen a second time. Harrison looked closely at Mrs. Hawthorne. The extent of her bruising and dry blood suggested that she was well beyond saving. For that, Harrison felt sadness. No woman, no person, should die under such isolated and dreadful circumstances. Harrison asked honestly and rather apologetically, "Forgive me, Mrs. Hawthorne, but I must know what happened to you and Marilyn Hawthorne." Mrs. Hawthorne replied: "Who are you? How do you know so much about us?" Harrison wanted to avoid a lengthy explanation, but believed this dying woman was entitled to some details. He responded to her inquiry, "My name is Harrison Rossetti. I am an agent of the United States government charged with the protection of the President of the United States." Mrs. Hawthorne closed her eyes and swallowed. She remarked, "I can see why you might be interested in Marilyn." She closed her eyes, shook her head and then spoke hysterically: "You've got to stop him! Please, you've got to stop him! Oh, Marilyn! Where is Clona?"

The beaten woman turned away from Harrison. He asked with urgency, "Stop who?" Mrs. Hawthorne did not turn toward the man. Harrison asked more emphatically, "Stop who Mrs. Hawthorne? Stop who?" The fading woman turned toward Harrison and responded to the gravity of his voice: "My husband. You must stop my husband." Anguish shot across the woman's face as if another discharge of torment exploded through her body. Although Harrison was affected emotionally by the woman's tortured state, he requested information nonetheless and he needed the details immediately. He touched softly the face of Mrs. Hawthorne and spoke gently: "Mrs. Hawthorne, Mary Lou, do you know if President Ashton is alive?" There was hope in Harrison's face and voice, but he began breathing quickly, almost inducing an acute panic attack.

He was afraid that this woman might have information about the demise of Elizabeth Ashton, details that he did not wish to hear. Mrs. Hawthorne did not respond immediately. Harrison showed his impatience: "Well, do you?" This was not a side of the kind man that Mrs. Hawthorne had experienced throughout their brief encounter this evening.

The badly beaten woman coughed and closed her eyes in pain. Upon opening her eyes, she peered directly at Harrison and spoke as best as she could with the physical insults on her person. "Mr. Rossetti, I was not included in the original plans of my husband to substitute Marilyn for the President." "Then you are aware of your husband's intentions?" interrupted Harrison. "No, not fully. I know that Clona was included, but I don't know the extent of her role or her whereabouts." Harrison knew obviously of Clona Hawthorne's self-imposed demise, but saw no reason to trouble Mary Lou further. He was, after all, unaware of her relationship with Clona. His thoughts focused once again on the dying woman's account. Her demeanor changed and ire arose as she continued, "My bastard husband had this done to me! I wouldn't agree to support him like Marilyn and Clona."

Mary Lou's anger taxed her diminished resources. She coughed again, but this time she spat up blood. Harrison removed his handkerchief from his back pocket and wiped the blood from her mouth. The dying woman cried, "I'm going to die, aren't I?" For a moment, Harrison did not know how to respond. He wanted to lie to spare the woman her fate, but decided to tell the woman what she didn't want to hear: "Yes, Mary Lou, you are dying. There is nothing that I can do for you here except avenge those who shortened your life. However, I can't do that unless you tell me what you know."

The dying woman nodded her head in inevitable agreement and continued her story: "My husband developed a growing paranoia over the years about the intrusion of government in his life. He complained frequently about taxes, the acquisition of his land against his will through eminent domain, the decay in the moral fabric of the Office of the President and politicians in general, liberals—his anger and defiance against the government grew irreconcilable." Mary Lou paused and asked in her weakened condition, "Please, I need some water." Harrison retrieved the bottle of wine and lowered it to her lips. She took several swallows of the liquid and weakly pushed it away. Harrison returned the bottle of wine to the floor and attempted to refocus the dying woman. Time was escaping and he did not know how long the woman would maintain consciousness. He asked again, "Where is President Ashton?" Mary Lou nodded her head and spoke although she began to wheeze: "I don't know. I don't know where the President is. I think she's still alive—as long as Marilyn is in the White House. Marilyn had so many physical features similar to President Ashton that it was not difficult to further clone her image through expert reconstructive surgery. Jacob told us that he could use the President as a hostage to negotiate Marilyn's release if the plan went sour. They must have her hidden in another building like this or on our ranch about 30 miles north of here." "They?" interrupted Harrison. "Jacob has a number of friends and hired hands on the ranch that feel the same way he does. He has gathered a small army. They are radical and dangerous men who readily exonerated violence where the end to them always justified the means."

The dying woman was breathing heavily now in short breaths. Harrison felt guilty about letting her die this way, but he knew no other course given the circumstances. He said sympathetically, "Who did this to you, Mary Lou?" The woman closed her eyes and looked anguished as if the question caused her to relieve her beating. Mary Lou opened her eyes as tears once again rolled down her face. Her tone was nasal as she spoke: "The more my husband explained his plans to Marilyn, Clona and me, the more I realized that he was insane, that he would do anything to attain his goal, including violence and murder."

The dying woman coughed and spat up more blood. Harrison again wiped her mouth and kept her as comfortable as possible. Mary Lou cleared her throat and continued, sometimes repeating herself, "Marilyn looked a lot like the President and a cosmetic surgeon completed the illusion. Clona was supposed to protect her and take care of anybody who got wise to her. I don't know where Clona is. I...I was...My husband wanted me to...he ordered me to misappropriate funds for munitions as well as forge papers to hide identities and penetrate building security systems. I did initially what was asked of me. I was Jacob's wife." The dying woman stopped abruptly and took a long breath before continuing. "What I was doing deeply troubled me. I couldn't sleep nights. I was a nervous wreck racked with guilt for the role I was playing in this conspiracy. My husband had concocted a campaign of hatred and vengeance for which he would stop at nothing. I became an unwilling pawn in his plan. I was no different from the other treacherous recruits except I was owned by the mastermind of the plot."

The woman paused. She was wheezing heavily now and blood oozed continually from her mouth. Harrison continued to do what he could which he realized was very little. Mary Lou spoke again, "I told him, I told him I couldn't go on doing this...being a part of something so villainous. I pleaded with him to abandon his plan and disband the militant army he was recruiting. I thought naively that my relationship with Jacob would place me in a position of influence, but his growing rage for what he believed was imposed upon his country blinded him to the point that there was no other paths to follow. He had committed himself even if such a resolution meant eventual imprisonment or death."

Mary Lou turned her head away from Harrison, perhaps in shame, as she continued, "I was no longer anything to him except a traitor, one of those individuals he planned to roll over at all cost. I misjudged him. I guess he no longer had feelings for me. A marital relationship of thirty years meant nothing...Oh [she cried]...meant nothing to him. I was no longer useful to him, but with the knowledge that I possessed, I was quite expendable. I pleaded that I would say nothing, but he understood how troubled I was over the unfolding events. As a reward for my loyalty, my bastard husband gave two of his recruits the privilege of eradicating a personal enemy of the cause. Jacob left and these two men began battering me with baseball bats. I was stunned and disoriented with each blow and somewhere in the process I became unconscious. I have drifted in and out of consciousness in the dark not knowing my whereabouts, but certain that wherever I was it would be my final resting place. I can't tell you how long I've been here, how long I've clung to a thread of life. Now you are here. I have spoken and can die in peace. I thank you for the kindness and benevolence not even my companion of thirty years would bestow on me. Avenge for me, sir, do not make my death a worthless one." The woman who had fought to tell her story was now gasping for breath. Blood flowed incessantly and the woman was choking on her own fluids. Harrison reached out and held her hands. He did not want her to die alone without the comfort of another. The irony did not escape Harrison. Here he was able to comfort a dying stranger, yet he was not able to comfort his dying friend, Josetta.

It was not long before Mary Lou took her last breath. The once anguished face now seemed serene. Harrison bowed his head and prayed for her peacefulness. However, he also avowed that he would avenge her death as she asked...as he promised.

Harrison released her arms and stared at the dead woman. He wanted to give her a proper burial, but he knew that he must return the surroundings to their previous condition. He could not risk leaving clues that suggested that somebody stumbled on the fate of this poor woman. Harrison lifted the sheet from Mary Lou. He bound her hands and legs and gagged her mouth, recreating the horrid scene. Harrison replaced the lid of the chest and corked the wine bottle before returning it to the shelf. He checked the sheet for blood and finding none, returned the sheet atop the furniture from where it came.

Harrison retraced his path to the other side of the boxes and returned them one-by-one to their original configuration. He knew that this building could not be his safe house. Harrison headed back toward the window upon which he entered the cellar. He shimmied up the wall and pushed himself through the window. It was wise of him not to have forced entry into the structure. Harrison turned on his flashlight and headed in the direction of his abandoned jeep. He experienced sadness over the woman's brutal death. However, Harrison had a mission to complete. He continued his long walk to his jeep as he mulled over in his mind what the dying woman told him. Harrison's good fortune came at a very high price.

Chapter 19

Prelude to Engagement

As Harrison approached his jeep, he looked carefully around the area to rule out that he might have been discovered, either by accident or by design. He climbed into his jeep after satisfying himself that the area was undisturbed. Harrison started the engine and slowly backed out of the area, as there was not sufficient space to turn his jeep around. It was considerably more difficult to see the path driving backwards and thus more treacherous than the drive in. Harrison got the break that he hoped for in Mary Lou Hawthorne. He did not want the opportunity wasted somewhere between this path and the ravine below.

Although it took a long time to retrace his path, Harrison had two women to avenge: Elizabeth Ashton and Mary Lou Hawthorne. Time was of the essence as sunrise was just several hours away. Harrison decided to forgo his initial plan of finding a structure that he could use has his safe house, his center of operation. He did not know how many men and women Jacob Hawthorne had already recruited. Perhaps no building in the area was safe and undisturbed. With this uncertainty and the life of President Ashton at risk, that is, if she indeed was still alive, Harrison determined that the canopy of nature would serve as his safe house. He was satisfied with the decision and felt secure knowing that his center of operations was mobile. Harrison would not risk being discovered due to maintaining a single focal point. He would stay constantly on the move. There were plenty of shrubbery and trees that could hide a mere mortal man.

Having made that decision, Harrison's operative tactics

would also change. He returned to the road leading to Sarhea and decided to scout out the ranch that the dying woman told him would be thirty miles to the north. The cloak of darkness would last for several more hours. Harrison knew, however, that such a vast operation by Jacob Hawthorne would not leave security to chance. He speculated that security would incorporate a large perimeter around the ranch and perhaps the entire town of Sarhea through the eyes of its inhabitants. Harrison would eventually have to go on foot and hide his jeep somewhere where it could not be discovered and traced. The veil of "Mr. Marshalli" would not hold up to the scrutiny of professional soldiers of fortune.

It is not likely, Harrison thought, that the domestic terrorists would randomly hide President Ashton in a structure similar to the one where he found Mary Lou Hawthorne. The high recognition factor of Elizabeth Ashton as President of the United States was too great a risk for discovery by a passerby let alone trained government and local law enforcement agents. Security around the President would be tight whether she was alive or assassinated. They cannot afford to lose their trump card in Elizabeth Ashton for indeed the confrontation would be over!

Harrison drove ten miles when he spotted a dirt road off to the left of the highway. He slowed down and steered his jeep off the beaten path onto the isolated route. Harrison crept along the path as it guided him deeper into a wooded area. He observed no buildings or structures although his perception was limited by the darkness. The path appeared to disintegrate before him as the forest of trees swallowed him and his jeep. 'This area indeed would make good cover' Harrison thought to himself. He looked for a spot to hide his jeep and equipment. He spotted another opening ahead and halted his jeep. Harrison left the vehicle and walked to the open area in front of him. The growth of brush disguised the area beyond the opening. Harrison decided that this was his place under nature's canopy and walked back to the jeep. He steered the vehicle to the opening and held the brush up on the driver's side allowing the vehicle to disappear into the mouth of the tamed jungle. Harrison drove slowly and as far as the disappearing path would permit him. He then stopped and jumped out of the jeep. Harrison reached to the rear of the vehicle and retrieved several briefcases and pieces of equipment. He cleared them away from the jeep and began covering the vehicle with brush, limbs and whatever else could be used as camouflage.

Harrison stood back to view his deception as the light of dawn's early morn began to peek through the darkness. It was unlikely that anyone would uncover the jeep unless they happened to walk directly upon it. Harrison opened the brief cases and unpacked his equipment. He would be mobile and travel fast necessitating that he also travels light.

Harrison flashed a broad beam of light on the equipment before him. He scrutinized all the items before making his choices of what gear he could not do without. He scanned visually the items several times before establishing a sense of confidence in his selections. Harrison reached out and chose the following items: a cellular phone with extra backup batteries; a flashlight with blinking red warning beam and high frequency radio waves that would be set at the megahertz designated by Mentor; an eavesdropping device with the range of fifty yards; a miniature video lens that could peer around corners and under doors; high-powered binoculars with night infrared capability; compass with magnetic north; glass cutters; electronic safe-cracking devices; a semiautomatic weapon; a handgun; a knife; a backpack complete with deadly hand grenades, light and sound percussion grenades, delayed fuses and incendiary devices; and a small pack filled with dry food rations and a supply of bottled water.

Harrison scrutinized the objects that he placed before him. He then reassessed his choices and was satisfied with his selection of armament and electronic equipment. Harrison gathered the unselected equipment and returned them to the jeep. He arranged the brush again to conceal the jeep and his equipment. Harrison returned to collect his gear and rations. He put on the large backpack of munitions and secured the backpack so that it fit comfortably. Harrison swung over his shoulders the food rations and water pack. They hung to the side at his waist. The remaining gear fit into a specially designed belt, freeing his hands for using high tech devices or weaponry.

Harrison took one last look around at his home base and marked the area's location on his map; however, he marked the area thirty miles due north of its actual geographical location in case the map should fall into unfriendly hands. Harrison grew nervous as dawn was quickly approaching and he would soon lose the protective cloak of darkness. Had Harrison the time, he would rest and stay put until evening. The stakes, however, were too high to play it safe and taking risks was now the order of the day.

Harrison decided to travel quickly and cover as much ground as possible before sunrise dawned in a full glow. He took out his compass and headed north expecting to find the ranch of Jacob Hawthorne as identified by one of his murdered wives. The overgrowth was perfect in providing Harrison concealment. He made whatever slight detours were necessary to hike through the wooded area. Harrison hoped that nature's canopy lasted for most of the hike northward. He knew that he could not travel in the daylight without some cover. Harrison repeatedly warned himself to 'remain alert' as the domestic terrorists had no intention of letting anyone waltz onto their property by accident or design. His stealth alertness started now, as he neither knew the expanse of the tentacles of the extremists nor their numbers. He did not know if they were ordered to 'shoot to kill' or possibly bring back all prisoners to interrogate them at whatever level necessary to gain their desired information.

Harrison knew that the sooner he located President Ashton, the sooner that they could both travel out of harm's way. If Elizabeth Ashton was still alive, he knew that she was capable and ready. President Ashton served in the Middle East conflicts, including Desert Storm in Iraq. She undoubtedly has assessed her situation and identified her options, including calculating the odds of escape and death. Harrison hoped that Elizabeth Ashton secured vital information about the terrorists' routine and modus operandi. She may have overheard their plans. In any case, what Harrison knew of President Ashton, she had considered her fate if his rescue mission failed.

Harrison was determined to make the President's rescue a success. Failure now would send a green light to all factions, extremists and terrorists that the White House was available for the pickings. They could plan insertions at will with little concern of retribution by the government. What Harrison did not know—could not know at the moment—was the exact extent of Mentor's success in concealing, misleading and duping the conspirators. He wondered how long Mentor could maintain his hoax of studying and implementing the seated President's ten point plan. The unraveling of the hoax also meant the end of Harrison's mission in securing the release of President Ashton and perhaps the demise of Mentor and himself. The attack by Clona Hawthorne before the start of this mission attested to the terrorist's sophistication, planning and surveillance. The domestic terrorists knew to expect something and have contingency plans in place. The assassinations of Hardware and Mentor were certainly one of those contingencies. Their deaths were necessary if the conspirators were to finalize their plan to infiltrate the Office of the Presidency. Undoubtedly, a ruse was already developed to explain their deaths and preserve their attack on the people of the United States from the highest office in the land. He believed that the only way to interfere with the terrorists' ultimate goal was to preserve the life of Elizabeth Ashton. With these thoughts weighing on his mind, Harrison wished he knew what Greg was doing and if his old friend was still alive.

Chapter 20

The Mirror of Ashton

Mentor spent the past several hours worrying about the status of Harrison and reviewing the ten-step plan forwarded to him by the President. The stakes were never higher to him in his twenty-five years of government service. It was Mentor's role to perpetrate a fraud on Capitol Hill that would deceive the treasonous conspirators sufficiently long enough for Hardware to resolve his mission.

Mentor was busy outlining short-term objectives and long-term goals in response to each of the ten steps. For the fifth time in the early morning hours, he reviewed the President's itemized solution to counteract domestic terrorism by assimilating domestic terrorism into American politics. Mentor attempted to formulate a believable response as directed by the President. He reviewed the ten steps for a sixth time:

"Step one: Review prison cases and release those dissident terrorists in federal prison whose crimes do not include direct acts of violence against the people of the United States;

Step two: Provide financial compensation to these individuals for time loss on the job and emotional reparation;

Step three: Discontinue federal wiretaps on suspected terrorists where there is no direct, concrete evidence of intention to commit a crime despite a positive past history of such crimes;

Step four: Direct the FBI and IRS to no longer use their strong arms in investigating individuals just because their views differ from our government's stance;

Step five: Develop a moderated committee whose membership includes people appointed because of their distinct dissident views to provide input to governmental activities, funding and law;

Step six: Arrange that such a committee is solely responsible and reportable to the President;

Step seven: Allow for equal access time in all broadcasting media, particularly during federal, state and local elections;

Step eight: Provide guidelines and sensitivity training to all branches of law enforcement in their exchanges with our country's dissident terrorists;

Step nine: Provide guidelines to local governments on how to develop and maintain open forums so that varying viewpoints can be heard, documented and implemented; and lastly,

Step ten: Reinitiate efforts to support vigorously the right of law-abiding American citizens to carry arms as provided in our Constitution.

Mentor's eyes grew tired and his head nodded slightly when he heard a knock at the door. "Come in" was his automated reply. The door opened slowly and the President walked into the conference room. She looked directly at Mentor and said rather ironically, "My, aren't we up late? Or are we up early?" He made direct eye contact with the President and then briefly averted his eyes to the surveillance camera mounted on the wall before returning his stare back to her. "Late, Madam President" responded Mentor sharply. "I was finishing outlining a plan for implementing your ten points in counteracting domestic terrorism" continued Mentor.

The President walked over to Mentor and took the working draft from his hand. She scanned the material quickly, nodding her head intermittently in polite approval. "Not bad," was the

President's reply. She added, "For a first draft. Very good work." "Thank you, Madam President. I hope it will meet with your approval."

The President smiled and then asked, "Where is Hardware? I thought you might have him working with you on such a major up taking." Mentor responded, "I sent him home for a rest. I want him alert later this morning to finalize this draft before sending it to your desk for your review and approval." Mentor hoped that the subterfuge would buy Hardware and himself some valuably needed time. The President looked at Mentor coyly and replied, "Very good. I'll look forward to your draft. Do try and get some rest." "Yes, I will. Thank you Madam President" responded Mentor. The President turned and was about to exit the room. She unexpectedly came back to Mentor and said sharply, "Be sure that Hardware is here tomorrow." Mentor nodded and the President left the room. He was alone once again to ponder a believable reply to an impossible plan.

Mentor hoped that he would hear from Harrison soon. Yet, he understood the need for silence and the risk that communication could bring to the mission. There would be no judicial judgment or appeal if the mission failed. Assassins would summarily execute Mentor and Hardware. He so wished that he could have briefed Harrison more fully or sent him assistance, but he knew that the risk of discovery was too great. Mentor's best-case scenario was for him to continue the deception in Washington although he recognized that time was not on his side. The President will eventually insist on seeing Hardware and Mentor will have to produce him.

Mentor reviewed what he had written in response to the President's plan. What he offered was plausible although he felt it was treacherous. Moreover, Mentor knew that at some point he would have to begin implementing his pending plan in order to continue his contrived hoax. He gazed at his watch and knew that whatever cloak of darkness used by Harrison was now fading away. The light of day soon would betray him. He hoped that Harrison's focus was not sidetracked by thoughts about Hannah and the loss of Pope Josetta. Mentor recalled that he had sent his friend on missions before when personal and, at times, tragic events unfolded. He knew from his conversations with Harrison how he felt about being absent from such events, the void he felt, and the guilt he carried—all because of his dedication to the security of the President. He understood that Harrison would take more risks than usual given the urgency of his task and daylight or not, he would continue his mission. Mentor signed heavily and nervously awaited a signal from his friend. The absence of such a signal was unthinkable to Mentor. He had relied heavily on Harrison's skills and cunning many times before. Mentor found himself in this familiar, uncomfortable position once again where the best he could do was wait. Mentor's ability to wait became less patient with age. Perhaps because the missions were more complicated and risky as they kept pace with the complex emerging American society—a society that contained so many factions with many conflictive viewpoints. Resolutions of such viewpoints also became less philosophical over the years giving away to rhetoric, restless conflict and physical violence.

Mentor reached into his pocket and looked at the special cellular device that was set at the frequency agreed upon for Harrison's contacts. A touch of a button verified that the signal was set correctly and operational. Mentor kept a vigil on the device before reminding himself that "a watched pot never boils." He returned the device to his pocket and glanced at the surveillance camera. Mentor decided he would remain in his office for now, composing his response to the President and eagerly awaiting a contact from Harrison.

Chapter 21

Hide and Seek

As Mentor labored in D.C., Harrison continued his trek toward the Sarhea ranch of Jacob Hawthorne. He hoped that Mary Lou Hawthorne was truthful on her deathbed, or at least candid about the location of their ranch. Harrison tired from his quick pace. His backpack and the equipment he carried further burdened him. Dawn was breaking as evidenced by light leaking through the scattered clouds. Harrison could see better now which also meant, unfortunately, that he could be better seen. So far, he witnessed nothing unusual and that worried him. If the ranch was nearby, a security force was in place and patrols were guarding the perimeter. Harrison worried and wondered if he had missed something or someone. Had he succumbed to a trap even before he began his search for Elizabeth Ashton? Was he the captured rescuer? Was he the knight who tripped before he mounted his horse?

Harrison stopped under some heavy brush. He breathed heavily from the pace that he maintained over the last several hours. Harrison bowed his head momentarily and caught his breath. He raised his binoculars and scoured the countryside around him. Harrison scanned the distant low and high ground. He looked for patrol and security clues near the trees and treetops. Unless well camouflaged, security equipment and personnel would be vulnerable to the magnified eye. Harrison's initial search did not reveal such clues. He considered the possibility that the dying woman did not betray her husband despite the brutality inflicted in sanctioning her murder.

Harrison focused his binoculars and searched again as

sunlight now draped nature's canopy. He was on the high plain looking down into a deep, rich green valley. In the distance Harrison saw a weatherworn home—picturesque to the eye and much like one seen in a movie or mounted on a postcard. It was a three-story home wrapped by a wooded fence that appeared coated in fresh white paint. To the east of the structure was a deep blue lake bordered by tall trees. To the west of the home was a large gazebo painted in bright yellow. It was open on two sides allowing for several steps heading downward to the trimmed lawn. Around the gazebo between the steps were many multicolor flowers and vines. The path leading to the house was wide and filled with stones. Tall trees also lined it. Taking the direct approach down the path indeed was out of the question, as it forded no protection.

Harrison continued his march through the brush and trees. He paralleled the road to the extent possible. Harrison estimated that twenty minutes had passed when he stopped. He placed his hand on a branch and moved it away from his path of vision. Harrison used his binoculars and peered toward the house. A number of steps reached upward to the large front door. Tall, white wooden pillars decorated both sides of the stairway.

Harrison's heart jumped suddenly as he focused on a heavily armed man leaning against one of the pillars. Above the man and secured to the pillar was a security camera. The murdered wife told the truth as this structure had to be the Hawthorne ranch house. Harrison took a long look at the scene before him. He then slowly released the branch so that it returned to its original position and provided its natural camouflage. Harrison's senses were at high alert as he proceeded with caution. He reminded himself of the main objective of his mission—the return of Elizabeth Ashton as the best-case scenario—or, sadly, the return of her body.

Harrison estimated that he was about a half mile from the ranch home. He knew that the armed personnel and security systems were not confined to the main structure. Now everything that Harrison saw that was pleasing to his eyes might be the source of his death. A single miscalculation or omission on his part would terminate the mission in failure with America's way of life, its democracy, hanging in the balance.

Harrison proceeded cautiously and guarded his every move, his every step. He inspected carefully the ground below him and the trees above. Suddenly, Harrison stopped in half step. A flash of reflected light caught his eye and revealed a thin wire below where his right foot was ready to step. Harrison retracted his foot and backtracked several steps. He bent down slowly so as not to disturb the ground around him. Harrison's eye followed the wire to a nearby tree. He walked aside the wire and discovered that it was attached to a security device, most likely tripping an audio signal if strained. Were Harrison trudging at night, he would be trapped and the mission exposed. As he investigated the security mechanism closer, he heard the nearby rustling of brush and branches. Some roaming animal perhaps? Harrison decided not to risk exposure on a guess and slowly backtracked behind some thick brush. The rustling sound grew louder and appeared headed right for him. He soon ruled out that it was a wandering creature. Two armed men were pushing their way through the brush. Had Mentor's subterfuge unraveled? Had the domestic terrorists uncovered Harrison's mission? Were these two terrorists on a scheduled patrol or looking specifically for him?

Harrison lunged immediately from a standing position to a kneeling one and found himself prone to the ground. He withdrew his weapon and screwed on the silencer. Harrison was prepared to defend himself as a last resort; however, he did not want a confrontation. If he survived the conflict, his opponents would be mortally wounded. If they failed to report, the ranch's security would advance to full alert making Harrison's task increasingly more difficult.

Harrison lay still, breathing shallow and quietly. He heard the men conversing although they were still too far away for him to understand what was being said. Harrison was reminded that this was not the first time he found himself in this posture. He thought briefly of the time that he first met Pope Josetta under similar circumstances, but quickly dismissed the memory in order to focus on the danger before him.

Suddenly, the two men stopped. They spoke and gestured to each other, then headed off in different directions. Was Harrison spared? Harrison moved his head as he tracked the two men walking in opposite directions. It was not long before the men were out of his range of vision. Harrison took advantage of the opportunity and began walking ahead. He walked in a crouched position to reduce the risk of discovery. He was concerned that if he remained, the two men may circle around him and approach him from behind.

Harrison continued his slow walk toward the ranch. He knew that any clues about President Ashton would come from there. Harrison gauged that he must navigate within fifty yards of the home if his electronic eaves dropping device was to be effective. He continued walking toward the home, carefully scanning the ground and trees for other security devices. At all cost, Harrison would avoid any contact with the extremist group.

Harrison stopped abruptly as he noticed a slight mound ahead on the ground. The dirt around the mound was clear of all footsteps, animal or human, and appeared as if it was swept purposely. Harrison approached the area carefully and knelt to the ground. He took out a knife and cautiously probed the earth around the mound. At first, the knife inspection revealed nothing out of the ordinary, nothing but dried dirt. Harrison gently poked closer to the swell when the probe stopped suddenly as it made contact with a metal surface. Harrison warily removed the knife and began moving the dirt slowly with his hands. The gradual unearthing revealed a small contact mine sufficiently lethal to blow off a man's legs. Harrison carefully returned the dirt and rendered the area to its near-original appearance in hopes of disguising his presence. He sighed as he realized that he was still several hundred yards away from the main ranch structure.

The uncovering of the mine forewarned Harrison that there was little room for error. A slight miscalculation or omission now was less likely to lead to his capture than to his demise. Harrison decided to stop and survey the property rather than risk a further incursion. He reached for his binoculars and scanned the area ahead of him to assess the level of security. Harrison's observations revealed multiple mounds rising from the ground. Several trip wires were also seen. Harrison directed his vision upward and at first saw nothing unusual about the tall trees. He increased the magnification of his binoculars, which exposed several platforms in the distant trees. Harrison increased the magnification once more and the platforms revealed several surveillance cameras.

Harrison thought over about the direct approach to the ranch, but again determined that it was not feasible. The risk was too high for exposure. He decided to backtrack about twenty yards and then proceeded forward at an angle that intersected one side of the ranch rather than the main house. Harrison gained new respect for Hawthorne's security layout and saw no reason to directly challenge it. He walked cautiously to the rear all the while rapidly sweeping his field of vision in hopes of uncovering other camouflaged devices and explosives.

The trek backward took longer than the journey forward; however, Harrison reached his destination about twenty yards behind his previous position. He scanned the territory at both angles to the main property and assessed which one was the better route. After several minutes, Harrison made his choice and began his trek forward once more. He paid greater attention to what was around him leaving nothing humanly possible to risk. Harrison's alertness was at its peak and he vowed not be denied on this mission.

Harrison's diagonal approach was a prudent one as he had yet to encounter any of the extremists. He did come upon a number of electronic devices that he skillfully evaded. Harrison estimated he was now within fifty yards southeast of the main house on the ranch. He saw a secluded area and made his stake out there. Harrison removed the backpack that was strapped to his shoulders and laid it opened on the ground. He put together the small pieces that comprised his eavesdropping device and aimed it toward the main structure. Harrison inserted the earpiece and began his patient wait.

Chapter 22

Do You Hear What I Hear?

Harrison estimated that he had lingered at his present listening post for about an hour when his patience was rewarded. "Yes, Mr. Hawthorne..." replied the unidentified voice into his ear. Harrison fixed the aim of his listening device and reached for his high-powered binoculars. His view was obstructed partially, but he made out two figures through a partly opened window. Harrison listened intently for the clues that he hoped would steer him on from this moment.

The voice of the other man, presumably Mr. Hawthorne, spoke: "Have we been in contact lately with the 'President'?" "No, sir" the unidentified man replied respectfully. The man continued, "Should we attempt to contact your wife, sir?" There was a moment of silence before the man identified as Mr. Hawthorne responded, "Yes, call the 'President' using our contact there." At that, the stranger said "Yes, sir" and left the room. Hawthorne sat at a table and began reading the newspaper. Harrison wished that he had a better view, but he did not want to jeopardize his vantage point for espionage. Harrison waited patiently as before, keeping alert to the noises and sights around him. He heard voices once again, but they were not emerging from his earpiece. Harrison glanced to the right where he saw three men walking in his general direction. He withdrew his electronic equipment and binoculars. Harrison laid flat on the ground, but raised his head sufficiently to track the three men. They stopped abruptly about fifteen yards away from him, but they did not raise their weapons. Harrison's breathing became heavier and faster. One of the three men offered cigarettes to his comrades. They each took a cigarette from the pack and were offered a light by the man holding the cigarette pack. The men smoked their cigarettes and engaged in conversation as they continued their patrol toward the ranch house. The terrorists' manner suggested that penetration by the enemy at this level was inconceivable by them. Harrison thought that this may prove to be Hawthorne's critical error upon which he might capitalize.

As the domestic extremists distanced themselves from Harrison, he arose gradually from the dirt, dusted himself off and assumed his previous stance to continue his espionage on the main house. He aimed his listening device directly at the window where he confirmed with his high-powered binoculars that Hawthorne was still seated at the table reading the newspaper.

Harrison continued to spy on the ranch as his magnified view remained unchanged. The listening device was deaf until the sudden buzz of a telephone intercom rang in the background. Hawthorne did not move, but spoke apparently into a speaker microphone. "Yes, what is it?" said Hawthorne. A voice from the intercom replied, "Software is on the line, sir." Hawthorne rose quickly from his chair. He picked up the telephone receiver and greeted the party on the line: "Are we scrambled?" Harrison did not hear the voice that replied. He continued to listen to the one-sided conversation: "Good! How are you, darling?" Harrison's eyes widened and his adrenalin rushed. Was the other party Marilyn Hawthorne? The sardonic use of Software disgusted Harrison, but he listened closely to Hawthorne's side of the exchange: "Nothing unusual here except that I have not heard from Clona for two days. Perhaps you can make some low-level inquiries through our contacts there without rousing suspicion." The voice of Hawthorne paused and then said in an altered tone of voice: "I'm afraid that she's dead by now. Very unfortunate, but she was too great a risk to keep alive." The voice paused again as Harrison struggled to draw a conclusion from what he just heard. Who was dead? Was it Mary Lou Hawthorne or Elizabeth Ashton? Harrison's heart raced at the thought of the possible demise of President Ashton. Was he too late? Was his mission already a failure?

Harrison listened intently for Hawthorne's next words. He did not have to wait long. "You have to pull this off, Marilyn. It already has carried a high price tag for both sides. One of my wives is dead. One of my wives is missing. The President of the United States is dead..." Harrison put down his binoculars and stood there frozen in time. He was stunned, yet fought to keep away the aftershock caused by what he heard. Harrison refocused his attention on the man who professed the murder of President Elizabeth Ashton.

"We still have a bargaining chip if our conspiracy is uncovered. They won't know that President Ashton is dead until it's too late." There was a pause as Hawthorne listened to the caller. Then Hawthorne replied, "I don't think so. We've had no infiltrations or attempted intrusions here at the ranch since you've begun your 'Presidential' role in Washington, my dear—and if they had gotten wind of our plan, they apparently have not established the link between us. After all, you're the spitting image of Ashton and the voice training sealed your impersonation. No, I'm sure of it. If they were aware of us, we would have heard from the government bastards by now. Don't worry dear. You are doing well. I've been watching some of your press conferences on television. If I didn't know who you really were, I'd swear that you were indeed President Ashton." After a brief pause, Hawthorne continued, "You won't hear from me again until the operation is over. We will begin tomorrow, so maintain a low profile and remember what we rehearsed as your response when 'main target' is set in motion. Goodbye, dear." At that, Hawthorne returned the phone to its cradle. He then left the room, out of Harrison's sight and hearing.

The stakes of this mission, which were high, just got higher. The risks, in turn, also escalated. Harrison must confirm the death of President Ashton and, upon doing so, make contact with Mentor to sanction the next phase of his mission. He must also inform Mentor that Hawthorne's campaign "main target" was scheduled for implementation tomorrow.

Harrison packed his equipment and walked slowly toward the main house. He knew that he had to infiltrate the ranch itself to uncover the clues that would lead to Elizabeth Ashton. He kept alert in an effort not to trigger any of the sensors or make unnecessary contact with the domestic terrorists.

Harrison stepped carefully around the trip wires and mines. He retreated in the brush at his first glimpse of patrols. What Harrison expected was the unexpected as he moved closer to the main ranch house. He was not disappointed as he stopped dead in his tracks for in front of him was a sentry post constructed high in the trees. The post was built circling the entire tree giving the guards a 360-degree panoramic view of the area. Harrison lowered himself to the ground and pushed himself on his stomach until well hidden in the thicket. He lay still and focused his attention on the sentry station. Harrison retrieved his binoculars and scanned the guard post in front of him. The magnified lens revealed two sentries heavily armed with sophisticated automatic weapons and a bazooka. The sentries stared back in the direction of Harrison as they too used binoculars to scan the area around them.

Harrison was immobilized in thought. He knew that there was no way around the post as the area of trees and bush were cutback considerably to afford the terrorists an enhanced view of their patrol area. 'Simple!' thought Harrison. He would walk under the post like he owned the place. Harrison needed to "borrow" temporarily the clothing of the day, which translated to assaulting one of the terrorists. The problem was that he seldom saw a soldier of fortune walking or patrolling the area alone. They were usually in groups of two or three men. Harrison would have to backtrack once again away from the observation of the sentry post. He pushed himself on his stomach for several yards before standing and walking back out deep into the woods. If Harrison had to accost two men— he would not try three men—his chance of survival would increase if he could take them by surprise and be unobserved by others or their sensory devices. He would have to choose the location of the ambush carefully and await patiently his opportunity.

So Harrison waited and prepared himself for the engagement. He took off his backpack and other "baggage" that would drag him down in a hand-to-hand conflict. He also took out his knife if his attack became "personal." Harrison knew that if the patrol included two men, he would have to chance dropping one dead immediately with a single, silent shot. The moment of shock and surprise would hopefully render the remaining terrorist off balance for a second quiet shot or the piercing of a cold steel blade.

Thirty minutes passed and Harrison saw no patrol. He kept alert and sharpened his senses. Harrison repeatedly checked his weapon perhaps for as much as good luck as performance. He rehearsed his plan of attack in his mind. His rehearsal was interrupted by the sound of footsteps snapping twigs and brush. Harrison drew close to the ground and turned his head toward the encroaching sound. His adrenalin rushed once again. He was unaware whether or not the approaching terrorists would make suitable targets. Harrison waited for his first glimpse of the patrol. What he saw surprised him. He could not believe his good fortune as a lone soldier approached him. Harrison crouched in an attack position ready to spring on the terrorist as he passed by.

The unsuspecting terrorist was whistling and appeared to be eating something. Harrison threw down his gun and readied his knife for battle. He was not going to take a chance of only wounding the extremist to have him shout out a warning. The terrorist grew closer. Harrison's crouch was now spring like, ready to pounce on the passing prey. The terrorist was within five yards now. Harrison was ready. His adrenalin rushed and was at its peak. The terrorist, on the other hand, had his rifle shouldered whistling as he marched into harm's way.

The moment arrived. Harrison sprang from his crouched position, knocking the terrorist and himself to the ground. Harrison did not linger and took advantage of surprise. He plunged his right-hand forward and stabbed the man several times in his heart. The doomed terrorist made no sound except the gasp of a dying man. Harrison withdrew the blade and pulled the dead man's body under the camouflage of the brush. He quickly took off the terrorist's jacket and shirt to minimize the absorption of blood. Harrison left nothing to chance and divested the man of everything except his underwear and the blood stained undershirt—clothes, jewelry, weaponry—all was transferred to Harrison.

Harrison tidied himself and began his march to the ranch. It was clear that the terrorist was connecting with the main road. Harrison heaved a heavy sigh and headed to the central path. He kept his rifle at the ready and had grenades attached to his waist. A small gun and knife were strapped to his legs hidden away. Harrison slowed his pace, as he did not want to appear overanxious or driven even though that was descriptive of his present state. He soon connected with the main road and walked due north to the ranch. Harrison kept alert for he knew the main road was undoubtedly mined and full of electronic sensors. Unlike his dead predecessor, Harrison did not know the exact locations of the devices, but he had to make it appear like he did when he came into view of the observation post.

Chapter 23

No Signature, Man!

Harrison saw the observation post in the distance and his adrenalin, which traveled like a roller coaster all day, increased once again. He scanned visually as much of an area as he possibly could look for any pattern in the layout of electronic devices and explosives. Harrison may be able to fool the terrorists in the sentry post, but such success would be short lived if he blew himself up several steps beyond the post.

Harrison continued his slow trek toward the main ranch. He spotted no pattern to the trip wires, mines and sensory devices. Harrison told himself to remain alert and rely on his senses to keep safe, an approach he depended upon many times. There was too much at stake to play it safe. He must confirm the death of President Ashton as confessed by Hawthorne.

The sentry post grew in size and intimidation as Harrison approached. He counted two men patrolling the circular wooden post. Harrison observed previously that the patrols waved to the sentries as they passed and he planned to mimic their actions. He would glance quickly to acknowledge the sentries, but attempt simultaneously to avoid visual detection. Harrison's walk became more deliberate as he neared the patrol station. He kept his head down to avoid identification by the magnification of a telephoto lens or binoculars.

Harrison checked to see that his rifle was ready for firing and patted his right side for access to his small automatic weapon. He felt prepared, but he had a sinking feeling that something was not right. Harrison continued his approach to the sentry post as both men on guard turned toward him. He was spotted, but hopefully not identified.

Harrison glanced up nervously once more. The position of the guards remained unchanged, but the sentinels now had their automatic weapons at the ready. Harrison walked within five yards of the station. He looked downward for the next several steps before glancing upwards once again. This time Harrison observed that one of the guards had his binoculars trained on him. He developed suddenly an uneasy feeling as he continued walking while looking downwards. He was about even with the tower when he looked upwards briefly and waved his right hand. Harrison neither heard anything nor stopped to await a response. He did not travel far before shots rang out and a spray of bullets skidded by his left side. Harrison stopped dead in his tracks. He knew that his next move was critical and would make the difference between life and death—his!

Harrison turned slowly and raised his hands in the air. One of the patrols called out in a menacing voice, "Stop right there! Do not move!" While one sentry kept a rifle trained on Harrison, the other made his way down to ground level. The guard carefully approached Harrison. He kept his weapon trained on him as the other sentry made his way down. Once the second terrorist approached, the first sentry lowered his weapon and began frisking Harrison. He grabbed Harrison roughly and stripped him of his weapons and equipment, unceremoniously casting them aside. The guard patted down Harrison and managed to find the small gun and knife hidden on his legs near his ankles. The sentry grasped Harrison and spanned him around so that he faced his enemies. One of the guards spoke, "Would you like to tell us who you are and what you are doing here?" Harrison evaded the question and asked one of his own, "How did you know that I wasn't one of you?" "No signature, man" said the sentry. "Signature?" echoed Harrison. He guessed that his question was rhetorical as neither terrorist responded. "Let's take a walk" was all that Harrison heard. With that, a gun at his back pushed him forward. Harrison continued his walk to the main ranch house except that his hands were raised now and he was deprived of his weaponry. He had not planned on confronting Hawthorne on this mission, but it appeared that such an introduction was now unavoidable. It took about five minutes for the group to reach their destination. With the terrorists at his back, Harrison walked up the stairway passing other guards who were stationed by the pillars. For a brief moment, he thought of attempting an escape. However, just as hastily, he realized that such an impulsive act would end in his death and abort any hope of determining the whereabouts of President Ashton or her lifeless body. As Harrison approached the large door to the main house, one of the terrorists commanded, "Stop!" He stopped as demanded while one of the guards walked around him and opened a sensory alarm box. The terrorist flipped several switches and opened the thick door in front of him. The guard behind him poked his gun in Harrison's back and motioned him forward. Harrison complied and walked through the enormous gateway that lead to a long, narrow corridor. As were the pillars outside, the corridor was lined with heavily armed terrorists stationed about every five yards. No one spoke, but the shove of the gun continued to motion Harrison forward to another large door. He was told to "Stop" once more as he neared the door. One of the terrorists activated an intercom system and awaited a reply. He did not have to wait long as the voice on the other side demanded, "Identify yourself." The guard complied and said, "Follower 1027; codename Software." Harrison was greatly irritated upon hearing the bastardization of President Ashton's codename. The electronic lock on the door opened with a metal clank. Harrison was pushed ahead and walked forward. The corridor gave way to an expansive waiting area. The spacious inner layout of the home belied the smaller appearance of its outer shell. Patrols guarded the waiting area as they did with every other area of the ranch. The sentries maneuvered Harrison toward another door and stopped. One of the patrols knocked on the door. The door opened and Harrison was pushed through it. He walked into another room and was shoved abruptly into an overstuffed chair. A guard stood on either side of him with their guns aimed menacingly at his head.

Harrison estimated that twenty minutes had passed before a tall gentleman entered the room from a hidden door—at least hidden on the side that he occupied. As the man moved closer, Harrison recognized him as the individual he had under surveillance several hours ago—the man who confessed the murder of Elizabeth Ashton. The man identified as Hawthorne.

Hawthorne stopped about halfway across from Harrison and motioned for one of the terrorists. The two men whispered back and forth before Hawthorne dismissed him with a wave of his hand. The leader walked up to Harrison and without notice slapped him across the face. Hawthorne smiled and said, "Welcome to my humble home, Mr…?" Harrison shook off the blow on his face and stared at Hawthorne. He did not reply or offer information. Hawthorne continued, "Oh, come now. We are not playing cloak and dagger here. You are trespassing on private property. You did not simply lose your way and stumble on my ranch. You killed one of my men, yes? You confiscated his clothes, yes? You know obviously that I am Jacob Hawthorne. You also may have some idea of the purpose of my organization, yes? You perhaps are looking for Software?"

Harrison wondered if Hawthorne also knew his name, social security number and blood type. "How did your patrol know that I was not one of you?" asked Harrison. "Easy my friend—no 'signature'" replied Hawthorne. He continued with a smile upon observing Harrison's quizzical look: "All my men have an identifier that is lined in their inner wear, their undershirts and briefs, and are read by laser. You showed no 'signature.' If you steal somebody's clothes, you should take them all." Hawthorne laughed heartily at his enemy's mistake. "Now, Mr...?" demanded Hawthorne once again.

Harrison saw no reason to play it coyly. A group with this sophistication would easily uncover his true identity. He responded, "Rossetti—Harrison Rossetti." "And you are here, Mr. Rossetti, to find your President?" said Hawthorne coyly. Harrison was perturbed to say the least that this buffoon consistently had the upper hand. He answered Hawthorne wittily, "Does it show on my face?" "Not at all, Mr. Rossetti. Not at all. You are an agent of the United States government. Your codename is Hardware. You are currently assigned special duties involving President Elizabeth Ashton, a.k.a. Software. Your supervisor's codename is Mentor. Shall I continue, Mr. Rossetti?"

Harrison was confounded by the information that Hawthorne possessed, not to mention angry and embarrassed. "No," was his weak reply. Hawthorne continued, "We've been expecting you. Our intelligence informed us that you would be paying us a 'visit' although we were not sure when or where. You'll find us very well prepared and informed, Mr. Rossetti. These characteristics are required for an organization and a mission such as ours." "And what would that be?" asked Harrison unconvincingly. "Oh, come now, Mr. Rossetti. The fact that you are here informs me that you know that the Elizabeth Ashton in power is not President Elizabeth Ashton. What you may or may not know is that my wife, Marilyn Hawthorne, is presently empowered as the President of the

United States. A perfect double wouldn't you say?"

Harrison did not say. He knew that he was a dead man given that Hawthorne was taking him into his confidence. Harrison would not be allowed to leave the ranch alive although he may be used as a bargaining chip if Elizabeth Ashton is indeed dead. "A perfect double, indeed" replied Harrison. "My compliments to your surgeon." "Yes, he did do a wonderful job, didn't he? Too bad he didn't live long enough to see the results of his skilled, sensitive hands." The implication was clear: the surgeon was an unnecessary risk and expendable.

Harrison had to get Hawthorne off balance and gain control of the unfolding events. He stated matter-of-factly, "Yes—and I'm sorry that Clona won't be returning home." Hawthorne's facial expression transferred instantaneously from jovial egocentrism to homicidal anger. "What the hell do you mean?" demanded Hawthorne. Harrison found his opportunity to seize control. He replied to the terrorist, "You're so good at deciphering information and predicting events, you figure it out!" At that, Hawthorne ripped the rifle from the hands of one of his guards and butted Harrison in the forehead. The blow was sufficiently hard that Harrison collapsed and tumbled to a heap on the floor. Hawthorne raised the rifle in anger once again, but stopped the attack as he started its downward plunge. Hawthorne breathed heavily as he barked out an order to his guards: "Take him to the cell, the one next to our 'guest.' If Mr. Rossetti gives you any trouble, kill him. How, I will leave up to your imaginations. Just make sure he dies slowly and painfully!" At that, the two guards that ushered Harrison into the ranch house grabbed the unconscious man by his hands and feet. They unceremoniously carried Harrison out of the room through a hidden panel door. The corridor on the other side of the opening traveled down a staircase and below ground level. They roughly placed Harrison in the cell, tossing him by his hand and feet to the dirt floor. One of the terrorists kicked Harrison in his side where the only response was a low moan. The guards closed the cell door resulting in an echo of clanging steel. The terrorists smiled at each other and headed up the stairway.

Harrison stirred slowly raising his right hand to his forehead. He did not immediately know where he was, but he knew he had a massive headache and felt blood on his forehead. Harrison did not attempt to sit up, but lay on the dirt floor. He began massaging his temples in an effort to help soothe his pain. Harrison was in no hurry to stand. The recent events were unfolding gradually in his mind and clearing his disorientation. Harrison stood slowly and repeatedly attempted to maintain his balance. He grabbed his head to stop the cell, or his head, or both from spinning. Harrison was uncertain about the passage of time. The cell and its surroundings were lit dimly. Harrison took an accounting of his interned environment and discovered there was little to count. He was in a cell and observed attached cells on either side of him. His cell was lit dimly by a single light bulb dangling from the ceiling. There was no furniture, no sleeping cot, no bathroom facilities—nothing, just an empty cell with steel bars on three sides and a brick wall completing side number four.

Harrison walked to the steel bars that formed the side of one of the adjacent cells. A single bulb hanging from the ceiling dimly lighted it. Like Harrison's cell, it was empty. He staggered to the other side that formed the side of an adjacent cell. It too was dimly lit by a single light bulb hanging from the ceiling. This adjacent cell also appeared empty except for a single piece of rectangular furniture about a foot away and parallel to the brick wall. Harrison thought nothing of the misplaced furniture at first as he continued to massage his temples. Several seconds later, he stopped his self-massage and his heart sank abruptly. Harrison thought that the piece of furniture seemed, at a distance, almost identical to the final resting place of Mary Lou Hawthorne. At that, Harrison collapsed to the dirt floor. His fatigue, lack of food and water, and physical abuse took their toll and he drifted out of consciousness.

Chapter 24

"Love, Modem"

Harrison was unaware of the passage of time as he awoke struggling to open his heavy eyelids. The starkness of his cell quickly brought to mind his circumstances. Harrison raised himself from the ground where he had slept. The cell was dimly lit as before denying Harrison clues as to the time of day or night. As he turned toward one of the adjacent cells, he was reminded of the coffin-like piece of furniture. Harrison walked toward the iron bars that formed a common wall between the two cells. He needed to view the contents of the "unoccupied" cell. Would he find Elizabeth Ashton in her final resting place like he discovered Mary Lou Hawthorne? Or were the contents empty and simply a cruel joke? For Harrison, the answer was in the adjacent cell and he was not.

Harrison walked the edges of the compartment looking for a weakness that he could defeat. The steel bars were solid and unyielding to the touch. Harrison walked past the jail cell door without giving it a second thought or a try. He was certain that his keepers simply did not leave his cell door unlocked. Harrison took several more steps and stopped. 'Or would they?' he thought to himself. He considered the kind of man that Hawthorne projected of himself. Harrison returned to the cell door and gave it a push. To his astonishment, the metal door squeaked and opened with a clank. Harrison walked out cautiously expecting one or more guards to be upon him, but they were not. His eyes widened as he now saw something that he did not see from inside his cell: stockpiles of munitions and other weaponry lining the walls of the dimly lit cellar.

Harrison walked to the adjacent cell. Would he be able to

gain entry there as quickly as he left his own cell? He reached the steel bars and pulled opened the door. The clank and squawks were much the same as before. He walked slowly to the only piece of furniture in the cell. Harrison bent down and felt carefully around it to rule out the setting of explosives. He did not want to make his demise any easier than he already has for his captors.

Harrison scrutinized the object and discovered nothing lethal. He opened the slide locks on each side and lifted the top. Harrison immediately put his hand over his mouth, as the stench was overwhelming. He tossed the top over the side and peered inside. Harrison's worst fears were confirmed as he looked down and saw what appeared to be Elizabeth Ashton. It was clearly her form and stature although some decomposition had taken place. Harrison saw something glittering around the neck of the corpse. He bent over and tugged on the gold necklace. As it pulled away from the body, a gold heart was revealed. He uncomfortably pulled the pendant off the poor soul and moved toward the light. An inspection of the locket revealed an inscription. Harrison moved the heart back and forth while squinting his eyes. It took several moments to read fully the inscription that said, "To my candidate and love of my life. Love, Richard." 'Richard Ashton,' thought Harrison, 'husband of Elizabeth Ashton.' He saw the medallion many times before at the White House. Mr. Ashton gave the locket to his wife at the time of her candidacy years ago for the Presidency of the United States as a memento of his love and support for her difficult challenge to the White House. Harrison thought for a moment, actually contemplated several explanations for what he found. However, there was one conclusion he could not explain away: here lay the body of Elizabeth Ashton, President of the United States.

Harrison bowed his head in respect and prayer. Yet, he hardly could contain his anger, as he was unable to defend his President. He was not given the opportunity to be in the line of fire. He realized that in a short amount of time two people that he knew closely died and he was not able to comfort them or their loved ones. Harrison raised himself and replaced the lid on the resting place of the President. He vowed, however, that this would not be Elizabeth Ashton's final resting place. If the President's death was to have any meaning, he would have to free himself from his present confines and expose Hawthorne and "main target." The battle for Harrison just got personal— very personal.

Harrison walked up the dimly lit stairway. He was not expecting to just walk out unscathed or even alive for that matter. Harrison figured that Hawthorne's men knew exactly what he had seen and precisely where he was headed. But why would Hawthorne take such risks? Is Hawthorne that much of an egomaniac that he believed he could wipe Harrison out of existence without a trace at any given moment? Was the planned discovery of the body of Elizabeth Ashton supposed to demoralize him to the point of impotence in carrying out his mission? Or entirely give up his mission?

Harrison knew that the completion of his mission and the recovery of the body of the President of the United States depended upon the success of contacting Mentor who could dispatch reinforcements. He had completed a major segment of his assignment by determining the sad status of the President. Harrison would need reinforcements to thwart Hawthorne's conspiracy to control or perhaps even overthrow the United States government and return the body of Elizabeth Ashton to her proper place.

Again, Harrison thought it was inconceivable that the domestic terrorists were simply going to allow him to walk away from the ranch and conclude his assignment. He wondered how far he would travel before they intervened. Harrison suspected it would not be long before he unearthed the answer. He continued walking up the staircase undetected. He stopped at the door that presumably led to his freedom or perhaps just a delusion. Harrison placed his ear to the door, but he heard nothing. He grasped the door handle and pushed open the gateway as quietly as he could. Harrison was bewildered that he had gone undetected although he observed security cameras mounted around the room. He wondered if Hawthorne wanted him to escape and relate the discovery of his murdered President. 'No,' he thought to himself. Hawthorne had nothing to gain from such a disclosure and everything to lose—not the least being the wrath of the American people and those around the world.

Harrison asked himself, 'Why was he still alive?' The egocentric nature of Jacob Hawthorne came to mind—something that he postulated before—the "thrills" of the game itself regardless of the risks. As Harrison stood alone deep in thought, he heard voices coming from outside the room. He darted to conceal himself behind the bar located on the eastside of the room.

Three men entered the room. Harrison could not see them, but one of the voices was unmistakably that of Hawthorne. He listened intently to their conversation hoping to gain understanding as to why he had not met a similar fate as President Ashton. One of the two insurgents spoke to Hawthorne: "We still don't understand why the government agent was still alive?" Hawthorne chuckled and challenged the men: "Why don't you ask Mr. Rossetti himself?" There was a brief pause before Hawthorne asked, "What do you say to that Mr. Rossetti?" Harrison's hopes of projecting stealth were dashed in an instant. He thought of no reason to remain hidden, as it was obvious that one of the three men knew he was in the room. Harrison stood up from behind the bar. The two terrorists trained their guns on the agent who was in the process of raising his hands in temporary surrender. "Well, I'll be…" mumbled one of the terrorists. Hawthorne turned slightly to acknowledge Harrison's presence and asked nonchalantly, "Won't you join us, Mr. Rossetti?"

Harrison was disappointed with himself for this was the second time that he was caught by this self-proclaimed leader. This experience was no more tolerable than the former one. He walked slowly to the end of the bar and around its corner. Harrison continued to walk slowly so as not to provide ammunition for receiving a bullet in his head. "Sit down, Rossetti" motioned Hawthorne. Harrison did as he was asked and seated himself directly across from the man he learned to despise.

"We were just talking about you, Hardware." The use of his codename disgusted Harrison even more so than hearing those of Software and Mentor uttered by the enemy. Harrison lost control and quipped, "How did a bastard like you make it this far?" Hawthorne did not react to Harrison's weak attempt to humiliate him. Hawthorne looked directly at the captive agent and said, "These gentlemen are confused because they can't understand why you are still among the living. Would you care to enlighten them?" 'Talk about egos,' thought Harrison. He believed the opportunity to redeem himself and possibly escape was handed to him if he judged correctly why he was still alive.

Harrison did not alter his focus on Hawthorne. It grew clear why he was still alive. Harrison put down slowly his tired arms, which yielded no reaction from the guards. "Because Hawthorne…" Harrison started confidently, "You're a sportsman who considers the game itself utmost in your hierarchy of operations. You're so confident that your men will terminate me before I step beyond the boundaries of your camp that you're willing to take what no doubt seems to you to be a reasonable risk. However, if you're wrong, I will have the pleasure of identifying you as the assassin of the President of the United States."

Hawthorne managed a nervous smile while slowly and deliberately clapping his hands. "Very good, Rossetti. You've captured the true me." Harrison was smug about his personality analysis of Hawthorne. He also felt partially vindicated despite his capture and predicament. Hawthorne turned to his men and queried, "Did you learn anything, boys, from Mr. Rossetti?" Hawthorne then turned toward Harrison and spoke, "Let there be no mistake, Rossetti, you will not leave this camp alive. Nobody has a clue except you that Elizabeth Ashton is dead—a secret that you will take with you to your eminent death." "Not much of a sport," countered Harrison. He smiled and continued, "I will be outgunned in personnel, material and electronics. You certainly don't think I'm that masterful, do you?"

Harrison attempted to appeal to Hawthorne's narcissism for he knew that there was no hope of singly defeating such a formidable force. Hawthorne thought momentarily about Harrison's taunts and then offered, "You may be right, Mr. Rossetti, you are not that good! What I'm willing to do for this exercise is to turn off our sensory electronics and," he paused briefly, "I will give you a map of the mines and other explosives," he paused briefly again, "and I will give you a fifteen minute head start. I think this is more than a generous offer. Wouldn't you say Rossetti?" Harrison's taunting had accomplished more than he expected from the vain warlord. He smiled mockingly at Hawthorne and said, "A very generous offer, indeed, Mr. Hawthorne. Perhaps I was wrong about you.

On the other hand, how do I know that a homicidal maniac like you who slaughters innocent men and women, including his own wife, will keep his word?"

Harrison quickly had second thoughts about what he said as the words echoed in his mind. The self-righteous terrorist leader was not amused. Hawthorne responded with ire, "You're becoming boring and redundant. You will die, Mr. Rossetti. Mark my words...and I will be the executioner! Now, get out of my home before I retract my more than generous offer and kill you here and now!" Hawthorne's angry eyes were trained on Harrison and unmoving. 'Perhaps he had gone too far,' thought Harrison. It would not be the first time that he had pushed the envelope of the window, but if the terrorists had their way, it would be the last time. Hawthorne's position remained frozen as he commanded his guards, "Get him out of here!" The terrorists, with their guns drawn, motioned Harrison to rise. Harrison walked with them and was escorted out of the main ranch house. They walked together up to the elevated guard post. The terrorist waved to the men on patrol at the post and stopped. They kept their weapons trained on Harrison and motioned him ahead. Harrison walked slowly keeping his hands down to his side. He expected to be dropped by a bullet at any moment and it was unsettling to think that this camp of hate and violence might be his final resting place.

Chapter 25

"Alpha - Bravo - Zulu..."

Harrison knew he had little time to exploit the circumstances that were handed to him. His only advantage, unbeknownst to his captors, was to return to the location from where he maintained surveillance on Hawthorne and ambushed the unsuspecting terrorist. He needed to find the very spot where he buried his survival equipment. Although time was at a premium, Harrison's rate of travel was tempered by the terrorist's camouflaged defenses. He told himself that he would be a fool to take Hawthorne at his word—perhaps a dead fool at that.

Harrison kept a watchful eye as he continued down the main path from the sentry post and the ranch house. He approached the cutoff from which he exited the forest area after killing the unsuspecting terrorist. Harrison kept a steady, but slow pace. At the same time, nothing and everything seemed familiar. Harrison traveled in a southerly direction, straining his senses to a high state of alertness. If he could get word to Mentor about the fate of Elizabeth Ashton and her final resting place, reinforcements would be dispatched and the extremists' camp secured. Then and only then could the impersonator—the mirror president—be exposed for whom she was and the government returned to its unsuspecting people. A subsequent investigation would be launched to ferret out Hawthorne's co-conspirators among government ranks.

Harrison knew that once he made the pivotal contact with Mentor, he would be considered expendable. His subsistence depended on his own espionage and survival skills. Perhaps Harrison would be a minor footnote to world history, but to

Hannah, he was an important part of an upcoming momentous event—their wedding. Harrison allowed himself a brief smile, something foreign of late. It was the first time he thought of his beautiful Hannah since he arrived in Sarhea. Although Hannah's image brought him brief respite and joy, he knew that such intrusions could cost him the honed edge he required for survival. As pleasing and satisfying were Harrison's thoughts of his fiancée, he dismissed them and concentrated on his upcoming plan of operation.

Harrison stopped and gazed at the line of trees and bushes to his right. It was here that he believed he exited to head directly for the main ranch house. Harrison stood and examined everything around him. He proceeded guardedly into the brush and searched for the area where he ambushed the terrorist. It was there that Harrison buried his equipment and there where he hoped it remained undisturbed.

Harrison continued his march forward being ever so careful to scan for trip wires and mines. The map given to him by Hawthorne was unmistakably incorrect. He estimated regrettably that his fifteen-minute grace period had expired. It was open season now assuming that the murderous insurgent leader was a man of his word. The double entendre of truth and murder cohabitating in the same person did not elude Harrison. Yet, he had no time to devote to resolving such ideological viewpoints.

Harrison sensed that he was near the area where he buried his equipment, his communication lifeline to Mentor and the munitions he required for his own survival. He continued forward several steps before standing frozen on the spot. Harrison heard voices coming up from behind him. Perhaps he did not receive the full fifteen minute's head start as promised by Hawthorne...or perhaps the patrols had a genuine map of all the mines and devices making travel assured and much faster for them. Harrison darted into some bushes and knelt to the ground. He peered through a small opening in the thicket and waited to discover not who, but how many terrorists were approaching his location. Although Harrison felt no consolation, he knew that whoever found him first will not likely be his executioner. That right undoubtedly belonged to only one man: Jacob Hawthorne.

As Harrison watched, he counted a patrol of four men. He no longer was kneeling, but lay supine to the ground. Harrison believed that he only needed five more minutes to discover his spot of hidden treasure. He must elude the patrol and decided to head in a different direction than planned. This was his only chance of escaping Hawthorne's hunters with the hope of doubling back to his present location. Harrison carefully withdrew and headed at an angle away from the patrol thereby reducing the odds that they would turn suddenly toward him. He knew, of course, that the odds were against him for another patrol might approach him from a different direction…and even if they did not, how long could his good fortune hold out of not being caught by a sensory device or blown apart by an explosive mine?

Harrison felt some relief, as the voices of the patrol grew increasingly faint in the distance. He had no time to waste and headed back to the location that contained his backpack and equipment. Harrison kept a vigilant eye out for trip wires and traps. He hoped to escape further contacts with the terrorist patrols. As Harrison walked through the brush and trees, he saw something familiar yet out of place against the greenery— a bright red berry bush near which he buried his backpack. Harrison quickened his pace as he continued to scan for lethal devices. He glanced around the area and neither saw nor heard the enemy. Of course, that did not mean that he was not under surveillance at this very moment. Hawthorne was not the kind of man who accepted defeat. Yet, neither was Harrison. He found his way to the spot by the bush where he recalled burying his equipment. Harrison grabbed a nearby thick dead tree branch and began digging. He stopped and looked up periodically to watch for unwanted company. Harrison dug at a frantic pace; well, at least as fast as one could with a rudimentary 'shovel.'

After five minutes of digging, Harrison hit the top of something familiar. It was his camouflaged dyed backpack. He stopped and glanced around once more to confirm his privacy. Harrison focused his attention on his backpack as he pulled it out of the ground. He patted off the excess dirt and then pushed the dirt into the hole. Harrison padded down the dirt and scuffed the ground around the hole with his feet attempting to make the area blend in with its surroundings. He thought there was no sense in helping his captors by leaving clues to his whereabouts or whereabeens. Harrison knew it was too risky to remain at his present location. He planned to move out as far as possible before attempting contact with Mentor. Harrison removed a semiautomatic weapon and a lethal knife from his backpack before securing the pack to his back. If he was to go, he was not going to go peaceably. Harrison planned to be on the defensive and avoid all contact with the terrorists if he was to have any opportunity of reaching Mentor.

The grasp of the weapon gave Harrison some needed confidence in regard to his odds for survival. He continued to head further away from the ranch house, stepping around devices and avoiding patrols as he went. Harrison estimated that he survived one hour beyond the threat of being killed personally by Hawthorne. The odds of survival were definitively not in his favor, but there were improving and he felt better about them. Harrison hiked for another thirty minutes and determined that it was time to chance communicating with Mentor. He selected a small area that provided concealment behind heavy brush. Harrison knelt down in the dirt and removed his backpack. He also placed his weapon down, but within easy reach of his right hand. Harrison looked around, twisting his head and neck to scan a full 360 degrees. There was nothing to be seen or heard to the unsupported human senses. To leave nothing to chance, Harrison withdrew his binoculars from the backpack and scrutinized the area as before. He followed a similar procedure with his audio surveillance equipment. Harrison heard voices, but they were muffled and distant.

Harrison satisfied himself that he was reasonably secure. He removed the portable short wave radio from his backpack. Harrison placed some leaves on the dirt to provide a platform for the radio. He pulled out the antenna as far as it would stretch and tuned the radio. Harrison dialed to 131.0 megahertz, the setting agreed upon earlier with Mentor prior to the start of the mission. He held the microphone to his mouth and called out a short string of code using the international aviation phonetic alphabet. The sequence in the code would verify to Mentor that Harrison was indeed the authentic source of the message, the legitimate agent Hardware: "Alpha – Bravo – Zulu – Alpha – Bravo – Zulu – Uniform – Sierra – Hotel – Whisky – Mike, over." His message brought no other reply but static. He repeated the coded sequence: "Alpha – Bravo – Zulu – Alpha – Bravo – Zulu – Uniform – Sierra – Hotel – Whisky – Mike, over." Harrison attempted to wait patiently although seconds seemed like hours under the present circumstances. He placed the mike to his mouth and transmitted once again: "Alpha – Bravo – Zulu – Alpha – Bravo – Zulu – Uniform – Sierra – Hotel – Whisky – Mike, over." Harrison waited eagerly for the voice of his dear friend, but received only static as before. He thought about the possibilities why Mentor did not respond: that Mentor was not in a position to respond; that Mentor was captured; or that Mentor was assassinated.

Harrison checked the cycle and confirmed 131.0 megahertz. He then sent the coded sequence for the fourth time: "Alpha - Bravo - Zulu - Alpha - Bravo - Zulu - Uniform - Sierra - Hotel - Whisky - Mike, over." Harrison listened with hopeful anticipation for the voice he wanted to hear. As static burned the air, he took his binoculars and scanned the area around him to avoid being surprised by the terrorists or Hawthorne himself. It was then that he spotted Hawthorne with a patrol of five heavily armed men. Upon careful observation, Harrison noted that one of the men carried a radio, perhaps a radio detector. Had Hawthorne assumed (rightly so) that his enemy had some kind of transmitter available to him? He could not be sure. Harrison thought he had little to lose if he moved out, as his transmissions to date have yielded nothing. He shut down the short wave and packed quickly his equipment. Harrison threw the backpack onto a grassy piece of ground. He snapped a branch off a tree and began brushing the dirt in hopes of eradicating any evidence of his presence. He gazed down at the disturbed area of dirt and decided that it blended in with it surroundings, hopefully offering no substantial clues to a passerby.

Harrison grabbed his backpack and secured it over his shoulders. As before, he headed away at an angle from the approaching Hawthorne and his men. It was imperative that he conceal himself once again and reinitiate his transmission to Mentor as soon as possible. Harrison maintained his alertness looking for hidden explosives and surveillance devices. These observations slowed him down, but he had no choice. He stopped briefly to view the enemy with his binoculars. They continued their patrol on their formerly identified course.

Harrison continued to watch the terrorists when his heart suddenly skipped a beat. Hawthorne and the man with the radio or radio detector continued on course, but the remaining four men spanned out roughly at equal angles. Harrison knew that the odds were low for escaping this kind of search pattern and even lower if other undetected patrols were nearby. He put away his binoculars and retrieved his weapon. Harrison continued on his course knowing that he would eventually have to take a stance and switch from a defensive to an offensive mode. As he continued his cautious pace, Harrison searched for another location that would temporarily camouflage him. Sending the transmission to Mentor now took top priority, even precedence over his own survival. Harrison could no longer avoid taking even greater risks.

Harrison continued his trek forward until he happened on a cavern. The cave entrance was crisscrossed with wood and appeared abandoned for quite a long time. Although it may provide concealment, the cave was too obvious a hiding place for serious consideration. Harrison began walking away from the cave when he stopped abruptly and headed back to its entrance. The cavern may indeed be too conspicuous, but it may provide a decoy and consume his enemy's time—time that he needed desperately.

Harrison removed easily the rotting wood covering the entrance. He retrieved a flashlight from his backpack. Harrison proceeded carefully, shining the light in front of him. He exaggerated his steps as he walked so that the imprints in the dirt would not be overlooked. Harrison did not walk in far as the terrorists were nearby. He retraced his steps backward to the cave entrance, carefully stepping lightly in the tracks that he made. Prior to exiting the cave, Harrison dropped several boxes of his food rations that were visible in the dim light. He hoped that he could deceive sufficiently the terrorists on the duped hunt and provide him time to escape.

Harrison exited the cavern and walked on the rocks forming the base of the cave in order to mask his footprints. As he reached a grassy area, he jumped from the side of the cave onto the leafy ground. Harrison took out his binoculars and searched the area. He spotted one of the terrorists in the distance heading in the direction of the cave. Harrison would not know immediately if his ploy succeeded. He hoped that the terrorist would contact other patrols to investigate the cave and tie up personnel in a wild goose hunt.

Harrison returned his binoculars to his backpack and headed away from the cavern. He continued his search for a spot that would conceal him to initiate another transmission to Mentor.

Chapter 26

Mirror, Mirror

Harrison estimated that twenty minutes passed when he finally came upon an area that provided the camouflage he needed. He noted a small opening in the brush. Harrison used both hands to push away a bush and soon find himself in a secluded area. Harrison released the backpack and dropped it roughly to the ground. He pulled out quickly his short wave radio and extended the antenna to its limits. Harrison grasped the mike and hurriedly transmitted the sequential security code without delay: "Alpha - Bravo -Zulu - Alpha - Bravo - Zulu - Uniform - Sierra - Hotel -Whisky - Mike, over." He shook his head in disgust as there was no reply and the airwaves were still replete with static.

Harrison was growing short of patience and retransmitted the security code that he hoped would link him with Mentor: "Alpha – Bravo – Zulu – Alpha – Bravo – Zulu – Uniform – Sierra – Hotel – Whisky – Mike, over." However, the familiar static crackled over the speaker. Harrison stood slowly to survey the area around him, but he saw nothing alarming. He knelt down and transmitted the security code again, adding a personal remark to the all familiar code: "Alpha – Bravo – Zulu – Alpha – Bravo –Zulu – Uniform – Sierra – Hotel – Whisky – Mike, over—damn it, Mentor!" Whether it was the timing of the message or his elegant personal remark (and Harrison did not care which at the moment), the static of the air waves was interrupted by a familiar, comforting voice: "Yankee – Zulu – Alpha – Yankee – Zulu – Alpha – Uniform – Sierra – Mike – Hotel – Whisky, over." There was a brief pause and the security code was repeated: "Yankee – Zulu –

Alpha – Yankee – Zulu – Alpha – Uniform – Sierra – Mike – Hotel – Whisky, over." Harrison responded, "Harrison here. It's good to hear your voice, Greg." "Yours too, Harrison" returned Mentor. Mentor continued: "What is your status?" "Not good" was Harrison's reply. He continued in a trembling voice, "The worst of it is that Hawthorne assassinated President Ashton. I saw her decomposed body. I…" Harrison choked on his words as images of Elizabeth Ashton's body flooded his mind. There was no immediate response from Mentor. Then the familiar voice said reassuringly and apologetically, "Harrison, that was not the President. Elizabeth Ashton is here. She is safe. She never left the oval office. No time to explain. The person you saw was Marilyn Hawthorne. Until this moment, only President Ashton and I knew that."

Static filled the air, as Harrison was too confused to formulate an immediate response. However, Mentor needed some critical information and asked urgently, "Harrison, where is Hawthorne's headquarters and what is the estimated strength of his organization?" Harrison was still in shock, but managed to provide Mentor with a summary report including the information he required about Hawthorne, his men, defensive sensory devices and explosives. He also noted Hawthorne's "main target" operation scheduled for tomorrow. Harrison could not keep from stumbling over his words as he asked Mentor: "But how? Why?" Mentor knew that he could not review the details of the mission and hoped his words would suffice for the moment: "I'm sorry, Harrison. It was necessary to convince the co-conspirators that they indeed kidnapped the real Elizabeth Ashton by sending you to search for her. You provided us the time we needed to track down and uncover Hawthorne's contacts here in Washington. I'm happy to say that their immediate threat has been compromised."

There was a brief pause and then came gravity in Mentor's

voice: "What is your status?" "Not good" was Harrison's reply. I've become the personal target of Hawthorne and he's determined to capture his trophy—dead or, well, dead. If you're a betting man, Greg, the odds are not in my favor." Mentor's response came quickly and assuredly, "The company men are on their way, Harrison. I ordered them in the air about one hour ago in anticipation of your contact. They will be redirected to your coordinates. Their ETA is about one hour direct flight time. You must hold on. Repeat. You must hold on." There was a pause before Mentor attempted to lighten the mood: "Besides, they have your paycheck!" The two men permitted a slight chuckle between them before Mentor broke into the airwaves: "I spoke with Hannah this morning. She is concerned about you, but she says to tell you that she is 'fine.' I'm sorry about the death of Pope Josetta. I know you were very close to him. It seems that each time I send you on..." Harrison abruptly broke through the airwaves: "Targets approaching. Will attempt to contact reinforcements. Hardware out."

Harrison ended the transmission and hurriedly replaced the devices in his backpack. He secured the pack on his back and focused his attention in the direction of the approaching voices. Harrison rose to a crouching position and pushed away the brush that interfered with his vision. The voices were distinct and sufficiently clear that he needed nothing more than his naked senses. Harrison observed three approaching men, one of whom was Hawthorne. The terrorist leader was armed this time and had his weapon drawn. Harrison estimated that at least twenty-five yards separated him from his enemy. He found himself in a dilemma that he had to resolve quickly: attempt to conceal himself from the militants or try to outgun the hunters.

The dilemma soon turned complicated and was no longer a

dichotomous decision. Harrison thought for a brief moment of a third possibility: the capture of Jacob Hawthorne. Such personal vengeance, however, would put him in the position of defying Mentor's direct orders and run the risk of perishing himself. People have already died at the hands of Hawthorne and countless others will lose their lives and political positions before this ugly chapter in America's history is closed.

Orders or no orders, Harrison decided that he could not pass up the opportunity afforded him. Hawthorne must be captured alive. Harrison believed that there was a higher risk of Hawthorne being killed in the melee of bullets fired by numerous agents than those discharged by a single man. Two quick shots would fall Hawthorne's guards leaving the leader alone to spray the brush that concealed Harrison with a volley of bullets. Perhaps Harrison would survive and capture Hawthorne...Perhaps.

Harrison was not afforded time to debate the issue as the three men grew closer, marching directly toward him as if they knew he was there. The issue was now moot as Harrison's survival depended upon quick, accurate action. His adrenalin rushed as his gun hand stiffened with uncertain anticipation. He was weighing his skills and training against those of the insurgents. Hawthorne hired skilled and merciless men or they would be of no use to him. Harrison squinted his left eye as his right arm and right eye funneled the line of fire. He aimed his weapon at the terrorist on the left and fired several bullets into the man's head. This savage kill was necessary. Harrison was uncertain as to whether Hawthorne's closet guards wore body armor. The guard on the left slumped sharply backward and dropped to the ground. One of two men was eliminated. Harrison quickly swung his gun toward the terrorist on Hawthorne's right. This time, accuracy was left to chance and he would use a larger target than the man's skull. Harrison aimed quickly and shot four rounds at the body of the terrorist, hoping that at least one bullet found its lethal mark. The terrorist stumbled to the side while shooting his weapon into the air. By now, Hawthorne had time to react and began emptying his rounds ahead of him at his unseen, yet known target. Harrison dove to the ground and attempted to roll his body away from the spray of bullets. Yet, the secluded area that he chose so carefully now seemed small and unyielding. Hawthorne continued to fire at will spending his rounds like there was no tomorrow...and perhaps for Harrison, tomorrow may never come.

Chapter 27

Back to the Hornet's Nest

If there was one thing worse than eating crow, it was ingesting dirt…and Harrison was consuming his fair share of the latter. Fortunately, Hawthorne did not know his precise position. Harrison's acrobatics were keeping him out of harm's way and the spray of bullets thus far. The random near misses made it clear to Harrison that his defensive mode would soon turn fatal. As he considered his options, the shower of bullets stopped abruptly. Harrison figured that Hawthorne was reloading his clip and would soon start the barrage again. Not willing to test his theory, Harrison shot up and began firing in the direction of Hawthorne. He caught a glimpse of the terrorist moving away, blasting rounds as he went. If Harrison thought he might capture Hawthorne, he must do it quickly. The cavalry had not yet arrived. However, Hawthorne's men were scattered across the acreage and undoubtedly heading toward the noise and confusion.

Harrison moved away quickly from his pinned down area and began a short end run in hopes of ambushing Hawthorne. He remained alert to the planted sensory devices and explosives, but worried more about the latter than the former. The sudden appearance of patrols that would shoot first and perhaps never bother asking any questions was also foremost in his mind. Harrison continued to move cautiously, but steadily, maintaining as fast of a pace as circumstances permitted. He was not long into his end run before he spotted Hawthorne slumped behind a pile of rocks. Harrison's heart jumped as shots unexpectedly rang out. However, they were not aimed at him. Hawthorne was firing rounds in the air attempting to signal his patrols for help. That would not do, thought Harrison. He continued his pace through the brush toward the treacherous man. No sooner was he concerned about Hawthorne's men, he spotted a group of insurgents, maybe seven or eight of them, heading toward their self-proclaimed leader. The men yelled out for their comrade in terrorism and were rewarded with a redundant "Over here!" in response.

Harrison realized that he was now outnumbered. His concern about disobeying Mentor's direct order was no longer a liability. For his own survival, Harrison chose to head back toward the ranch house. Hawthorne and his men likely assumed that he would continue making his way toward the ranch's perimeter, not back in the direction of the hornet's nest. It was exactly that kind of thinking that kept Harrison alive all these years—doing the unexpected, betting against the odds. Just how long he could extend his play before the "house" demanded its due was uncertain.

Harrison heard gunfire in the distance, but not sufficient fire to suggest that the Mentor's marauders had arrived. It was more likely that Hawthorne and his men were shooting blindly, hoping to bag Harrison purely by chance. Harrison figured that Hawthorne was cursing his "benevolence" of providing him with an opportunity at freedom instead of just killing him on the spot when afforded the convenience. No matter. Hawthorne's loss was Harrison's gain.

Harrison continued his cautious, but steady pace toward the ranch house. He kept a close eye on the ground beneath his feet and the trees above him. Harrison could ill afford to alert the terrorists of his whereabouts as their emotional rage would mean certain and immediate execution. He still heard sporadic gunfire in the distance, but was stopped by a closer vision. Harrison crouched lower as he spotted ten-to-twelve militants patrolling guard near the ranch house. Perhaps he sold

Hawthorne short in his tactical savvy. The main path to the house was blocked formidably. Harrison could not remain in his present location, as terrorists in retreat from the attack by government agents would overrun him eventually.

Harrison angled away from the front of the ranch house to test the defenses around its perimeter. He hoped that Hawthorne's shield was more penetrable elsewhere. However, pregnable or not, it was critical that he infiltrate the ranch and uncover physical evidence of Hawthorne's conspiracy against the United States government. The hidden safe in the room where Hawthorne first discovered him was a good place to begin his search.

Harrison's reconnaissance soon paid off as the eastern part of the ranch house was patrolled by only two visible men. He crouched and observed their movements to determine how best to eliminate them. Harrison watched as the two men separated and walked away from each other by 20 yards before they turned and closed their gap once again. He was still in terrorist dress and planned to replace one of them as they separated. Harrison chose the terrorist on the north end as a group of bushes would be an ideal place to hide the man's limp body.

Harrison maneuvered his position to the eastside of the ranch house. Timing would be critical both in jumping and stabbing his assailant. Harrison withdrew his knife from its hidden holder and firmly grasped it. He had to surprise the terrorist and cover his mouth before the sounds of death escaped him and warned his partner. Harrison crept closer to his target and readied his stance. He calculated that fifteen feet separated him from his victim, the distance for which he must stalk his foe.

Harrison checked his watch. His reinforcements were still about 20-25 minutes out given Mentor's estimates. The two patrolling men stopped as they met each other once again and began conversing. Harrison waited patiently for the men to split. They seemed to deliberate for a long time before leaving each other once again. Harrison stood ready and did his best to observe both men. He could not attack the terrorist unless his colleague continued to maintain his attention in the opposite direction.

Harrison's adrenalin soared as the hand-to-hand battle approached. He stole one more glance at the other guard before quickly stalking his victim. Harrison approached the terrorist from behind. He placed his hand around his impending prey's mouth while simultaneously stabbing the man in his back and twisting the blade of steel. The terrorist wanted to scream, but was made incapable of broadcasting his pain or warning. Harrison quickly pushed the collapsing body of the terrorist in the nearby brush. He grabbed his victim's red bandana and rifle. Harrison nimbly wrapped the bandana around his head and shouldered his rifle. He continued walking forward on patrol realizing that about six feet remained before he would stop and turn as he witnessed previously. At the patrol perimeter, he turned around and began his walk toward the unsuspecting insurgent. He was unsure how close he could come to the terrorist before he realized that Harrison was not who he pretended to be. As Harrison paced his walked toward the unwitting sentry, he readied his knife once again. Their facial features became more distinct as they approached. Harrison turned his head away from time-to-time as if watching for an unforeseen enemy and hopefully disguising his direct profile from the advancing sentry. He glanced forward once again for any signs of recognition from the enemy, but deciphered none. The terrorist continued his approach apparently oblivious to his fate.

Harrison glanced away again estimating that twelve feet

separated him from the terrorist. He firmly grasped the knife in his right hand that was hanging stiffly down his side. His adrenalin surged as he returned his view to the approaching guard. However, Harrison kept his head down and eyes upward seeking signs of betrayal. The two men were soon upon each other when the insurgent spotted Harrison. The guard attempted to aim his rifle at Harrison. However, Harrison had the upper hand and brought his right-hand forward and into the chest of the militant. The sentry emitted only muffled sounds as the mortal knife lacerated the man's heart, spilling blood profusely. The terrorist collapsed quickly to the ground. Harrison withdrew his knife from the dead man and dragged his body toward the ranch house. He dropped the body down one of the lower level window wells and headed toward a side door of the ranch house.

Harrison slowly opened the door and walked guardedly into the house. An eerie silence greeted him as he looked quickly for any signs of the enemy. Harrison surmised that most of the terrorists were guarding the front of the house and the perimeter of the ranch from the impending government forces. He made his way toward the main sitting room and the safe that hopefully held the evidence to expose Hawthorne and his conspiracy. The silence continued as Harrison paced his way through the ranch.

It was not long before Harrison reached the main sitting room where he had unsuccessfully penetrated the ranch just hours ago. He walked over to the wall opposite the bar where he observed Hawthorne placing papers in the safe. Harrison stood in front of the wall and pushed his hand gently over the wallpaper feeling for the panel that provided passage to the vault. It did not take long to expose the panel and safe. Harrison had neither the time nor the equipment to ascertain the correct position of the tumblers, but instead withdrew a small container from his pocket that contained plastic explosives. He carefully removed the explosive and pressed it around the tumbler of the safe. Harrison stuck a small fuse in the explosive and lit it. He ran quickly across the room to protect himself behind the bar. Harrison did not have to wait long for the loud blast. He hurried across the room back to the safe and withdrew every document that he found. Harrison discovered and left a considerable amount of money untouched in the safe. He retraced his path to the side of the ranch house from which he made his entrance. Harrison knew that the blast would bring nearby guards and patrols, but he was in no position to fight the multitudes. He glanced at his watch and was encouraged that Mentor's reinforcements would soon penetrate the ranch's perimeter. Harrison reached the outer door and stopped. He opened it quietly and glanced outside. He saw no visible guards or sentries. Harrison quickly left the house and ran toward the opposite cover of brush and trees. As he paused to consider his next move, he heard the crackle of weaponry in the distance. There was no doubt in his mind that Mentor's reinforcements began infiltrating the perimeter of the terrorists' camp. Harrison buried quickly the documents that he retrieved from Hawthorne's safe. He marked the area so that he could easily recognize it once the impending battle was over. Harrison ran back to the ranch house. He was determined to make the house unusable as a fortress for the insurgents who were likely to retreat to the ranch when overrun by government agents.

Harrison entered the ranch house through the now familiar side entrance. He heard voices inside the house, but they were muffled. Harrison's goal was simple: head for the lower level where he was imprisoned and the corpse of the President of the United States, a.k.a., Marilyn Hawthorne, lay in repose. More important, the lower level was home to an arsenal of weaponry and explosive devices. Harrison was determined to set the explosives—if time permitted. He grabbed a pack from the arsenal and quickly counted the number of bombs and timers, noting ten of each. Harrison decided that the number of detonators was sufficient to destroy the home. He glanced toward the cell where the body of Hawthorne's wife rested, but he saw nothing. Harrison ran to the remaining cells and observed nothing. They were all inexplicably empty.

Harrison had no time to ponder the whereabouts of what Hawthorne suspected was the President of the United States. He knew that he had to work quickly and began by setting one of the charges in the middle of the arsenal. He glanced at his watch and knew that only ticks of the clock were left before the retreating terrorists entered the ranch house and blockaded themselves in the well-armed fortress. Harrison shook his head and exclaimed, "Damn!" as his hand on the timer trembled slightly when he set the clock for ten minutes. He grabbed the remaining nine explosives and ran quickly up the staircase. Harrison headed toward the main sitting room and set several explosives there. He set their timers for eight minutes. Harrison then headed toward the rear of the ranch house hoping to plant charges there as well. However, his progress was restrained by the voices of terrorists who were plotting their own strategy. Harrison counted seven men and knew that their presence impeded his plan. These terrorists would have to be eliminated if Harrison was to succeed.

Harrison exclaimed, "Damn!" Once again he knew that the explosive would have to be timer-set much like a grenade, five seconds or less, if he hoped to terminate his targets. Harrison set the timer for only three seconds. He calculated he had a second to throw back his arm, a second for the explosive to transverse the air, and a final fatal second to descend among the unsuspecting militants. There could be neither any error nor time left over for reaction. The explosive had to cause immediate death to result in an inescapable conclusion. Harrison took a deep breath and set the explosive in his hand for three seconds. He took another deep breath and exhaled as he released the timer. Harrison quickly drew back his arm and pause momentarily looking like a quarterback passing for the final "Holy Mary" play of the game. The man-made grenade sped through the air and hit one of the terrorists. The device exploded as it descended to the ground, killing or seriously wounded the insurgents who were plotting their counter-offensive.

Harrison estimated that he had about three minutes before the arsenal below him carved its path through the floor beneath his feet. He hurried to the main entrance of the ranch house and set two more charges. Harrison latched the main door to help delay what penetration might occur. He thought momentarily as he realized that his own life was now at risk—a risk perpetuated by his own hands. Harrison headed toward the side exit and found himself at the door. The charges would explode in a few tics and he knew that he must run for cover. Harrison darted out the door and only took half dozen steps before the first of the multiple explosions tore through the ranch house.

Chapter 28

The Confrontation

"Holy hell!" exclaimed Harrison as he escaped from the erupting and disintegrating ranch house. He was uncertain whether he could outrun the flying rubble, but he was not going to take the time to calculate his odds. Harrison ran at Olympic speed knowing that he had to win this qualifying sprint if he was to finish his mission. Pieces of the ranch house fell all around him, entrapping him in a circle of fiery debris. Harrison continued his quick pace, but was knocked to the ground by flying wreckage that hit him from behind like a whaler's harpoon. His forward progress ended abruptly and he thought that his life might as well. Harrison found himself in the dirt and in a defensive posture as he covered his head with his hands. He hoped to shield himself from the persistent hail of exploding debris. Despite the seriousness of his circumstances, Harrison found himself thinking of the clip from the "Wizard of Oz" when the home of Dorothy came falling down on the wicked witch of the west. He recalled the line, "Be gone before somebody drops a house on you!" Harrison would like to 'be gone;' however, his vulnerability was exposed, as he lay shrouded in the dust.

Small pieces of fiery debris continued to pummel Harrison, but the quantity and intensity were lessening. He slowly removed his hands from his head and turned his face away from earth's soil. Harrison peered toward the ranch house. What he saw amazed him as the ranch house was leveled to the ground. The home had lost its structure and it was anybody's guess as to what rested in the twisted heap.

Harrison raised himself from the ground. He did not have

time to survey the destruction for the crackling of gunfire was almost upon him. Harrison took cover near the area where he buried Hawthorne's documents, evidence he hoped would help expose the depth of the domestic terrorist's plot and help identify its covert players. He gazed toward the direction of weapons fire and observed the first retreating terrorists. They ran in the direction of the ranch to what they hoped was their safe house. The insurgents progressed forward for about ten yards before simultaneously turning 180 degrees and firing rounds seemingly into the uninhabited forest. For his part, Harrison took aim at the retreating militants, determined to kill or wound as many of them as he could in hopes of sparing the lives of his colleagues. He aimed and fired at will, dropping one terrorist after another. The volume of insurgents increased considerably as the battle line of government reinforcements came into Harrison's view. He continued to fire rounds into the retreating patrols when he observed Hawthorne separating himself from his main force and heading in an eastward direction.

Harrison believed that the handwriting was on the wall for the retreating insurgents. They soon would be captured or killed by Mentor's government forces. Harrison was determined to thwart Hawthorne's escape from the quagmire that the terrorist created *via* suspicion and hate. He began his pursuit by angling toward the fleeting Hawthorne. Hawthorne, himself, was isolated now with no patrols to support or protect him. Harrison wanted him alive to face the executable charges of conspiracy against the government of the United States and the murder of federal agents. He did not want to "cheat the hangman." Yet, Harrison knew that Hawthorne would not simply roll over and allow himself to be captured. Moreover, if Hawthorne dies, he will take many federal people with him. Harrison knew that Hawthorne would choose death to imprisonment and trial if permitted the choice.

Harrison grew closer to Hawthorne as gunfire continued to echo in the background. His weapon was drawn and in position to defend himself. Hawthorne stopped suddenly causing Harrison to dive abruptly to the ground. He lay on his stomach with his right hand extended forward and weapon aimed. Through the twigs and leaves, Harrison stared at his confused opponent. Hawthorne's plan of retreat likely included his ranch house, an option deleted by Harrison's sabotage. As abruptly as Hawthorne stopped, he was on the move and withdrawing at a fast pace.

Harrison was determined not to lose his prey and continued to stalk Hawthorne. Hawthorne was oblivious to Harrison's presence as his focus was steered to the invasion of his property, his private property, by government forces—the same government he hoped to cripple if not topple with his conspiracy. How indignant Hawthorne must feel given his political platform to have his personal property violated by the very individuals he opposed!

As Harrison continued to pursue Hawthorne, a barn-like structure came into view. It was clear that Hawthorne was heading for the barn. He likely hid instruments of destruction or equipment for escape in the structure. Harrison knew that their final confrontation must occur now before Hawthorne had an opportunity to implement his final solution.

Harrison stopped briefly and surveyed the area ahead of them. Hawthorne was heading for the front of the barn, but Harrison noted a small side entrance as well. This was his opportunity thought Harrison. As Hawthorne disappeared into the structure, he darted toward the side entrance. Harrison glanced around making sure that he was as isolated as he felt and observed no retreating terrorists or advancing government agents. He opened the barn door quietly and vanished inside.

The structure appeared more expansive indoors than its outer shell intimated. It was dimly lit inside. Harrison heard someone and that someone had to be Hawthorne. He made his way forward through multiple arsenals that lined the inner walls of the barn. Land mines, explosives, rifles—everything a well-fortified army required were stockpiled. Although such weaponry impressed Harrison, he was not prepared for what he saw in a clearing just ahead. There, basking in the dim light, were a number of Abrams tanks and the man preparing to board one of them was no other than Hawthorne himself.

Harrison had to act quickly. If Hawthorne's plan of retreat, escape or counteroffensive included this offensive might, a number of agents would die in the field. Unaware of Hawthorne's specific plan, Harrison did not delay his confrontation with the terrorist leader. He walked ahead with his gun drawn, cradling his gun with both hands so as to increase his aiming accuracy. Harrison wanted to avoid battling Hawthorne from within the confines of a tank. He paced ahead quietly much like a lion approaching his prey. Harrison was upon Hawthorne in seconds. The terrorist was totally unaware of his enemy's approach. Now that Harrison had the upper hand, he commanded in an even voice: "Stop, right there, Hawthorne." The warned terrorist did not turn around, as the voice was too familiar. "Mr. Rossetti, I presume. This is becoming quite tiring, you know." With these words, Hawthorne turned around slowly and fired off several rounds in the direction of his unseen, yet known enemy. Harrison's experiences with Hawthorne had taught him of his cunning. He was already in a crouched position as the bullets whistled by overhead. Harrison squeezed off several rounds himself. One of the bullets found its mark as Hawthorne grabbed his stomach and winced in pain as he bent over. Hawthorne managed to shoot off several more rounds as he attempted to retreat, bent over, to the front of the tank.

Harrison pursued quickly the wounded terrorist. He knew that there was nothing more dangerous than a wounded animal and Hawthorne had nothing to lose. Harrison approached the back of the tank and looked around the side toward the vehicle's front. He neither saw nor heard anything. Harrison cautiously walked by the side of the tank, exposing himself to whatever danger was ahead of him. He was breathing heavily and sweat was streaming down his face. Harrison licked his lips and continued stalking Hawthorne. He had reached the tank's midpoint and continued his pace with his gun aimed forward. Harrison slowed his pursuit as he neared the tank's front. He still neither heard nor saw anything. He glanced at the tank's big cannon before returning his gaze toward the front of the tank. Harrison's destiny would soon be sealed as he reached the forward part of the tank. He stopped to listen for anything that would betray his enemy's presence and position, but was offered nothing. Harrison's heart pumped faster and the sweat now rolled down his face. He crouched again and inched his way forward when he found himself flush with the front of the tank. Harrison took a deep breath and exhaled quietly. He then jolted around the front of the tank prepared to fire at will. However, his target was not there.

Hawthorne who leaped jumped Harrison suddenly from the top of the tank. Harrison dropped his gun as he was knocked to the ground. He looked upwards and saw Hawthorne bearing down on him with an iron bar. Harrison rolled quickly to his left as the iron weapon smacked the ground just inches from his head. Hawthorne withdrew the weapon and aimed for a second blow at his head. Harrison rolled back to his right as the iron bar nearly missed his scalp.

Hawthorne jumped atop Harrison and attempted to choke his victim by laying the iron bar across his throat. The terrorist pushed with all his strength. Harrison gasped for air and grabbed the iron bar. He pushed back at Hawthorne with all his might placing the weapon in a tug-of-war. The two men struggled with their respective strengths witnessed by the strain on their faces and the bulging of the blood vessels.

The battle continued for several minutes before Harrison gained the upper hand. Harrison pushed Hawthorne aside and grabbed his own neck as he gasped for oxygen. Hawthorne dropped the weapon and ran off into the darkness as best he could given his injuries. Harrison inhaled large breaths of air as he sat up. He gathered his gun and scanned the barn for Hawthorne. As Harrison turned and walked toward one of the tanks, Hawthorne stepped out. Harrison dove to the ground as gunfire echoed and bullets whizzed by his head.

As Harrison judged the direction of the gunfire, the unmistakable sound of a tank filled the silence. Hawthorne managed to climb in and start one of the tanks. The Abrams tank, second in line, was steered out of its resting place. Harrison rose and ran quickly after the fleeing tank. Hawthorne was slowed due to the maneuvering required inside the barn. However, Harrison knew that once the tank cleared the munitions, the tank would escalate to full-throttle. If Harrison was going to stop Hawthorne, he had to climb on the tank now. Harrison extended himself in a burst of speed and found himself directly behind the tank. He climbed on the rear of the armored vehicle as Hawthorne increased to ramming speed. Hawthorne, the tank and Harrison smashed through the locked barn doors. Harrison held on tightly as splintered wood fell to either side of the tank's cannon.

Hawthorne found himself speeding on open range unaware that an unwelcome passenger was holding on for dear life. Harrison's strength was tested as the tank dipped and jumped over the rough terrain. He slowly pulled himself forward attempting to reach the passageway that led to Hawthorne. Suddenly, the tank dipped down a gully and Harrison lost his left-hand grip. There he dangled with his right hand the only link between life and death. Harrison struggled to return his left hand to its grip as his body was bounced around by the rough ride. After several tries, Harrison managed to regain his left-hand grip.

Harrison continued his movement forward and finally reached the hatch. He reached for his gun and determined he would take no chances this time. He positioned himself in such a way that he could open the hatch and fire simultaneously. Harrison waited for leveled land and was soon afforded the opportunity. He opened the hatch and leaned inside the tank. Harrison view was that of Hawthorne's back. He gave no warning, but fired three rounds at the terrorist. Hawthorne's body fell to the side. Harrison climbed quickly into the bowels of the tank and moved to switch off its engines. He gained control of the metal beast and brought it to a stop.

Harrison turned toward his mortally wounded prey. Hawthorne moved his head to align his vision with his victorious enemy. Blood was oozing from his mouth and his ears. The dying man managed a sly smile as he addressed the victor in a strained and garbled voice: "You think you've won, but your President is dead! Our cause will survive me." Harrison smiled back and retorted: "You and your cause are dead! Your misguided followers will be exposed, imprisoned or executed. You will be remembered as a small footnote for your crime, nothing more." Harrison paused momentarily and then continued in an assured tone of voice: "Oh, by the way. President Ashton is quite alive and well in Washington. I'm afraid that it is Marilyn Hawthorne who is dead, not the President...and I have avenged the death of Mary Lou!" A look of shock drained the face of the dying man. He uttered nothing as the life force left his body.

Harrison bolstered his gun and climbed out of the tank into the light of day. The sun shone brightly despite the smell of stale gunpowder in the air. Limited gunfire could be heard in the distance and attested to the defeat of the insurgents by government forces. Harrison leaned against the tank and tried to reflect on the recent turn of events. However, it was Hannah who entered his thoughts—'See you soon, my love...'

Chapter 29

Friendly Capture

Harrison was lost in thought over Hannah when an unknown government agent approached him. The agent was unaware of Harrison's credentials. She brought her rifle to bear on her unidentified colleague and said in a menacing voice, "Don't try anything and you might still be alive in five seconds!" Harrison offered no argument and raised slowly his hands as he eyed the barrel of the rifle several feet away. After all, he had no identification and was dressed as the enemy. The youngish agent would believe nothing he would say. Senior agents at their field headquarters would identify Harrison. Until then, he planned to remain calm and follow orders. He did not offer that Hawthorne lay dead in the tank or that documents lay buried attesting to the scope of the conspiracy, but would soon convey that information to the agent in charge.

The government agent ordered Harrison to keep up his hands and walk in front of her. The agent motioned him away from the smoldering ranch house and toward the outer perimeter of the ranch property. Harrison offered, "You do know that there are trip wires and land mines scattered about, don't you?" The young agent swallowed hard and commanded, "Keep your mouth shut!" Despite the agent's surface coolness, Harrison glanced at the woman and observed her looking about. A childish grin came across Harrison's face as if just pulled a boyish prank.

The two agents, apparent enemies on the surface, were in truth colleagues. Harrison was relieved that the physical battle had ended although he knew that the debate of ideologies would continue to divide his country. For his part, Harrison was overjoyed to learn of the safety of the President of the United States. He was uncertain as to why Mentor concealed the true identity of the President—that is, the President was indeed the Software, the real Elizabeth Ashton, not her mirror self, a.k.a. Marilyn Hawthorne. Yet, Harrison knew from experience not to question Mentor's judgment in such matters as his reasoning was usually justified. He was not going to debate such issues now. Harrison just wanted to rest and rejoin his fiancée—to hold Hannah safely in his arms, to feel her warmth, to see her smile...

Harrison continued to walk ahead of his 'captor' with his hands raised. The agent behind him trained her rifle as he himself was instructed. They continued their steady pace in the heat for what Harrison estimated was thirty minutes. As they approached the perimeter of the late Jacob Hawthorne's ranch property, Harrison gazed upon the camp of the federal agents. He noted a number of helicopters and army jeeps. Harrison, still with a rifle at his back, was directed toward a tent that was used for processing the insurgents. Next to the tent was a prison-like structure created hastily from fencing and barbwire.

Harrison strained his eyes in the hope of finding someone who knew his identity. The thought of being imprisoned with the terrorists did not appeal to him. Harrison knew that one of the insurgents was bound to recognize him and then he would be unrecognizable following their brutal and perhaps fatal beating. The agent guarding Harrison ordered him to stop at the entrance to the tent. The guard at the tent and Harrison's 'escort' saluted each other. They were then ushered into the tent and found themselves facing the commander of operations, Nathan Zachary, codename Ops. All of a sudden Harrison felt like smiling as he greeted the commander, "Nathan! Thank God there's somebody here who knows me." Harrison reached out to grasp the extended hand of Ops who greeted Harrison in return: "Harrison! Good to see you. We weren't sure of your condition or even if you were alive. We've been searching for you since we've arrived here. Mentor was very specific about that." Then, the friendly commander spoke to Harrison's 'escort:' "You can put that rifle down, Williams. He's one of us actually." The female agent guarding Harrison blushed and apologized needlessly as she lowered her rifle for the first time. Ops introduced the two strangers: "Harrison, meet your 'captor,' Toni Williams. Ms. Williams, this is Harrison Rossetti." The two strangers shook hands as friends. Williams then excused herself and left the tent.

Ops smiled and said, "She's a good agent. I should give her an immediate promotion if she kept you at bay all this time!" The men permitted a laugh between them. Harrison attempted to defend his honor: "I just played along so I wouldn't get shot!" The men laughed again. Harrison continued, "On a more serious note, you'll find Jacob Hawthorne dead in a tank on the very spot where agent Williams 'captured' me. You'll pass a barn on the way to the tank and find quite a huge arsenal of explosives and munitions, including numerous tanks. You may also find the body of one of his wives, Marilyn Hawthorne—a dead ringer for Elizabeth Ashton. I first discovered her body in the cellar of the ranch house, but it was not there when I returned to the house to destroy its use as a fortress for the insurgents." Ops interrupted, "A nice piece of work. You saved a number of lives with that one." Harrison thanked Ops and continued, "You'll find another one of Hawthorne's wives, Mary Lou Hawthorne, in the basement of an old dilapidated structure about thirty miles south of town. She was also brutally murdered by Hawthorne's command. She was able to direct me to the ranch and provide some background information before I watched her die slowly in anguish." Harrison looked down sickened by the past image of Mary Lou's unmerciful death. He continued, "I was terribly relieved when Mentor told me that it was not Elizabeth Ashton who lay dead."

Harrison shuddered as he was visibly shaken by the events and images of the past few days. He was surrounded by death and destruction, but very much wanted life and future—a future with Hannah. Harrison desired Hannah now—Oh, God, how he wished she was in his arms. How Harrison wanted to forget the struggle...How he wanted to cling to life...How his senses desired to reach out and touch softness, to see beauty, to smell her sweet fragrance, to hear the voice that calmed him.

Suddenly, Harrison's stream of thoughts was interrupted by the call of his name. It was Ops who was trying to intrude upon Harrison. The invasion was sufficient as Harrison raised his head and looked at the concerned man. He then spoke, "I'm sorry, Ops. I was somewhere else." "With Hannah?" queried Ops with a knowing smile. Ops continued, "Mentor left very specific instructions on how to get you back to Washington. Your 'captor,' agent Williams, will drive you back to Great Falls which will give you about three hours of rest and sleep. Target One will be refueled and ready for your flight back to Washington. Mentor will conduct the debriefing and let you in on a surprise." Normally, the thought of a surprise enticed Harrison, but he was too tired right now to consider the prospects. Ops suggested that Harrison rest while he made arrangements for his trip back to Great Falls and Target One. Harrison countered, "As much I want to Ops, I took some important documents from Hawthorne's safe before the ranch house exploded. I buried them nearby and must retrieve them for Mentor." "No problem," returned Ops. He ordered a jeep for Hardware to retrieve the papers.

Chapter 30

Briefing and Debriefing

Harrison retrieved Hawthorne's documents and laid down for some sleep. His catnap was interrupted by a familiar feminine voice. For a moment, it sounded like Hannah as his mind wandered in the twilight haze between sleep and consciousness. The voice was persistent and becoming clearer. "Mr. Rossetti! Mr. Rossetti!" Harrison opened his eyes to find agent Williams softly shaking him. "Mr. Rossetti! Mr. Rossetti!" continued her voice. Harrison breached the border into consciousness and focused on the person attached to the voice. "Mr. Rossetti! The chopper is fueled and checked out for flight. We're ready to fly to Great Falls."

Harrison struggled to raise himself and wiped his face as if to brush the sleep from his eyes. "Fly?" inquired Harrison. "Yes, sir" replied Williams. She continued, "We were going to drive, but direct orders from the President are to get you back to Target One and Washington by the quickest route available." Harrison shook his head in acknowledgment and gazed at the beauty of Williams. She, in part, reminded him of Hannah and that pleased him.

Harrison and his colleague left the tent and headed for the area consigned to the copters. There were three helicopters ready for flight. The combined noise of the rotating blades was deafening. The two agents found themselves shouting at each other in order to communicate. Harrison was given a flight helmet as he climbed into the lead chopper. Agent Williams entered the craft and buckled herself in for the flight. The noise level faded somewhat as the helicopter's doors were closed. Agent Williams turned toward Harrison and offered,

"You'd better get some sleep, sir. We will be in Great Falls in about ninety minutes. Unfortunately, this will cut your sleeping time in half." A tired Harrison nodded and positioned himself for sleep.

The copter rose vertically and then headed south for the flight to Great Falls, Montana. Although Harrison thought he might not be able to sleep, the steady hum of the copter blades created 'white noise' and blocked out other annoying sounds. His tiredness pushed him to sleep within several minutes. Agent Williams glanced at her retired passenger and smiled.

The flight to Great Falls was void of surprises—something that Harrison would have appreciated if he were awake. Agent Williams landed the craft next to the hangar protecting Target One at Malmstrom Air Force Base. The sounds of the electrical instruments and her transactions with the control tower did not disturb Harrison's stream of unconsciousness. The blades of the chopper began whining as their rotations were slowed by friction. Agent Williams initiated her shut down procedures "by the book." She calculated that if she followed them "by the book," she bought Harrison fifteen more minutes of sleep before he had to assume the role of pilot for his trip back to D.C. aboard Target One.

Williams noted that it took seventeen minutes to shut down "by the book." She leaned over to Harrison and gently shook him, a role to which she had become accustomed. She called out his name: "Mr. Rossetti! Mr. Rossetti!" Harrison awoke abruptly and readily assumed a defensive position not realizing that he was safely tucked within the chopper's casing. He heard a female voice plead: "It's OK sir. We're back in Great Falls." Harrison regained his footing in consciousness and acknowledged Agent Williams.

The two agents stepped out of the helicopter. Harrison thanked Toni Williams and apologized for his boring demeanor. He walked toward the hangar that housed Target One. He greeted the officer in charge and proceeded aboard the jet. Harrison decided that a quick shower and change of clothing were in order. He sensed he was a bit gamy. Well, actually, a whole lot gamy—given the circumstances of the past forty-eight hours. Harrison stepped into the shower, a pleasurable convenience on Target One, and sighed as the water stream droplets bounced off his chest providing a warm, healing massage. His mind drifted to the times Hannah and he had spent together in showers around the world. The recurring fantasy was an erotic one for Harrison although lacking in intensity with the absence of Hannah. He permitted his consciousness to drift as the steamy stream beaded his naked body. Harrison leaned against the shower wall for support and relaxation. Time passed without notice. "Damn!" uttered Harrison as the warm water turned cold. He quickly finished his shower and toweled himself dry. He dressed in suitable clothing knowing that he would be briefed and debriefed by Mentor and perhaps President Ashton back in Washington.

Harrison finished dressing and went into his office. He faxed a message to Mentor that he will take off shortly with his ETA set at 10:00 P.M. Washington time. Harrison then attempted to contact Hannah in Rome, but was truly disappointed that there was no response. He was looking forward to her infectious smile…her sultry voice…her exciting touch…the physical and emotional presence that she brought to their relationship.

On that note, Harrison smiled and brought Target One's engines on line. He went through the pre-flight checklist and began taxiing to the airstrip. "Target One to control tower. Target One to control. Taxiing to runway 290. Over." There was a brief pause before the tower responded: "This is the control tower, Target One. You are clear for taxiing." Harrison steered his jet to the runway and proceeded to turn the plane for takeoff into the wind. Harrison halted the craft and examined his instrument readings before radioing the tower: "Target One to control. Target One to control. Permission to leave Malmstrom A.F.B. and Great Falls, Montana." "Roger that, Target One" replied control. "Visit again and God's speed." "Thank you" replied Harrison. "Target One out." He throttled the engines to a high-pitched whine sending Target One accelerating down the runway. The jet lifted off at which point Harrison sighed with relief. As Target One gained altitude, he altered course and headed easterly toward Washington, D.C.

Harrison engaged the autopilot once Target One's heading was corrected and it was flying at the designated altitude. He pushed his body back into the pilot's seat using 'feet' power and stretched his arms as high as the cockpit cabin permitted. Harrison let out a big yawn, but reminded himself that he recently had a catnap.

The flight to Washington was uneventful—something that Harrison has appreciated more and more through the years. Within three hours, Harrison landed at Dulles Air Force Base as ordered. He was told that a limousine would be sent to take him directly to the White House. Harrison taxied to the hangar designated by the tower. He guided Target One into the sheltered structure as directed by the hand waving ground crew. Harrison brought the jet to a stop and powered down the engines. He quickly left the cockpit, foregoing the shut down checklist, and debarked the plane.

Harrison no sooner left Target One when a limousine drove up to the hangar and stopped to the side of him. The driver walked to the passenger side and opened the rear door for him. To Harrison's pleasant surprise, Mentor extended his hand as he stepped into the limousine. His friend and supervisor spoke first: "Congratulations, Harrison. Your mission was a success. On a more personal note, I'm glad to see that your safe and apparently all in one piece. Welcome home." Greg and Harrison allowed themselves a personal moment as each firmly shook hands and smiled broadly while maintaining eye contact. Their professional survival permitted them to enjoy their lasting friendship.

Hardware handed to Mentor the documents that he secured from Hawthorne's safe. Mentor thanked his agent and commented, "These should be quite damaging to the conspirators." Mentor paused and spoke again, "Harrison, I know you're tired. However, I also know you have many questions and we also need some answers. We are headed for the White House where we will meet with the President to brief and debrief you." "I understand, Greg" was Harrison's brief reply. He wanted to say more, but he was indeed tired and had not debriefed himself of the past days' events and their significance. Harrison closed his eyes and leaned his head back deeply in the seat. Mentor allowed his agent his space for now knowing that the debriefing would be long and arduous. The two men sat quietly for the remainder of the trip. Mentor too decided to allow himself some shallow sleep as he lay back into the seat.

The trip understandably seemed long for both men who had exercised their minds and bodies to their limits and beyond. They would not sleep now, but at the very least they could rest their eyes and perhaps their thoughts. Images would be fleeting and not be allowed to remain long in consciousness. Their briefing and debriefing would come soon enough. For Harrison, it would provide him the opportunity to learn the clandestine background aspects of the mission as well as relive the events of the past forty-eight hours.

The trip to the White House was uneventful. It just seemed

terribly long. The limousine reached its destination carrying its important passengers. As the car drove up to a side entrance, the two men stirred and tried to wipe the tiredness from their bodies. They stretched at the allowable limits given the confines of the limousine. Harrison was first to leave the car followed closely by Mentor.

The two tired men entered the White House and presented their credentials to the guard on duty. Mentor and Hardware took the elevator to the second floor. Mentor motioned Hardware into the conference room. Hardware entered the room to find President Elizabeth Ashton sitting at the conference table wading through report papers. The President turned around at the opening of the door as Harrison spoke with a smile: "The real President Elizabeth Ashton, I presume." "Hello, Harrison," greeted the President. "Welcome home," she said warmly.

The two men sat down at the table opposite President Ashton. Mentor greeted the President and started the formal proceedings: "Well, I wasn't sure at times that this moment would ever come, but I'm glad we're finally together. The past several days crawled like months and were intense for each of us during the course of this mission. But the success of this mission, largely through Harrison's efforts, has helped to preserve the democracy of the United States and the office of the Presidency. And whatever the terrorists' 'main target' plan that was scheduled for implementation tomorrow, it is now neutralized by our infiltration of the militant faction."

"I want to echo my sincere congratulations as well, Harrison, on your successful mission" added President Ashton. "On a more personal note," she continued, "I want to thank you both for carrying out your duty to your government. I apologize, Harrison, for keeping you in the dark about my reported 'kidnapping.'"

Harrison offered, "There is no need to apologize, Madam President. I learned a long time ago not to question Greg's judgment in these matters." Harrison looked at Greg and raised his eyebrows to underscore his statement, as was his manner. He continued, "You can't imagine how I felt when I discovered your body, er, the corpse of Marilyn Hawthorne and then have Greg wipe away my shock, grief and loss with his revelation that you were still among the living."

Mentor interrupted, "We're sorry, Harrison, but security and success of the mission depended on secrecy." Mentor paused briefly and then continued, "Let me lay it out for you, Harrison. An attempt to kidnap President Ashton did happen in Helena, Montana. She was attending a day conference and evening fundraiser. It was only fate that kept the President from being kidnapped and assassinated. Software and her personal bodyguard, Agent Jack Roberts, returned to the President's suite to pack for the trip back to Washington, D.C. that evening. Agent Roberts felt ill most of that fateful day. He requested to be excused for a moment to relieve himself in the restroom. Unknown to Software or her agent, the mirror president, a.k.a., Marilyn Hawthorne and her personal guard were making their way to the Presidential suite. It must have been relatively easy for the aliases to pass through security with her mirror image of Software."

President Ashton interjected and continued; "You can imagine my startle when Marilyn Hawthorne and her look-a-like bodyguard entered my suite. The shock of the moment paralyzed me. This is what the terrorists counted upon and used to gain an upper hand over me. They were very professional, said nothing and did not waste any time. Her bodyguard quickly gave me a shot. My scream was short-lived and I suspected heard by no one. The drug they gave me acted quickly. But there I was wrong. Agent Roberts, who was relieving himself, heard my fading scream. As related later to me by Roberts, the two terrorists were preparing me for transportation to who knows where when he darted out of the restroom, surprised them and got the drop on them. Agent Roberts called Mentor and advised him of the situation. He also summoned a security agent and my personal physician who traveled with me to Montana. Fortunately for me, I was given a strong sedative and nothing more."

President Ashton rested and Mentor continued the story: "By the time I received the call, Software was resting comfortably. Roberts related to me the recent turn of events. From that moment on, we decided to keep matters secret because there really wasn't any other way to play it. At President Ashton's request, we didn't even tell her husband. The story of Modem's discovery that the President was not the President was a ruse. Sorry, Harrison." Mentor paused and then continued; "I knew we were given a golden opportunity to play things out with control in our hands. We knew that anybody with the sophisticated intelligence to get themselves uninvited into the same room safeguarding the President of the United States would be a chronic threat to our nation's security and the office of the Presidency itself. The key to our plan was secrecy and convincing the terrorists that they succeeded in this phase of their operation. With the help of the President's physician, we were able to revive Software and shared with her the events leading up to her sedation. It was at this point that Madam President and I decided to give them what they came for. President Ashton understood the risks to her personal safety, but she insisted that the charade be played out to expose the conspirators in the plot. Instead of the mirror President taking the place of Elizabeth Ashton, it was Software who took the place of the mirror conspirator—'mirror, mirror' at the White House."

President Ashton continued the chronicle: "I really did not see that I had any choice, Harrison. I knew that my safety was compromised severely and going undercover for their side, if you will, would swing the balance of surprise and control to us. According to my physician, the drug dosage given to me was not far from lethal. We assumed they did not plan immediately to murder me in case something went awry and they needed a hostage—a high-priced hostage. I'm not happy about this part, but Mentor convinced me of the necessity to give my mirror twin the lethal dose of the same drug hoping that the conspirators believed they miscalculated the dosage. Marilyn Hawthorne was dead before she left the Presidential hotel suite. We got enough information from her accomplice that my, er, her body would soon be recovered from the hotel. I was to be contacted by her accomplices in the dissident organization. We placed her guard under arrest for conspiracy and hid him away in solitary confinement. He will await trial like his co-conspirators. We finished packing to head back to Washington and left my mirror twin looking peacefully 'asleep' in the bed with my clothes, jewelry and other personal effects."

Mentor picked up the story from there: "We did not attempt any degree of surveillance at the risk of exposing what we had discovered. We knew that any organization that could carry out such planning with their sophistication had to be well-organized and broad in membership, perhaps even agents, congressmen and staff in D.C. If we exposed the conspirators at that moment, the identification and extensiveness of their membership would never have been known. It was obvious by Marilyn Hawthorne's mirror image of the President that it was their intention to substitute her for Software. We also suspected that they would contact who they believed was their mirror President. Such contacts would build the base of our list of conspirators that would eventually lead to the exposure of their organization for its treasonous intentions. It did not take long before President Ashton heard from the conspirators and we began building our list. When we gathered sufficient information to identify a general target, I contacted you and the operation was set into motion."

Software and Mentor had finished their detailed briefing. Harrison spoke, "I appreciate the specific information and certainly understand why secrecy was critical. You were both right. I might have done things differently if I knew that you, Madam President, was alive and well in Washington. I perhaps would not have taken the risks that I did to uncover the plot behind Jacob Hawthorne. Now, I suppose that you want to hear the rest of the story. Mentor looked at his watch and smiled, "If you've got the time, Harrison...If you got the time."

Software, Mentor and Hardware managed a tired smile. Mentor and the President listened intently to Harrison's recounting of the past forty-eight hours. It was well into the early morning hours before the debriefing ended. Harrison asked, "Is there anything else I need to detail?" "Not at this time," responded Mentor. "I think we have enough information to begin our official investigation and issue indictments and subpoenas. The papers that you secured from Hawthorne's safe were, shall we say, very detailed." Harrison reflected and then commented, "You know that it was a good plan strategically speaking. Had it been successful [he paused] I dread to think of what would have happened."

On that note, Harrison excused himself and walked out of the conference room. He requested a government car and then exited the White House. Harrison began his short drive to his apartment. "Oh, damn" he said aloud. Harrison realized that he forgot to ask Mentor about the surprise that he reportedly was going to give him. He shrugged his shoulders and yawned often as he drove back to his apartment.

Chapter 31

How Many Surprises?

Harrison looked at his watch as he pulled into his apartment complex and noted that it was four in the morning. He parked his government vehicle (something, by the way, he would never trade for his own) and walked the few steps to his apartment. Harrison unlocked his door and turned on the corridor light. He walked into his usual backlog of mail and newspapers that always greeted him upon his return. What would he do without his charming neighbors, Al and Diane Adzn, who tracked his frequent comings and goings? However, there was nothing in either pile of materials that magnetically drew him to it, especially at four o'clock in the morning.

Harrison started undressing as he walked toward his bedroom. He stopped suddenly and noticed that his bedroom door was closed. This is not how he left it; in fact, he never closes his bedroom door. Harrison withdrew his weapon from its back holster. Perhaps Mentor did not identify all the conspirators from his mission. He walked slowly up to the door and stood silently. No noise echoed from the room to betray its occupant. Harrison gently put his left hand on the doorknob and turned it slowly. He was careful not to alert anyone to his presence. The doorknob unlatched without a sound. As the door yawned, there was a dim light shining from inside the room. Harrison entered the room and observed a figure lying in his bed. In a split second, he dropped his gun and ran to the bed. "Hannah! Hannah!" he shouted excitedly. If Harrison's shouts did not wake Hannah, the ripples of the mattress from his swan dive to the bed did. "Harrison" she shouted back. The two lovers clenched and held their embrace tightly as if they would soon be torn apart. They kissed deeply and continued to hold each other, saying nothing to disturb the moment. Harrison's tiredness left him as all that was Hannah revived him.

Harrison broke their silence and embrace by asking, "How is the future Mrs. Hannah Rossetti?" For her part, Hannah smiled and said nothing. She wanted nothing but to continue their hug. Their embrace increased in sensualness as the lovers' feelings became more erotic toward each other. Harrison finished undressing, as did Hannah. Nothing now came between their bodies. Harrison sighed as he felt the warmness of Hannah's body against him. They continued kissing and caressing each other at erotic speed, their pheromones unleashed and pushing the two lovers into reckless abandon.

Their caressing excited their erogenous zones and the aroma of sex accelerated their lovemaking. Heartbeats and panting quickened their pace as the silence was pierced with low moans. The art of foreplay took a back seat to their engaging pheromones. Hannah massaged her lover's manhood as Harrison suckled on his lover's breasts. They rotated intermittently taking turns at being the dominant lover. Hannah and Harrison moaned and panted so much that the two functions began to interfere with each other. As Hannah continued rubbing her lover, Harrison's hand slipped from her breast and down to her womanhood. The two lovers approached frenzy as their mutual massage hastened their eroticism.

Neither lover could hold back now. Lust and physiology caught and surpassed love and romance. Harrison and Hannah mounted each other as their sighs turned to cries. The agony on their faces belied the pleasure they received from their bodies. The lovers thrashed about, their momentum undaunted and unleashed by their mix of sweat and sexual scent. Their excitement spurred their joint thrusts as Harrison's felt his stirring. Hannah moans became longer and deeper as she reached the beginnings of her orgasm. The two lovers stimulated each other beyond the road of no return. At the peak of arousal, neither could hold themselves back as their orgasms were now self-perpetuating. Their thrusts became stronger until Harrison's body stiffened. He was nearing the point of ejaculation as Hannah continued her inner massage of his manhood with her own engaging orgasm. Her strokes became longer and slower as both lovers approached their orgasmic climaxes. Harrison could hold back no longer. His body twitched as his sperm rose and crossed wetly into Hannah. They continued their mutual massage until their eroticism was satisfied and faded. Then, Harrison and Hannah lay still. Their panting and breathing continued their quicken pace, but their bodies relaxed. The physical twitching and thrusting of moments ago were gone, but the love and romance between the two lovers lingered. Hannah and Harrison kissed each other warmly, softly as they maintained their sexual connection. They fell asleep quietly in their embrace as if recent events never transpired.

It was late morning when Harrison and Hannah awoke. The two lovers faced each other in bed and simply smiled. The scent of their sex and the afterglow of their pleasure permeated the room. Harrison stroke Hannah's hair and said, "What a great surprise to find you here. I tried to call you in Rome on the flight back to Washington, but there was no answer." Hannah interrupted, "There was no answer, my love, because your friend Greg put me on a flight so that I could see you, touch you once again upon your return to Washington." A sense of seriousness grew on Hannah's face as she spoke sadly,

"I'm sorry about Josetta, Harrison. He so much wanted to see us together. I know how much you wanted to be with him, to comfort him—to comfort me." Harrison said nothing, but nodded and fought to halt the swelling of tears.

Hannah felt her lover's grief and attempted to override the sadness. She asked, "Was the mission successful?" Harrison switched gladly his thoughts and attached emotions. He replied, "Yes, very successful. It will take considerable time to tie up loose ends, but that operation was assigned to other agents. Now, Mrs. Rossetti..." Harrison was interrupted by Hannah's protest: "It's still Miss Littleton for three more days, so watch yourself Mr. Rossetti!"

The engaged lovers' laugh was interrupted by the piercing ring of the phone. Harrison reached over and picked up the receiver. "Harrison Rossetti," he said. "Hardware," came a familiar voice from the other side. "I hope you have rested well and enjoyed the 'surprise' that I arranged for you" said Mentor. "Yes, I'm grateful for your arrangement and allowing us some time together." Harrison then said in a more serious tone, "You addressed me by my codename, Mentor. Is there any significance to that?" "I'm afraid so," said Mentor reluctantly. "I know Hannah and you are getting married in three days, but..." "Oh, no" interrupted Harrison...

Other Books by the Author to be published by CCB Publishing

Beginnings

Beginnings is based on the lives of Greg and Charly that propels the reader on an emotional roller coaster, as events unfold in their lives, including the more absurd and humorous aspects of life. *Beginnings* traverses the singledom lives of Greg and Charly and bring them together. The global benchmarks that help define them and a people unfold for each decade of their lives. We all encounter collectively many beginnings and beginnings of the end. We share them for they are part of what we call the human condition. Man and wife experience many beginnings and beginnings of the end, as Greg and Charly discover—some predictable, some unexpected. Some beginnings are critical moments in our lives as they forever change us for better or worse—they bring us together or tear us apart. They are intimately tied to human relationships as they strengthen or weaken the stuff that binds us.

Twelve Upon A Time...

A kindergarten-elementary aged children's book...each monthly story is unique and illustrated by the original drawings of children whose interpretation of the words can only be seen through their eyes. The stories are written to assist the imagination of children and to strengthen the parent and child bond through the sharing of heartwarming, silly, absurd and believably impossible tales.

242

Side Stepping the Rules: Broken or Not

There are many books about the dating relationships of men and women written by women, but men write few. Well, take heart, for now is the parody book that presents the sensitive man's guide for escaping the clutches of the woman who thinks she's Mrs. Right. And it must work because it seems like the author has been single forever!!!